THE PRAIRIE FLOWER;

OR,

ADVENTURES IN THE FAR WEST

BY EMERSON BENNETT.

AUTHOR OF "THE FOREST ROSE," "THE BANDITS OF THE OSAGE," "THE TRAITOR," "OLIVER GOLDFINCH," "KATE CLARENDON," ETC., ETC.

> But O, the blooming prairie,
> Here are God's floral bowers,
> Of all that he hath made on earth
> The loveliest.   *   *   *
> This is the Almighty's garden,
> And the mountains, stars, and sea,
> Are nought compared in beauty,
> With God's garden prairie free.

NEW EDITION, REVISED AND CORRECTED BY THE AUTHOR.

CINCINNATI:
PUBLISHED BY U. P. JAMES,
No. 177 RACE STREET.

Entered, according to act of Congress, in the year 1850,

BY J. A. & U. P. JAMES,

in the Clerk's office of the District Court of the United States, for the District of Ohio.

Printing Statement:

Due to the very old age and scarcity of this book, many of the pages may be hard to read due to the blurring of the original text, possible missing pages, missing text, dark backgrounds and other issues beyond our control.

Because this is such an important and rare work, we believe it is best to reproduce this book regardless of its original condition.

Thank you for your understanding.

DEDICATION.

TO

Frank Major, M. D.

OF
COVINGTON, KENTUCKY.

DEAR SIR:—In selecting your name to grace this page, I feel I am only doing an act appropriate to the esteem in which I hold and the friendship that I feel for you. And to me this inscription seems the more appropriate, that our acquaintance was formed in the sick-room, and at the bedside of one near and dear to me, while I was engaged in writing the closing scenes of the pages which follow. My child, an only child, was lying at the point of death; and you were called, in your professional capacity, to visit him. The kindly interest you manifested in his welfare — the close and almost constant attendance you gave him — the high professional skill you displayed in his behalf — and last, though not least, your *success*, under God, in snatching him, as it were, from the very jaws of death — led me to admire your talents as a physician, and, together with one who had been, like myself, nearly prostrated with affliction, at the thought that our only child must go from us, to regard you as truly a "friend in need." The friendship thus begun, and since continued, I trust will be lasting; and as a remembrancer of the many pleasant hours we have spent together, exchanging ideas and traveling over the bright and fertile fields of imagination, I carably inscribe this work to you.

THE AUTHOR.

INTRODUCTORY.

As almost every one who takes any interest in a book, has some desire or curiosity to know how or why it came to be written, and as there are some things of which he desires to speak particularly, the author, compiler, or editor of Prairie Flower, (whichever you please, reader,) has, after due consideration, decided on giving the information alluded to, in an introductory note to the present volume. While engaged in writing for the press, a tall, dark-visaged, keen-eyed individual entered his sanctum, early one morning, bearing in his hand a bundle of no inferior size. Having stared around the apartment, as if to assure himself there was no mistake, he coolly took the only remaining seat, when the following conversation occurred.

STRANGER.— Mr. Scribblepen, I presume?

AUTHOR.—My name, sir!

STRANGER.—He-e-m! (A pause.) Write novels, presume, Mr. Scribblepen?

AUTHOR.—When I have nothing better to do.

STRANGER.—(After a little reflection.) Found them on fact, eh?

AUTHOR.—Sometimes, and sometimes draw rather freely on the imagination, as the case may be.

STRANGER.—How would you like the idea of writing one THAT SHOULD CONTAIN NOTHING BUT FACT?

AUTHOR.—(Becoming interested and laying down his pen.) Have no objections, provided there is fact enough, and of a nature sufficiently exciting to make the story interesting to the general reader.

STRANGER.—(Smiling complacently, and tapping his bundle.) Got the documents here, and no mistake. Every word true, I pledge you my honor. Promise to work them up faithfully, and they are at your service.

AUTHOR.—(In doubt.) But how am I to know they contain *only* facts?

STRANGER.—You have my word, sir!

AUTHOR.—Did you write them? Do they comprise a journal of your own adventures?

STRANGER.—(A little testily.) No matter about either! They contain nothing but facts, and that is enough for any reasonable man to know.

AUTHOR.—But how am I to know this? You must remember you are a stranger to me, sir!

STRANGER.—(Coloring, and carelessly placing his hand upon the breech of a pistol, barely seen protruding from beneath his waistcoat.) I allow no one to doubt my word, sir!

AUTHOR.—(A little nervous, and not caring to doubt such *powerful* testimony.) O! ah! I see—it is all right, of course.

STRANGER.—(Again smiling pleasantly.) So you will undertake the job, Mr. Scribblepen, and give facts in everything but the most important names?

AUTHOR.—I will try.

STRANGER.—(Placing the package upon the table and rising as if to go.) You can have them, then. All I ask is that you will be a faithful chronicler. The names I wish changed, you will find marked. I have a desire to see the whole in print, and you may take all the profit and whatever credit you please, so you keep fact in view. The incidents are romantic, and sufficiently exciting for your purpose, without embellishment. I shall keep an eye upon the publication, and you *may* see me again, or you may not: I make no promises. Good morning, sir!

AUTHOR.—(Rising to bow him out.) But your name, stranger, if you please?

STRANGER.—(Hesitating.) I am called the Wanderer. Good morning, Mr. Scribblepen!

AUTHOR.—Good morning Mr. Wanderer! (Returns to the mysterious package, opens, examines it, begins to read, gets interested, and goes to bed the night following minus dinner and supper.)

Having shown you how he became possessed of the *facts* of the story, the author would say a few words more as regards the characters set forth in the following pages, he would state, that, *being all real,* some represent a class, and some an individual only. Prairie Flower is of the latter, *and is drawn from real life.* That the proceedings of herself and tribe may appear mysterious, and, to some, at first thought, (her locality and everything considered) out of place, the author does not doubt; but he believes that no one who is conversant with Indian history, and especially with that relating to the Northwestern Tribes and the Moravian Missions, during the early settlement of Ohio, will find in this character or her tribe anything that may be termed overstrained or unnatural. That she is a marked character, distinct and peculiar, and liable to be misconstrued by those who do not take every thing into consideration, but allow a first fancy to have full sway—he admits; but at the same time would desire such to withhold an expression of opinion, until they shall have read to the end, when he trusts they will find the explanation satisfactory.

With these remarks, and the simple statement that the reader may look upon the scenes described as *real,* the author would take his respectful leave for the present, hoping the reader may find, if nothing else of interest, information regarding life in the Far West, sufficient to repay a perusal.

CINCINNATI.

ADDITIONAL.

The foregoing was affixed to the first edition of "PRAIRIE FLOWER," which appeared in 1849, and which, though a large one, was exhausted in a little over three months. And the Author would here take occasion to say, that the success this work has met with from the reading community — the high mark of popular favor which has been bestowed upon it by an intelligent and discriminating public — together with the friendly notices it has received from the Press, and the eulogistic remarks of correspondents, both known and unknown to the Author, from all parts of the country — have been the green OASES in the desert of life of one who toils only to please, and who herewith returns his humble thanks to each and all, coupled with his regrets that the work in question is not more worthy of the eulogiums that greeted its first appearance.

To those unknown friends at a distance who have made kindly inquiries by letter, concerning the strange individual from whom the author obtained the manuscripts referred to in the foregoing note — as also in reference to the present whereabouts of "Prairie Flower" herself, and others — but which a press of business has prevented him from answering as he otherwise would have done — the author takes occasion to say, to one and all, that as respects the "*Wanderer,*" having never heard from him since, he congratulates himself on having given no offense, in working up the materials he furnished; and that, with regard to Prairie Flower and the rest, he knows nothing additional to the facts recorded in the following pages.

CINCINNATI, O.

THE PRAIRIE FLOWER

CHAPTER I.

THE PROPOSITION — THE RESOLVE — HO! FOR OREGON.

"Ho! for Oregon — what say you, Frank Leighton?" exclaimed my college chum, Charles Huntly, rushing into my room, nearly out of breath, where I was cosily seated, with my sheep-skin diploma spread before me, engaged in tracing out my legal right to subjoin the magical initials, M. D., to my name. "Come, what say you, Frank?" queried my companion again, as I looked up in some surprise.

"Why, Charley," returned I, "what new notion has taken possession of your brain?"

"Oregon and adventure," he quickly rejoined, with flashing eyes. "You know, Frank, our collegiate course is finished, and we must do something for the remainder of our lives. Now, for myself, I cannot bear the idea of settling down to the dry practice of law, without at least having seen something more of the world; and by all means I would not settle here in the east, where lawyers are as plenty as stubble in a harvested rye-field, and, for the matter of that, to make the comparison good, just about as much needed. You know, Frank, we have often planned together, where we would go, and what we would do, when we should get our liberty; and now the western fever has seized me, and I am ready to exclaim — ho! for Oregon."

"But, Charley," returned I, "consider; here we are now, snug in old Cambridge, and Oregon is thousands of miles away. It is much easier saying, ho! for Oregon, than it is getting to Oregon. Besides, what should we do when there?"

"Hunt, fish, trap, shoot Indians, anything, everything," cried my comrade, enthusiastically, "so we manage to escape ennui, and have plenty of adventure!"

"I must confess," said I, "that I like the idea wonderfully well — but ——"

"But me no buts!" exclaimed Huntley; "you will like it — I shall like it — and we will both have such glorious times. College — law — pah! I am heartily sick of hearing of either, and long for those magnificent wilds, where a man may throw about his arms without fear of punching anybody in the ribs. So come, Frank, set about matters — settle up your affairs, if you have any, either in money or love — and then follow me. Faith! man, I'll guide you to a real El Dorado, and no mistake."

The words of my companion produced a strong effect upon my naturally restless mind. Nothing that he could have proposed, at that moment, would have suited my inclination better than such a journey of adventure; and no companion would I have chosen in preference to himself. We had been playmates together in infancy, we had studied together in youth, and, for the last four years, had been chums at old Harvard University — he studying law and I medicine. True, by the strict discipline of the University, we were not entitled to occupy the same apartment, on account of our different studies; but the influence of our connections made us privileged personages; and the professors winked at many things in us, that in others would have been grave offences. The substance of the matter is, we began our studies together, roomed together, and each completed his course at the same time.

From childhood up, I had loved Charles Huntly—or Charley, as I more familiarly termed him—as a brother; and this fraternal feeling I knew he as warmly returned. We walked together, played together, sung together—ever took each other's part on all occasions, whether right or wrong—and, in fact, for our close intimacy, were dubbed the Siamese twins. We were both only sons of wealthy parents. My father was a wholesale merchant in Boston; so was his; the only difference in their occupations being, that the former dealt in dry goods, the latter in groceries. Now there was another strong tie between young Huntly and myself. He had an only sister—a sweet, modest, affectionate creature, some three years his junior—whom I loved with all the ardent passion of a fiery, impetuous youth; and was, I *fancied*, loved in return. Be this as it might, my passion for his sister he knew and encouraged; and this, as I said before, only added a stronger link to the chain of our friendship.

In age, Charles Huntly was my senior by nearly a year, and was now a little turned of twenty-one. In stature we were much alike—both being about five feet and ten inches, with regular proportions. In complexion we differed materially — he being light, with light curly hair; and I dark, with hair black and straight. In personal appearance my friend was remarkably handsome and prepossessing. His beauty did not consist in the mere perfection of features—though these were, in general, very fine—so much as in the play and expression of the whole countenance, where every thought seemed to make an instant and passing impression. His forehead was high and broad, and stamped with intellect, beneath which shone a bright, blue eye, that could sparkle with mirth, or flash with anger, as the case might be. The contour of his face was a something between the Grecian and Anglo-Saxon, though the nose was decidedly of the former cast. His skin—fine, smooth, and almost beardless—gave him an appearance so boyish that I was often mistaken for his senior by many years—a matter which generally irritated him not a little, as he had a strong repugnance to being thought effeminate. His temperament was strongly nervous. At heart he was truly noble and generous; but this, by those who did not know him intimately, was very frequently overlooked in his hot and hasty temper. None was more ready to resent an insult, or redress a wrong; and as he was very tenacious of his own honor, so was he of another's. If you insulted him, you must take the consequences, and they would not be slow to follow, unless ample apology were made, in which case his hand was ever open for friendship. If he did you a wrong, and became convinced of it, he could not rest until he had sued for pardon. He was wild at times in his notions, headstrong, hot-brained, and, in general, a great enthusiast. Whenever anything new took possession of his mind, it was the great all-in-all for the time being; but was very apt to pass away soon, and be supplied by something equally as great, and equally as evanescent.

Such, as I have just enumerated, were the striking points in the appearance and character of Charles Huntly; and though in the latter we were much alike, yet we seldom quarreled, and then only to make it up the next time we met.

Now, as Charles remarked, in language which I have already quoted, we had often, during our leisure moments, laid out plans of adventure for the future, when our collegiate course should be finished. But the plan of to-day had been always superseded by the one of to-morrow, so that, unless we resolved on something steadily, it was more than probable that the whole would result, simply, in speculating visions of the brain. The last proposition was, of course, the one which opens this chapter; and which had, perhaps, less weight with me at the moment, from my remembering the failure of all the others. Still, there was one thing in its its favor which none of the others had had. We had completed our studies now, and were at liberty, if we resolved on it, to carry our project into immediate execution, before it should become trite; and besides, nothing before had seemed so fully to meet the views of both in every particular. Adventure was our delight in every shape we could find it; as several powerful admonitions and premonitory warnings from our tutors, for various little peccadilloes—such as tying a calf to the bell rope, playing the ghost to old women, upsetting beehives, and robbing hen-roosts—might well attest. But there was, notwithstanding, a drawback, which made me hesitate when my friend interrupted me. He was of age, but I was not; and my father might not be willing to give his consent, without which I certainly would not venture. Another: I loved Lilian Huntly; and should I go and leave her, she might get married in my absence—a result which I felt was not to be endured.

While I sat, with my head upon my hand, buried in thought, rapidly running these things over in my mind, my companion stood watching me, as if to gather my decision from the expression of my countenance.

"Well, Frank," said he, at length, "it seems you have become very studious all a once. How long is it going to take you to decide on accepting so glorious a proposition?"

"How long since the idea of it entered your head?" I inquired.

"Ten, fifteen, ay, (looking at his watch) twenty minutes. I was down for the purpose of getting a hack, to take us over to the city, when the thought came across me like a flash of lightning, and I turned and hurried back, to ——"

"See me before you altered your mind," interrupted I, completing his sentence.

"Confound you, Frank—wait till I have done. I hurried back, I say, to let you share the bright prospect with me."

"Humph! prospect indeed!" said I, with a laugh, merely for the purpose of annoying him; for I saw, by his whole demeanor, that he was decidedly in earnest. "And a prospect it will ever remain, I am thinking, a long way ahead. You are joking, Charley, are you not?"

"No, by all the bright cupids of fairy realms, I swear to you, Frank, my dear fellow, I never was so serious about any thing in my life, since the time when I played the ghostly tin-pan drummer to the edification of old Aunt Nabby."

"But allowing you are in earnest, you have overlooked two important points in asking me to accompany you."

"Ha! what are they?"

"My father, and Lilian."

"Tut, tut, tut, Frank—don't be a fool!"

"That is exactly what I am trying to guard against, Charley. Shall I assist you a little?"

"Pshaw! stuff! nonsense!—what have your father and my sister to do with it?"

"Why, the first might refuse his consent to my going; and the last might consent to have my place filled in my absence."

"Well," answered Charley, "as to your father, I will pledge you my word that he will give his consent; and for Lilian, that she will await your return, if it be six years hence."

"You will?" cried I, jumping up so suddenly as to upset the table on to the toes of my companion; "you will pledge your word to this, Charley?"

"A plague on that table and your great haste!" muttered Huntly, hobbling about the room, and holding his bruised foot in his hand. "Yes, I will pledge you my honor to both, if you will say the word."

"Enough! here is my hand on it," I cried.

Down went the bruised foot, and the next moment I felt the bones of my fingers crack under the powerful pressure of those of my enthusiastic friend.

"Now, Frank," he almost shouted, capering about the room for joy, "you are pledged beyond a back-out."

"On condition you make your pledge good."

"I will do it or die."

"Then enough is said."

"Hurrah, then, for a hack!" cried Charles Huntly, darting out of my room and down a flight of stairs, to the imminent danger of his neck: "Hurrah for a hack! and ho! for the Rocky Mountains, Oregon, and the far, Far West!"

CHAPTER II.

PREPARATION—LOVE—JEALOUSY—SEPARATION AND DEPARTURE.

It was a clear, starlight evening in the month of May, that I found myself slowly nearing the fine mansion of Benjamin Huntly, to behold my sweet and dearly loved Lilian, perhaps for the last time. I felt strangely, as I had never felt before. A week had elapsed, and all had been arranged for my departure, at an early hour on the following morning. The consent of my parents had been reluctantly yielded to the powerful eloquence and soft persuasion of my enthusiastic friend. Already had my trunks been packed, and my purse filled, for the long separation. Already had I listened to the parental advice of my father, and seen the tears of sorrow in my beloved mother's eyes. The struggle of consent, but not of parting, was now over; and I was wending my way to the house of my friend, to take leave of one, at the thought of whom my heart ever beat rapidly. As I said before, I felt strangely. I was about to bid adieu—a long, perchance a last, adieu—to all the bright scenes of my childhood—to friends near and dear to me—to father and mother —and, last, though not least, to the idol of my purer thoughts.

It is hard, very hard, to leave the scenes of our youth for the first time—to venture forth, we scarce know whither, like a feather borne unconsciously upon the strongest current of air. However much we may plan in secret—however strikingly we may draw the pictures of adventure in the rosy colors of anticipation—however great may be our inclination to go and see the world for ourselves; yet when the time of separation comes—when we are about to cut the cord that binds us to all we have ever seen and loved—the heart grows sad, and soft, and we feel as if staggering under the weight of some impending calamity.

Thus I felt, and a great deal more which I cannot describe, as I paused for a moment upon the steps of Lilian Huntly's dwelling, to compose my agitated nerves and appear calm and collected. Why was it that my agitation should now only increase? Why could I never appear before her as before any other I had ever seen— cool and collected? Why must my heart always flutter so, and my usually free-coming words stick chokingly in my throat, or congeal upon my lips? Was it because I loved her? I would have given half my expected inheritance to talk to her freely as I could to others. I had often tried it, but in vain. I always made a fool of myself, and I knew it. I fancied Lilian knew it too; and this only added to my embarrassment. My heart and my self-esteem whispered me I was loved; but my bashful fears told me the contrary. I had never tested her, and now I was about to do it. If she loved me, she would plainly show it the moment of separation. I was shortly to be made happy or miserable, or miserably happy; for if she loved me, I should be happy in knowing it—unhappy in the thought of a long parting. I trembled as I thought, until my knees smote each other as did Belshazzar's.

At last, desperate effort, I assumed a courage I did not possess, and, ascending the steps, rang the bell. In another minute I was ushered into the parlor, and the servant who admitted me was already gone to summon my fair judge. I gazed around upon the beautiful paintings which adorned the walls, but without seeing them. I felt like a guilty culprit about to hear his doom. Could money, at that moment, have purchased me easy assurance, I would have had it at any price. I remained in suspense some five minutes, when the door opened and Lilian entered—entered like a fairy being into her golden realms.

Heavens! how lovely! I had never seen her, or ought else, look so enchantingly sweet before. In complexion and features, Lilian strongly resembled her brother—save that everything was more soft, more effeminate, more exquisitely beautiful. Her skin was fair, and clear as alabaster, with a slight tint of crimson upon each cheek. Her features were all of the finest mold. Her large, soft, clear blue eyes, were rendered extremely fascinating by long, drooping, delicately fringed lashes. In their depths was a soul of tender thought, feeling, and love; and, most joyful discovery! they were now swimming in tears. She loved me then, and had been weeping at the thought of my leaving her! The expression of her sweet countenance, too, was sad. Her plump, cherry lips were just parted, as if about to speak, displaying two rows of beautiful pearls. Her light hair was arranged *a la mode*, and a bright, glowing diamond sparkled on her forehead. Her exquisitely faultless form was arrayed in the emblem of purity, a snow-white dress, which almost made me fancy her an etherial, a spiritual visiter.

She advanced with a timid step, and held out her snowy, dimple hand. She tried to speak, but language failed her. I tried to do the same, with a like success. I made a step toward her, and her hand touched mine. Heavens! what emotions thrilled me! I was beside myself with the deepest joy I had ever felt. I forgot formality, caution, prudence, everything—and before I knew what I was about, or how I did it, my lips were pressed to hers. The pressure was returned, one moment, and then she sprang away, blushing and confused. Think what you may of it, reader, that was one of the happiest moments of my life.

I was the first to break the silence, and I trembled as I did so.

"I have come, Miss Lilian," I stammered, "to—to——"

"I understand," she murmured, faintly, sinking into a seat: while slowly the tears, that could not be suppressed, stole down her now pale cheeks: "I understand: I am about to lose a—a—brother, and a—a—friend."

Friend! heavens! how cold that word! It should be clipped by every lexicographer and sent out of existence! Friend! Why it chilled my blood, and for the moment made me an enemy of the language which harbored it. Was there, then, no other term —one a little more endearing?—and if so, why did she select one so cold!— Perhaps she meant it! Perhaps her grief was only for the loss of a brother, and—if I must use the hateful term—*a friend!* In that case she could not love me. I had once more made a fool of myself. But I would not do so again. I would let her see that I could be as indifferent as herself. She should not have cause to boast in after times—perhaps when wedded to another—how much I loved her, and how she pitied me. No! I would be cold as marble—ay! as a Lapland iceberg. These thoughts went through my mind rapidly; and scarcely a minute's pause succeeded, before I said, coolly enough, heaven knows:

"Yes, Miss Huntly, I have come to bid you a last farewell, and have but a few spare moments to do it in."

I looked at her indifferently as I spoke, and oh! what would I not have given to recall those words! Her soft, blue eyes turned full upon me, with a mingled expression of surprise and reproach, which I shall never forget. Her cheeks grew more deadly pale than ever; and her lips quivered, as she sighed, almost inaudibly, my name. There was no withstanding this; and on the impulse of the moment, I threw myself at her feet, and exclaimed:

"O, Lilian! sweet Lilian! I have wronged you. You love me, Lilian—you love me!"

She did not answer, but her look spoke volumes, as her eyes modestly sought the ground, and a slight flush beautifully tinted her cheeks. I seized her hand rapturously, and pressed it warmly. She did not return the pressure, neither did she seek to avoid it. I was in raptures, and I felt a soul of eloquence on my lips.

"I wronged you, Lilian," I said, passionately. "I thought you were cold-hearted, because you called me friend. But I was mistaken, I see! I was expecting a warmer term; but I had forgotten it was not your place to use it first. Lilian, dear Lilian—permit me so to call you—I am about to go far away; and God only knows when, if ever, I shall return. Pardon me, then, if I improve the present moments, and speak the sentiments of my heart. I have known you, Lilian, from a child; but I have known you only to love and adore. You have been the ideal of my boyish dreams, either sleeping or waking. The perfection of divine beauty, with me, has had but one standard—your own sweet, faultless face and form. Every happy thought of my existence, has some how had a connection with yourself. I could not picture happiness, without drawing you in glowing colors, the foremost and principal figure. I have thought of you by day, dreamed of you by night, for many years—have longed to be near you, have worshiped you in secret, and yet have never dared to tell you so till now. Whenever tempted to do wrong, your lovely face has been my Mentor, to chide and restrain me. I have loved you, Lilian—deeply, passionately, devotedly loved you, with the first, undefiled love of an ardent temperament—as I never can love another. I am about to leave, and I tell you this, and only ask if I am loved in return. Speak! let your sweet lips confirm what your looks have spoken, and I am the happiest of human beings!"

I ceased, and paused for an answer. While speaking, the head of the fair being at whose feet I kneeled, gradually, unconsciously as it were, sunk upon my shoulder, where it now reposed in all its loveliness. She raised her face, crimson with blushes and wet with tears. Her hand, still held in mine, trembled—and her lips, as she essayed to speak.

"O, Francis!" she at length articulated—then there came a silence.

"Say on, Lilian, and make me happy!"

"No, no!" she said, quickly, looking hurriedly around her, as if fearful of the presence of another. "No, no, Francis—not now—some other time."

"But you forget, dear Lilian, that I am about to leave you—that there may never be a time like the present! Only say you love me, fair one, and it is all I ask."

"But—but——" she stammered, and then paused.

"Ha! then I have after all mistaken friendship for love!" I returned, quickly, starting abruptly to my feet, and feeling some slight symptoms of indignation.

Again her soft, reproachful eye met mine, and every angry impulse vanished before its heavenly ray.

"You mistake me, Francis," she said.

"I—I——" another pause.

Again was I at her feet, ashamed of my hasty display of jealous temper.

"The word is trembling upon your lips, Lilian," I exclaimed; "speak it, and——"

At this moment, to my astonishment and chagrin, the door suddenly opened, and an elegantly dressed gentleman, some five or six years my senior, highly perfumed with the oil of roses and musk, took one step over the threshhold, and then, perceiving me, drew quickly back, evidently as much surprised and embarrassed as myself. Meantime, I had sprung to my feet, with a whirlpool of feelings in my breast, impossible to be described—the predominant of which were anger, mortification and jealousy. Lilian, too, had started up, and turned toward the stranger (stranger to me) with an embarrassed air.

"I crave pardon," said the intruder, coloring, "for my seeming rudeness in appearing thus unannounced. I found the outer door ajar, and made bold to step within, without ringing, not thinking to meet with any here save the regular members of the family."

"Then you must either be a constant visitor, or no gentleman, to take even that liberty," I rejoined in a sarcastic tone of some warmth.

The face of the intruder became as scarlet at my words, and his eyes flashed indignantly, as he replied, in a sharp, pointed tone:

"I *am* a regular visiter here, sir! but *your* face is new to me."

"Indeed!" I rejoined, with an expression of contempt, turning my eyes upon Lilian, as if for an explanation.

She was trembling with embarrassment, and her features alternately flushing and paling, like the rapid playings of an auroro borealis. She hastened to speak, to cover her confusion, and prevent, if possible, any further unpleasant remarks.

"This—this—is Mr. Wharton, Francis," she stammered: "a gentleman who calls here occasionally. Mr. Whar—Wharton, Mr. Leighton—an old friend of mine."

Of course the rules of good breeding required us to bow on being thus formally introduced to each other; and this we did, but very stiffly, and with an air of secret hate and defiance. That moment we knew ourselves to be rivals, and consequently enemies; for it was impossible there should be any love between us. As for myself, I was powerfully excited, and indignant beyond the bounds of propriety. Hasty, passionate, and jealous in my disposition, I was unfit to love any one; for to me,

"Trifles light as air,
Were confirmations strong as proofs of holy writ."

in consequence of which I only loved, to be miserable, and render the object loved equally so.

I exchanged no more words with Wharton, but turning to Lilian, I said, with all the coolness my boiling blood would allow:

"So, then, the riddle is solved. Had you been frank enough to have informed me that you expected *particular* company to-night, I should certainly, ere this, have ridden you of my presence."

"O, Francis," cried Lilian, with an imploring, reproachful look, from eyes moist with tears; "you are mistaken!—indeed, indeed you are!"

"O, yes, of course," I replied, bitterly, as I coolly drew on my glove, and prepared to take my final leave: "Of course I am, or *was*, mistaken; but I shall not be likely to be again immediately, I presume. Farewell, Miss Huntly!" I continued, coldly, rudely extending to her my gloved hand, "I shall probably never see you again, as I leave at an early hour in the morning."

O, what a look she gave me at that moment, of sweet, heart-touching, mournful reproach—a look which haunted me for days, for weeks, for months, for years—a look which, were I an artist, would peradventure be found upon every face I painted.

"Francis!" she gasped, and sunk fainting and colorless upon a seat.

This, in spite of my jealous feelings, touched me sensibly, and I was on the point of springing to her aid, when Wharton passed me for the purpose. I could stand no more—the devil was in me—and with a scarcely suppressed imprecation upon my lips, I rushed out of the apartment.

In the hall I met my friend Charles.

"Ha! Frank," he exclaimed, "you seem flurried. What has happened?"

"Ask me no questions," I replied, pointing with my finger to the apartment I had just quitted. "Give my kind regards to your parents, and bid them farewell for me."

"But stay a moment."

"No! I must go;" and I seized my hat and made for the door.

"All ready for the start in the morning. I suppose, Frank?"

"Ay, for to-night, if you choose," I replied, as I hurried down the steps leading to the street.

I paused a moment, as my feet touched the pavement, and as I did so, heard the voice of Huntly summoning the servants to the aid of his sister. I waited to hear no more, but darted away down the street, like a madman, scarcely knowing, and caring less, whither I went.

Such was my parting with Lilian Huntly.

At last I found my way home, and softly stealing to my chamber, threw myself upon the bed—but not to sleep. I slept none that night. My brain was like a heated furnace. I rolled to and fro in the greatest mental torture I had ever endured.

Morn came at last, and with it Charles Huntly, all prepared for the journey. I ate a morsel, pointed out my trunks, sighed a farewell to my parents, jumped into the carriage, and was whirled away with great rapidity.

Charles looked pale and sad, and was not loquacious. I wanted him to talk—to speak of Lilian—but he carefully avoided any allusion to her. I was dying to know how he left her, but would not question him on the subject. I inquired how he left the family, however, and he replied:

"Indifferently well."

"Well," sighed I, to myself, "she loves another, so why should I care?"

Half-past seven, and the rushing, rolling, rumbling cars, were bearing us swiftly away. Fifteen minutes more, and the city of our nativity had faded from our view, perhaps forever.

We were speeding onward—thirty miles per hour—westward ho! for Oregon.

CHAPTER III.

REFLECTIONS — THE GREAT METROPOLIS — THE WORLD IN MINIATURE — THE NATIONAL THEATER — ALARM — FIRE — AWFUL PERIL — PROVIDENTIAL ESCAPE, ETC.

Steamboats and railroads! what mighty inventions! With what startling velocity they hurry us along, until even the overcharged mind almost feels it lacks the power to keep pace with their progress. Whoever has passed over the Boston and Providence route to New York, will understand me. One mile-post succeeds another with a rapidity almost incredible; and ere he, who travels it for the first time, is aware that half the distance is completed, he finds himself in view of the capital of old Rhode Island.

So it was with myself. I had never been from home, and knew little of the speed with which the adventurer is carried across this mighty continent. I had heard men speak of it, it is true; but I had never realized it till now. Perhaps I was longer on the road than I imagined. When the heart is full, we take but little note of external objects, or the flight of time — time which is bearing us to the great ocean of eternity. My mind was oppressed and busy. I was thinking of home, of fond parents I had left behind, and all the joys of childhood, which I could never witness again. A thousand things, a thousand scenes, which I had never thought of before, now crowded my brain with a vividness that startled me. They were gone now — forever gone! I had bid them a last adieu. With one bold leap, I had thrown off youth and become a man — a man to think and act for myself. My collegiate days, too, were over — days which memory now recalled with sad and painful feelings.

True, my playmate, my fellow student, my chum, my *friend*, was by my side. But he, too, was sad and thoughtful. He, too, was thinking of home and friends, the domestic happy fireside, and all that he had left behind. His wonted gaiety, his great flow of spirits, his enthusiasm, were gone; and he was silent now — dumb as a carved image in marble.

I gazed upon him, and my thoughts grew heavier, sadder. He was now so like Lilian — sweet, loved, but ah! discarded Lilian! How could I avoid thinking of her, when I gazed upon the pale, sad features of her only brother! I *did* think of her; of how I had left her; and now that miles were gaining between us, I bitterly accused myself of injustice. Why did I leave her so abruptly, and in such a condition? My heart smote me, I had wronged her — wronged her at the moment of parting, and put reparation out of my power. Why had I done so? Why did I not part with her as a friend? If she did not love me, it was not her fault, and I had no right to abuse her. I had acted hastily, imprudently, unjustly. I knew it — I *felt* it — felt it keenly; and, oh! what would I not have sacrificed for one, even one, moment with her, to sue for pardon. Alas! alas! my reflections on my conduct had come too late — too late.

Thus I thought, and thus I felt, while time and progress were alike unnoted, uncared for. What cared I now for time? what cared I now for speed? My mind was a hell of torture almost beyond endurance, and I only sought to escape myself, but sought in vain.

"Passengers for the steamboat," were the first sounds that aroused me from a painful reverie.

I looked up with a start, and lo! I was in the heart of the city, and hundreds were round me. The cars had ceased their motion, and one destination was gained. At first I could not credit my senses. There must be some mistake — we were in the wrong city! But I was soon convinced of my error; and found, alas! that all was too truly, too coldly correct; for on the impulse of the moment, I had counted on a return to my native soil, and — and — I will not say what else.

I roused my friend, who also looked wonderingly about him as if suddenly awakened from a dream, and heaved a long, deep sigh — a dirge to buried scenes and friends away. Mechanically we entered a carriage, were hurried to the boat, and soon were gliding over the deep blue waters of Long Island Sound.

Early the next morning I beheld, for the first time, the lofty spires of that great Babylon of America, ycleped New York. What a place of business, bustle, and confusion! What hurrying to and fro! What rushing, scrambling, crowding, each bent on his own selfish end, and caring nothing for his neighbor, but all for his neighbor's purse! How cold the faces of the citizens seem to a stranger! There are no welcome smiles — no kind greetings — all are wrapped up in their own pursuits: and he feels at once, although surrounded by thousands, that he is now indeed alone, without a friend, save such as can be *bought*.

On the ocean, on the prairie, or in the forest, man is not alone; he does not feel alone; for he is with Nature in all her wildness—in all her beauty; and she ever has a voice, which reaches his inner heart, and, in sweet companionship, whispers him to behold her wonders, and through her look up to the Author of all—her God and his! But in the great city it is different—vastly different. Here all is artificial, studied, and cold; and as we gaze upon the thousands that throng the streets, and mark the selfish expressions on the faces of each, we feel an inward loathing, a disgust for mankind, and long to steal away to some quiet spot and commune with our own thoughts in silence.

Such were my reflections, as the rumbling vehicle whirled me over the pavements to that prince of hotels, (in name and wealth at least) the Astor House. True, I had been born and brought up in a city; but still these matters had never forced themselves so strongly upon my mind as now. I was a stranger in a strange city, and, with my otherwise misanthropic feelings, I doubly felt them in all their force.

The window of the apartment assigned me at the Astor House, looked out upon that world-renowned thoroughfare, Broadway. Dinner over, I seated myself at the casement and gazed forth. What a world in miniature was spread before my eyes! What a whirlpool of confusion and excitement! Before me, a little to my left, was the Park—its trees beautifully decorated with the flowers and leaves of spring, and its many winding walks thronged with human beings. From out its center rose the City Hall—the hall of justice. Along one side ran Broadway—along the other, Park Row, but shooting off at an angle from the main thoroughfare of the former—both crowded with carriages of all descriptions, from the splendid vehicle of fashion, with its servants in livery, and its silver-trimmed harness, down to the common dray — crowded with footmen, from the prince to the beggar, all hurrying and jostling together. Here sauntered the lady and gentleman of fashion, robed in the most costly apparel money could procure, bedecked with diamonds and gold, sapphire and ruby; there, side by side, on the same pavement, almost touching them, stroled the poor, forlorn, pale-faced, hollow-eyed mendicant, partially clothed in filthy rags, and perhaps actually dying for a morsel of food. Great Heaven! what a comment on humanity!

I have mentioned only the extremes; but fancy both sexes—of all grades, sizes, and nations between—and you have a picture which no city on the American continent save New York can present.

The evening found my friend and myself at the National Theatre—then new, splendidly decorated, and in successful operation. It was crowded almost to suffocation with the *elite* of the city. Rounded arms and splendid busts, set off with jewels—rosy cheeks, and sparkling eyes, were displayed on every hand, by the bewitching light of magnificent glass-tasselled chandeliers. But of these I took little note. My attention was fixed upon the play. It was that impassioned creation of Shakspeare, Romeo and Juliet. My mind was just in a condition to feel the burning words of the lovers in all their force; and I concentrated my whole soul upon it, listened every word, watched every motion, to the exclusion of everything else. The first and second acts were already over, and the last scene of the third, the parting between the lovers, was on the stage. A breathless silence reigned around. Every eye was fixed upon the players—every head inclined a little forward, to catch the slightest tones of the speakers. Already had the ardent and unfortunate Romeo sighed the tender words:

"Farewell! I will omit no opportunity
That may convey my greetings, love, to thee;"

and the answer of Juliet,

"O, think'st thou, we shall ever meet again?"

was even trembling on her lips—when, suddenly, to the consternation and horror of all, there arose the terrific cry of,

"Fire! fire!—the theatre is on fire!"

Heavens! what a scene ensued—and what feelings came over me! Never shall I forget either. In a moment all was frightful confusion, as each sought to gain the street. Startling shrieks, appalling yells, and hideous groans, resounded on all sides. Hundreds, I might say thousands, rushed pell-mell to the doors, to escape the devouring element, which, already lapping the combustible scenery, was seen shooting upward its lurid tongues, and heard hissing, and snapping, and crackling, in its rapid progress over the devoted building. I grasped the arm of my friend, and cried: "Rush, Charley, for your life!" and sprang forward.

The next moment I felt myself seized from behind, and the voice of my friend shouted in my ear:

"Hold! Frank—we must save her!"

"Whom?"

"Yonder! See! they have crowded her back!—and now—great God! she has fallen over into the pit!"

I looked in the direction indicated by the finger of Huntly, and beheld a beautiful female, vainly struggling to reach the door. As he spoke, a sudden rush forward crowded her back to the railing which divided her from the excited mass of beings in the pit. One moment she balanced on the railing, and the next, with a cry of terror, fell upon the heads of those below. At any other time she would have been cared for; but now all were wild with terror, and thought only of themselves; and instead of seeking to aid, they allowed her to sink under their feet. Save my friend and I, no one seemed to heed her. With a cry of horror, I leaped forward to rescue her from a horrible death. But my friend was already before me. One bound, and Charles Huntly was among the wedged mass below, and exerting all his strength to reach the prostrate form of the lady, who was now being trod to death under the feet of the rushing multitude. I would have sprang over the railing myself, but I saw it would be useless; one was better than two; and I paused and watched the progress of my friend with an anxiety better imagined than described.

So dense was the mass, so closely wedged, that for a time all the efforts of Huntly to reach the unfortunate creature were vain; while the glaring light, and the roar of the flames, as they eagerly leaped forward to the dome over head, rendered the scene truly dismal and awful.

At length the crowd grew thinner, as it poured through the open doorway; and renewing his exertions, my friend shortly gained the side of the unknown. He stooped down to raise her, and I trembled for his safety, for I saw numbers fairly pressing upon him. With a Herculean effort, that must have exhausted all his animal powers, I beheld him rise to his feet, with the fair unknown seemingly lifeless in his arms. I uttered a cry of joy, as he staggered toward me with his burden.

"Quick! quick! this way—give her here!" I shouted, bending over the railing and extending my arms toward her.

Huntly staggered forward, and the next moment my grasp was upon her, and she was in my arms.

"Fly! Frank—fast—for God's sake! and give her air!" gasped Huntly, in a faint, exhausted tone.

I cast one glance at her pale, lovely features, on which were a few spots of blood, from a contusion on the head, and then darted over the benches to the door, bidding my friend follow, but looking not behind.

The boxes were now empty, and the doors but slightly blocked, so that I had little difficulty, to use a stage expression, in making my exit. The street, however, was crowded with those just escaped, and others attracted hither by the alarm of fire. All was excitement and dismay. Parents were rushing to and fro, seeking their children—children their parents; wives and maidens their husbands and lovers, and vice versa.

I pushed my way through the crowd as best I could, with my lovely burden in my arms, and at length reached the opposite side-walk, where I paused to rest, and, if possible, to restore the fair one to consciousness. As I began chafing her temples, I heard a female voice shriek, in agonizing tones:

"Good God! will no one save my child — my only child — my daughter, — the idol of my heart!"

I looked around me, and beheld, by the light of the burning building, a middle-aged female, richly clad, only a few paces distant, violently wringing her hands, in mental agony, and looking imploringly, first at the already trembling structure, and then into the faces of the bystanders, as if in search of an answer to her heart-rending appeal.

"Oh God! oh God! save her! save her! — she must not, shall not die! I will give a thousand dollars for her life!"

A thought struck me. Perhaps she was the mother of the senseless being I held; and instantly I raised her in my arms and darted forward.

"Is this your daughter, lady?" I cried, as I came up.

She looked wildly about her — one painful glance — and then, with a shriek, sprang to and threw her arms around the fair creature's neck, and burst into tears.

"God! I thank thee!" were the first articulate words from her now quivering lips. "I have got my daughter again!" and snatching her from my arms, she pressed kiss after kiss upon her lips, with all the wild, passionate fondness of a mother. "Ha! is she dead?" she cried, with a look of horror, appealing to me.

"Only fainted," was my reply, made at a venture, for I dared not confirm my own fears.

"Yes! yes! God be praised! — I see! I see! She is returning to consciousness. But this blood — this wound?"

"A slight fall," I answered.

"And you, sir — you? I promised a thousand dollars. Here is part, and my card. Call to-night, or to-morrow, at —— (I failed to catch the name) and the balance shall be yours."

"I did not save her for money; in fact, I did not save her at all — it was my friend," I replied, taking from her extended hand the card, but refusing the purse which it also held.

"And where is your friend?" she asked, breathlessly.

Heavens! what a shock her words produced! Where was my friend, indeed! I looked hurriedly around, among the swaying multitude, but saw nothing of Charles Huntly. A terrible thought seized me. Perhaps he had not made his escape! I cast one glance at the burning pile, and, to my consternation, beheld the flames already bursting from the roof. Had he escaped? — and if not! — great God, what a thought! I waited to say, to hear no more, but turned and rushed into the swaying mass, shouting the name of my schoolmate. No answer was returned. I shouted louder — but still heard not his well known voice. Great God! what feelings came over me! — pen cannot describe them. Onward, onward, still I pressed onward, and shouted at every step — but, alas! no answer.

At length I reached the door of the theatre leading to the boxes. It was filled with smoke, passing outward, through which I could catch glimpses of the devouring flames, and hear their awful roar. One pause — an instant only — and with his name upon my lips, I darted into the shaking building. I gained the boxes, and found the heat of the flames almost unbearable. They had already reached the railing nearest the stage, and overhead had eaten through the roof, from which burning cinders were dropping upon the blazing benches in the pit. The smoke was stifling, and I could scarcely breathe. I looked down where I had last seen my friend, and beheld a dark object on the floor. I called Huntly by name, in a voice of agony. Methought the object stirred, and I fancied I heard a groan. The next moment I was in the pit, bending over the object. Gracious God! it was Huntly! From some cause he had not been able to escape. Instantly I raised him in my arms, and, with a tremendous effort, threw him into the boxes. I attempted to follow, but failed. The smoke was proving too much for me, and the heat becoming intense. Again I tried, with like success. I began to feel dizzy, and faint, and thought I was perishing. I sank back and looked up at the roof. I could see it trembling. A few moments, and it would be upon me. God of Heaven! what a death!

At this moment of despair, I felt a current of air rushing in upon me. It revived me, and I made a third attempt to clamber into the boxes. Joy! joy! I succeeded. I caught hold of Charles, and, with my remaining strength, dragged him to the door, and into the open air. Some five or six persons now rushed to my assistance, and in another moment I had gained the opposite side of the street. As I did so, I heard a thundering noise behind me. I turned quickly round, and no pen can describe my feelings when I understood the cause. The roof of the building had fallen in, and bright sheets of flame, and burning cinders, were shooting upward on the dark pall of the arching heavens. I had just escaped with my life; and if ever I uttered a prayer of sincere gratitude to the Author of my being, it was then.

As I stood gazing upon the remainder of the structure, I saw the walls totter; and ere I had time to move from the spot, the front wall went down, with a thundering sound, and lay a pile of smoking ruins—a part falling inward, and a part outward. The heat was now excessive; and as I sought to bear my unconscious friend further from the fire, the side walls plunged inward, leaving only the back wall standing. This now seemed to waver—totter—and then, great Heaven! it fell outward, upon an adjoining building, crushing in the roof, and, as I afterward learned, killing one of its inmates almost instantly.

By this time Huntly had begun to revive, and in a few minutes he was perfectly restored—the smoke and his exertions, only, having overcome him. He stared around him for a moment in wonder, and then seemed to comprehend all. Grasping my hand, with a nervous pressure, he exclaimed:

"Thank God! we are all saved; though I thought all was over with me. I see, dear Frank, I owe all to you. But the lady, Frank?"

"I left her safe in the arms of her mother."

"Thank God, again, for that! But who is she? and where does she live?" and I felt the grasp of Charles tighten upon my arm.

"I know neither; but I have her mother's card here."

"Quick! quick! give it me!" cried Huntly, with an impatience that surprised me.

But I was mistaken; I had not the card, it was lost; and with it, all clue to the persons in question. With an expression of deep and painful disappointment, my friend turned away.

"But we may yet find them," I said; "they were here a few minutes since"

"Where, Frank—where?"

"Yonder;" and I hastened to the spot where I had left them; but to the disappointment of myself, as well as Huntly they were gone.

I made inquiries of all around, but nobody had seen, or knew any thing of them.

"Always my luck, Frank," said Huntly, with a sigh; and jumping into a hack, we were shortly set down at the steps of the Astor.

That night I dreamed of fire—of rescuing Lilian Huntly from the flames.

Early the next morning we were once more upon our long journey — swiftly speeding toward the far, Far West.

———o———

CHAPTER IV.

THE OHIO — THE HIBERNIAN — ARRIVAL IN CINCINNATI—A FIRE—A FIGHT—NARROW ESCAPE—THE JOURNEY RESUMED.

It was a calm, beautiful day, that found myself and friend on the hurricane deck of a magnificent steamer, and gliding swiftly down the calm, silvery waters of that winding, lovely, and romantic stream, the Ohio, or La Belle Riviere. We had passed through Philadelphia, Baltimore, and Pittsburgh, without stopping, and were now speeding over the waters of this river on our journey to the Far West. Never had I seen a stream before so fascinating in all its attractions. On my right was the State of Ohio—on my left, those of Virginia and Kentucky; and on either hand, beautiful villages, farms, and pleasure grounds, with tree, blade, and flower in the delightful bloom of a pleasant spring. Here was a hill clothed with trees, reaching even to, overhanging, and mirroring their green forms in the glassy tide; there a smiling plain, stretching gracefully away from the river's bank, teeming with the growing products of the husbandman; while yonder a beautiful lawn, anon a village, or a pleasant farmhouse, rendered the whole scene picturesque and lovely beyond description.

The longer I gazed, the more I felt my spirits revive, until I began to resume something of the joyousness of by-gone days. A similar effect I could perceive was beginning to tell upon my friend. The first keen pang of leaving home was becoming deadened. We were now in a part of the world abounding with everything delightful, and felt that our adventures had really begun. We thought of home and friends occasionally, it is true; but then it was only occasionally; and mingling with our feelings, were thoughts of the present and glorious anticipations for the future. We were strong, in the very prime of life, and bound on a journey of adventure, where everything being entirely new, was calculated to withdraw our minds from the scenes we had bid adieu. The future is always bright to the imagination of the young and inexperienced; and we looked forward with delight to scenes on and beyond the broad and mighty prairies of the west.

"Well, Frank," said Huntly, at length, with something of his former light-hearted air, "what think you of this?"

"It is superlatively beautiful," I exclaimed, with enthusiam.

"I agree with you there, Frank," he replied; "but then this will all sink into insignificance, when we come to behold what lies beyond the bounds of civilization. O, I am in raptures with my journey. What a beautiful land is this West! I do not wonder that emigration sets hitherward, for it seems the Paradise of earth."

"Ay, it does indeed."

"But I say, Frank, there is one thing we have overlooked."

"Well, Charley, what is it?"

"Why, we must engage a servant to look after our baggage; and so let us employ one with whom we can have a little sport. I am dying for a hearty laugh."

"But that may not be so easy to do," said I.

"Pshaw! don't you believe a word of it. Now I have been standing here for the last ten minutes, laying my plans, and if you have no objection, I will try and put them in operation."

"None at all," I returned; "but let me hear them first."

"Do you see that fellow yonder, Frank?" pointing to a rather green-looking specimen of the Emerald Isle.

"I do. Well?"

"Well, I am going to try him; so come along and see the result;" and with this Huntley strode to the stern of the boat, where the son of Erin was standing, with his arms crossed on his back, gazing around him with an air of wondering curiosity.

He was a rare specimen of a Paddy, and bore all the marks of fresh importation. His coat was a wool-mixed gray, with bright metal buttons, and very short skirts. His pants were made of a greenish fustian, the upper portion of which barely united with a very short vest. Heavy brogans encased his feet, and a hat, with a rim of an inch in width, all the worse for wear, beneath which his sandy hair came low upon his brow, covered his head. A large mouth, pug nose, ruddy cheeks, and bright, cunning gray eyes, denoted him daring, witty, and humorous. In fact, he was Paddy throughout, dress and all; and being a strong, hearty fellow, was just the one to suit us.

"Well, Pat, a handsome country, this," said Huntly, in a familiar tone, as he came up to him.

"Troth, now, ye may well say that same, your honor, barring the name of Pat, which isn't mine at all, at all, but simply Teddy O'Lagherty jist," replied the Hibernian, with great volubility, in the real, rolling Irish brogue, touching his hat respectfully.

"Beg pardon, Teddy—though I suppose it makes little difference to you what name you get?"

"Difference, is it, ye're spaking of? To the divil wid ye now, for taking me for a spalpeen! D'ye be afther thinking, now, I don't want the name that me mother's grandfather, that was a relation to her, barring that he was'nt her grandfather at all, but only her daddy, give me?"

"O, well then, never mind—I will call you Teddy," said Charles, laughing, and winking at me. "But I say, Teddy, where are you bound?"

"Bound, is it, ye're asking? Och! I'm not bound at all, at all—but frae as the biped of a chap ye calls a toad, that St. Pathrick (blissings on his name!) kicked out o' ould Ireland, for a baastly sarpent, an' it was."

"Did St. Patrick wear brogans when he kicked the toad so far?" asked Huntly, gravely.

"Brogans!" cried Teddy, with a comical look of surprise, that any one should be so ignorant: "Brogans, ye spalpeen!—beg pardon! your honor I mane—why he was a saint, a howly saint, ye divil—beg pardon! your honor—and didn't naad the hilp of kivering to kaap the crathurs from biting him."

"O, yes," said Huntly, feigning to recollect; "I remember now, he was a saint; and of course he could kick anybody, or anything, whether bare-footed or shod."

"He could do that same—could St. Pathrick," replied the Irishman; "and as asy too, as your honor could be afther swollering a paaled praty, barring the shoking if yees didn't chaw it handsomely."

"A fellow of infinite jest; I like him much," said Huntly to me, aside, with a smile. "I must secure him—eh, Frank?"

"Certainly, by all means," I replied, in the same manner; "for his like we ne'er may see again."

"But if you are not bound, Teddy," continued Huntly, addressing the Irishman, "pray tell me whither you are going?"

"Faith, now, ye've jist axed a question which meself has put to Teddy O'Lagherty more'n fifty times, without gitting a single straight answer."

"Then I suppose you are, like us, on a journey of adventure."

"It's like I may be, for a divil of a thing else me knows about it."

"Would you like to get employment?"

"Would a pig like to ate his supgher, or a nager like to stael?" answered Teddy, promptly.

"How would you like to engage with us now?"

"Truth, I've done many a worse thing, I'm thinking, your honor."

"No doubt of it, Teddy."

"But what d'ye want of me, your honor?—and where to go?—for I'm liking travel, if it's all the same to yees."

"So much the better, for we are bound on a long journey;" and Charles proceeded to explain our intentions, and in what capacity the other would be wanted.

"Och!" cried Teddy, jumping up and cracking his heels with delight, to our great amusement; "it's that same I'd be afther saaking, if ye'd a axed me what I wanted."

"Think you can shoot Indians, eh Teddy?"

"Shoot, is it? Faith, I can shoot any thing that flies on two legs. Although I sez it myself, what shouldn't, but let me mother for me, I'm the greatest shooter ye iver knew, I is."

"Indeed! I am glad to hear it, Teddy, for I presume we shall have plenty of shooting to do. But what did you ever kill, Teddy?"

"Kill, is it? Troth, now, ye're afther heading me wid your cunning."

"Well, then, what did you shoot?"

"A two-legged bir-r-d, your honor."

"Well, you killed it, of course?"

"Killed it! Agh! now ye're talking. Faith, it wouldn't die. I shot it as plain as daylight, right fornenst the back-bone of its spine; and would ye belave it, divil of a shot touched it at all, at all—the ugly baast that it was."

"Well, well, Teddy, I think you will do," said Huntly, laughing; and forthwith he proceeded to close the bargain with the Irishman.

Our trip proved very delightful, and in due time we arrived at Cincinnati, where it was our design to spend at least a day. It was a beautiful morning, when we rounded the first bend above the city, and beheld the spires of this great western mart glittering in the sunbeams. The levee we found lined with boats, and crowded with drays, hacks, and merchandise; and every thing bespoke the life and briskness of immense trade. Taking rooms at the Broadway Hotel, we sauntered forth to view the city, and evening found us well pleased with our day's ramble.

It was about eleven o'clock on the night succeeding our arrival, that, having returned from a concert, we were preparing to retire to rest, when the alarm of fire, accompanied by a bright light, which shone in at our windows, attracted our attention.

"Ha! here is another adventure, Charley," I exclaimed, replacing my coat, which I was in the act of taking from my shoulders. "Come, once more forth, and let us see what we can discover that is new and startling—for to-morrow, you know, we leave."

"Not to-night, Frank," answered Huntly, yawning and rubbing his eyes. "I'-faith, man, I've seen enough of fire to last me for a long time; and O, (yawning again) I am so sleepy."

"Then I will go alone."

"Well, go; for myself, I'll to bed and dream about it. But I say, Frank," pursued Huntly, as I was on the point of quitting the room, "have you secured your pistols about you?"

"No."

"You had better."

"Pshaw! I do not want them: I am not going to fight."

"Nevertheless you had better go armed, in a strange place like this."

"Nonsense," I replied, closing the door, and hurrying down a flight of stairs, and into the street.

A thought struck me, that I would take Teddy along; but upon second consideration I resolved to go alone.

There was but little difficulty in finding the fire, for a bright flame, shooting upward on the dark canopy above, guided me to it. Passing up Broadway to Sixth street, I turned down some four or five squares, and discovered the fire to proceed from an old, two-story wooden building, which had been tenanted by two or three families of the poorer class. At the moment when I arrived, four engines were in active play, and some two or three others preparing to join them. The water was not thrown upon the burning building—for that was already too far gone—but upon one or two others that nearly joined, which were smoking from the heat. Many household articles had been thrown into the street, and these were surrounded by the fire-watch; while an Irishman and his wife, with a daughter of sixteen, were running to and fro, and lamenting in piteous tones the loss of their home and property.

"Och! howly mither of Mary! was the like on't iver saan?" cried the matron, some forty-five years of age, whose tidy dress bespoke her a rather thrifty housewife.

"Niver, since the flood," blubbered her husband, dolefully.

"What an' invention is fire!" again cried the mother.

"Tirrible crathur it is," rejoined the daughter.

"Och, honey, don't be despairing now!" said a voice, which I fancied I recognized; and turning toward the speaker, to my astonishment I beheld Teddy, in the laudable act of consoling the afflicted damsel.

"Teddy!" I shouted.

"Here, your honor," returned the Hibernian, looking around in surprise, and advancing to me with an abashed air.

"What are you doing here, Teddy?" I continued. "I thought you were at the hotel, and asleep."

"Faith! and it's like I thought the same of your honor, barring the slaap," rejoined the Irishman, scratching his head. "I seed the fire, your honor, and I thought as maybe there'd be some females that'd naad consoling; and so, ye see, I gathered meself hitherward, as fast as me trotters would let me."

"And so you make it your business to console females, eh?" I asked, with a smile which I could not repress.

"Faith, now," answered Teddy, "if it's all the same to yourself, your honor, I'm a female man, barring the dress they wears."

"Well, well," said I, laughing outright in spite of myself, "go on in your good work—but mind you are at your post betimes in the morning, or you will be left behind."

"It's meself that'll not forgit that same," answered the other, as he turned away to rejoin the party in distress, and add his consolation.

At this moment I felt myself rudely jostled from behind; and, turning quickly round, found myself hemmed in by a crowd, in which two men were fighting. I endeavored to escape, and, in doing so, accidentally trod on the foot of a stranger, who turned furiously upon me, with:

"What in —— (uttering an oath) do you mean?"

"An accident," said I, apologetically. "You're a liar!" he rejoined; "you did it a purpose."

I never was remarkable for prudence at any time, or I should have been more cautious on the present occasion. But the insulting words of the stranger made my young blood boil, until I felt its heat in my face. Without regard to consequences, and ere the words had fairly escaped his lips, I struck him a blow in the face, so violent that he fell back upon the ground.

"Another fight!" cried a dozen voices at once: "Another fight! hurrah!"

In a moment I regretted what I had done, but it was too late. I would have escaped, but the crowd had now formed around me so dense, that escape was impossible. Besides, my antagonist, regaining his feet, his face covered with blood, was now advancing upon me furiously. There was no alternative; and watching my opportunity as he came up, I dexterously planted the second blow exactly where I had the first, and down he went again.

"A trump, by ——!" "Give it to him, stranger!" "He's a few!" were some of the expressions which greeted me from the delighted bystanders.

But I had a short time to enjoy my triumph—if such a display of animal powers may be termed a triumph—for the next moment I beheld my adversary again approaching, but more warily than before, and evidently better prepared for the combat. I was not considered a bad pugilist for one of my age, nor did I in general fear one of my race; but as I gazed upon my advancing foe, I will be frank to own that I trembled for the result. He was a powerfully built man, six feet in stature, had a tremendous arm, and an eye that would quail before nothing mortal.

"By ——! young chap," he exclaimed, as he came up, "you've done what nobody else has of latter years. Take that, and see how you'll like it;" and with the word he threw all his strength into a blow, that fell like a sledge hammer.

I saw it, and prepared to ward it. I did so, partially, but its force broke my guard, and his double-jointed fist alighting upon my head, staggered me back and brought me to my knees. With all the suppleness I was master of, I sprang to my feet, only to receive another blow, which laid me out upon the flinty pavement. For a moment I was stunned and confused; but regaining my senses and feet, I prepared to renew the contest.

"I say, stranger," said my antagonist, motioning his hand for a parley, "you're good blood, but you haint got quite enough of the metal to cope with me. You're only a boy yit, and so just consider yourself licked, and go home, afore I git cantankerous and hurt you a few."

But I was not in a condition to take his advice. True, I was bruised and fatigued, and should have rested satisfied to let the affair end thus. But my worst passions had now got the better of my reasoning powers. I fancied I had been insulted, disgraced, and that nothing but victory or death could remove the stigma. I saw some of the spectators smile, and some look pityingly upon me, and this decided my course of action. My temper rose, my eyes flashed, and my cheeks burned, as I thought of the insulting words of the other.

"Some men live by bullying," I replied, pointedly; "and I suppose *you* are one of them; if not, you will keep your advice till one of us is the victor."

My opponent looked upon me with a mingled expression of surprise and rage.

"Fool!" he cried, "do you dare me again to the fight? By ——! I'll whip you this time or die!"

"Make your words good," I retorted, springing forward, and pretending to aim a blow at his head.

He prepared to ward it, and, in doing so, left his abdomen unguarded. He saw his mistake, but too late to retrieve it; for instead of striking with my fist, I only made a feint, and doubling with great dexterity, took him with my head just below the pit of the stomach, and hurled him over backward upon the ground. He threw out his hand, caught me as he fell, and drew me upon him.

Now came the contest in earnest. I had a slight advantage in being uppermost, but how long it would last was doubtful, for throwing his arms around, he strove to turn me. I seized him by the throat, and clung there with the tenacity of a drowning man to a rope. He made a desperate effort to bring me under, but still I maintained my position. The force of my grasp now began to tell upon him. He strangled, and I could sensibly perceive he was growing weaker. At length, just as I was about to relax my hold, for fear of choking him to death, he suddenly threw up one hand, buried it in my hair, twined a long lock around his finger, and the next moment placed his thumb to my eye, with a force that seemed to start the ball from its socket.

Great Heaven! what a feeling of horror came over me! I was about to lose an eye—be disfigured for life. Death, I fancied, was preferable to this; and instantly releasing his throat, I seized his hand with both of mine. This was exactly what he desired; and the next moment I found myself whirled violently upon my back on the rough pavement, and my antagonist uppermost. I attempted to recover my former advantage, but in vain. My adversary was by far too powerful a man. Grasping my throat with one hand, with such a pressure that everything began to grow dark, he partly raised himself, planted a knee upon my breast, and with the other hand drew a long knife. I just caught a glimmer of the blade, as he raised it to give me a fatal stab; but I was too exhausted and overmastered to make any resistance; and I closed my eyes in despair, and felt that all was over.

Suddenly I heard the voice of Teddy, shouting:

"To the divil wid ye, now, for a blathing spalpeen, that ye is!" and at the same moment I felt the grasp of my opponent leave my throat, and his weight my body.

With my remaining strength I rose to a sitting posture, and saw Teddy dancing around me, flourishing a hickory shelaleh over his head in the scientific manner of his countrymen, and whooping, shouting, and cursing, in a way peculiar to himself.

By some means he had been made aware of my danger, and, like a noble fellow, had rushed into the crowd and felled my adversary, with a blow so powerful that he still lay senseless upon the ground.

"And who are you, that dares thus to interfere?" cried a voice in the crowd, which found immediate echo with a dozen others.

"Who am I, ye blaggards?" roared Teddy: "Who should I be but a watchman, ye dirthy scull-mullions, yees!— Come," he cried, seizing me by the collar, "ye'll git a lock-up the night for this blaggard business of disturbing the slumbers of honest paaple afore they've gone to bid, jist."

I saw his ruse at once, and determined to profit by it, and make my escape. To do this, I pretended, of course, that I was not the aggressor, and that it was very hard to be brought up before the Mayor for a little harmless fun.

"Harmless fun!" roared the cunning Irishman. "D'ye call it harmless fun, now, to have your throat cut, ye scoundrel? Come along wid ye!" and he pretended to jerk me through the crowd, which gave way before him.

We had just got fairly clear of the mass, when we heard voices behind us shouting:

"Stop 'em! stop 'em!—he's no watch."

"Faith, they're afther smelling the joke whin it's too late," said Teddy. "But run, your honor, or the divils will be howld of us."

I needed no second prompting; and with the aid of the Irishman, who partially supported me—for I was still weak—I darted down a dark and narrow street. For a short distance we heard the steps of pursuers behind us, but gradually one after another gave up the chase, until at last we found our course left free.

It would be impossible for me to picture the joy I felt at my escape, or my gratitude toward my deliverer. Turning to the Irishman, I seized his hand, while my eyes filled with tears.

"Teddy," I said, "you have saved my life, and I shall not soon forget it."

"Troth, your honor," replied Teddy, with a comical look, "it was wor-r-th presarving—for it's the best and ounly one yees got."

I said no more, but silently slipped a gold coin into his hand.

"Howly mother! how smooth it makes a body's hands to be buithered," observed the Irishman, as he carefully hid the coin in his pocket.

Deep was the sympathy of Huntly for

me, when arrived at the hotel, I detailed what had occurred in my absence; and as deep his gratitude to the preserver of my life.

"Frank," he exclaimed, grasping my hand, "henceforth you go not alone, in the night, in a strange city."

The next day, though stiff and sore from my bruises, I found myself gliding down the Ohio on a splendid steamer, bound for St. Louis, where, in due time, we all arrived without accident or event worthy of note.

CHAPTER V.

THE PRAIRIE — SUNSET SCENE — REFLECTIONS — OUR FIRST CAMP — COSTUME — EQUIPMENTS — THE TRAPPERS, ETC.

The prairie! the mighty, rolling, and seemingly boundless prairie! With what singular emotions I beheld it for the first time! I could compare it to nothing but a vast sea, changed suddenly to earth, with all its heaving, rolling billows. Thousands upon thousands of acres lay spread before me like a map, bounded by nothing but the deep blue sky. What a magnificent sight! A sight that made my soul expand with lofty thought, and its frail tenement sink into utter nothingness before it. Talk of man—his power, his knowledge, his *greatness*—what is he? A mere worm, an insect, a mote, a nothing, when brought in compare with the grand, the sublime in nature. Go, take the mighty one of earth—the crimson-robed, diamond-decked monarch, whose nod is law, and whose arrogant pride tells him he rules the land and sea—take him, bring him hither, and place him in the center of this ocean of land—far, far beyond the sounds of civilization—and what does he become? Talk to him then of his power, his greatness, his glory; tell him his word is law—to command, and he shall be obeyed; remind him of his treasures, and tell him now to try the power of gold! What would be the result? He would deeply feel the mockery of your words, and the nothingness of all he once valued; for, alas! they would lack the power to guide, to feed, or save him

from the thousand dangers of the wilderness.

Similar to these were my thoughts, as I stood alone, upon a slight rise of ground, and overlooked miles upon miles of the most lovely, the most sublime scene I had ever beheld. Wave upon wave of land, if I may be allowed the expression, stretched away on every hand, covered with beautiful, green prairie-grass, and the blooming wild flowers of the wilderness. Afar in the distance I beheld a drove of buffalo quietly grazing; and in another direction a stampede of wild horses, rushing onward with the velocity of the whirling car of modern days. Nearer me I occasionally caught glimpses of various other animals; while flocks of birds, of beautiful plumage, skimming over the surface, here and there alighting, or starting up from the earth, gave the enchantment of life and variety to the picture.

It had been a beautiful day, and the sun was now just burying himself in the far off ocean of blue, and his golden rays were streaming along the surface of the waving grass, and tinging it with a delightful hue. Occasionally some elevated point like the one on which I stood, caught for a moment his fading rays, and shone like a ball of golden fire. Slowly he took his diurnal farewell—as if loth to quit a scene so lovely—and at last hid himself from my view beyond the western horizon. Then a bright, golden streak shot up toward the darkening dome of heaven, and, widening on either hand, gradually became sweetly blended with the cerulean blue. Then this slowly faded, and took a more crimson color; then more purple; until, at last, a faint tinge showed the point where the sun had disappeared, while the stars began to appear in the gray vault above.

I had stood and marked the whole change with that poetical feeling of pleasant sadness which a beautiful sunset rarely fails to awaken in the breast of the lover of nature. I noted every change that was going on, and yet my thoughts were far, far away, in my native land. I was thinking of the hundreds of miles that separated me from the friends that I loved. I was recalling the delight with which I had, when a boy, viewed the farewell scenes of day from some of the many romantic hills of old New England. I pictured the once cheerful home of my parents, which I had forsaken, and which now peradventure was cheerful no longer, in consequence of my absence. I fancied I could see my mother move to the door with a slow step and heavy heart, and gaze with maternal affection toward the broad the mighty west, and sigh, and wonder what had become of him who should have been the stay and support of her declining years. I thought, and I grew more sad as I thought, until tears filled my eyes.

Mother! what a world of affection is compressed in that single word! How little do we, in the giddy round of youthful pleasures and folly, heed her wise counsels! How lightly do we look upon that jealous care with which she guides our otherwise erring feet, and watches with feelings which none but a mother can know, the gradual expansion of our youth to the riper years of discretion! We may not think of it then, but it will be recalled to us in after years, when the gloomy grave, or a fearful living separation, has placed her far beyond our reach, and her sweet voice of sympathy and consolation, for the various ills attendant upon us, sounds in our ear no more. How deeply then we regret a thousand deeds that we have done contrary to her gentle admonitions! How we sigh for those days once more, that we may retrieve what we have done amiss, and make her sweet heart glad with happiness. Alas! once gone, they can rarely be renewed—and we grow mournfully sad with the bitter reflection.

My mother—my dearly beloved mother—would I ever behold her again! Should I ever return to my native land, would I find her among the living! If not—if not! Heavens! what a sad, what a painful thought! and instantly I found my eyes swimming in tears, and my frame trembling with nervous agitation. But I would hope for the best; I would not borrow trouble; and gradually I became calm. Then I thought of my father—of many other dear friends—and, lastly, though I strove to avoid it, I thought of Lilian—sweet, lost, but ah! dearly loved Lilian. I could see her gentle features, I could hear her plaintive voice—soft and silvery as running waters—and I sighed, a long,

deep sigh as I thought. Would I ever behold *her* again? I might, but—(my blood ran cold) but—wedded to another. "Ay! wedded to another!" I fairly groaned aloud, with a start that sent the red current of life swiftly through my veins.

I looked around me, and found it already growing dark. The beautiful scene I had so lately witnessed, was now faded from my sight; and the gloomy howl of a distant pack of wolves, reminded me that I was now beyond civilization, in the wilderness of an extensive prairie. I looked downward, and within a hundred yards of me beheld the fire of our first camp on the prairie; and with a hasty step I descended the eminence and joined my companions.

"Ah! Frank," said Huntly, as I came up, "I was beginning to fear something had happened you, and you can easily imagine my feelings. Why did you absent yourself so long?"

"I was on yonder eminence, enraptured with the glories of the sunset scene," I replied, somewhat evasively.

"Ah! was it not a splendid sight?" he rejoined, enthusiastically, with sparkling eyes. "I too beheld it with rapture, and regretted that you were not by to sympathise with me in my poetical feelings. But come, supper is preparing, and so let us regale ourselves at once, and afterward take our first sleep in this magnificent wild."

As I said before, this was our first camp on the prairie. On our way hither we had joined a party of four hunters or trappers, and in consequence our number was now augmented to seven. We had thrown off the lighter and more costly apparel of the settlements, and were now costumed in the rougher garments worn by the hunters of the Rocky Mountains. This consisted of a frock or hunting-shirt, made of dressed buckskin, and ornamented with long and parti-colored fringes. Our nether garments were of the same material, ornamented in the same manner, and on our feet were moccasins. Round the waist of each was a belt, supporting a brace of pistols and a long knife, the latter in a sheath made of buffalo hide. A strip of leather passing over our right shoulders, suspended our powder horns and bullet pouches under our left arms. In the latter we carried flint and steel, and small etceteras of various kinds, that had been mentioned as being useful where we procured our fit-out. Among other things, we had taken care to secure plenty of ammunition, tobacco and pipes, together with an extra supply of apparel for the cold regions toward which we were journeying, all of which were snugly stowed away in our large buffalo skin wallets—called by the trappers "possibles," or "possible sacks"—which were either attached to or thrown across our saddles.

In the description just given, I have been speaking of our party alone—namely, Huntly, Teddy and myself—without regard to the trappers, who were costumed and equipped much like ourselves, with the exception that instead of horses their animals were mules; and in place of one apiece, they had three. They, however, were bound on a regular trapping expedition, and carried their traps with them, and took along their mules for furs; while we, going merely on adventure and not speculation, had only taken the animals upon which we rode. Our horses and appendages, what we had, were all of the finest description; and our long, silver-mounted rifles drew many a wistful look from our newly made companions. In joining them, our chief object was to learn their habits and customs in the wilderness, before we ventured forth upon our own resources; and by being somewhat liberal in supplying them with tobacco and many small things of great value to the trapper, we secured their friendship and favor at once.

The trapper of the Rocky Mountains is a singular being. Like the boatman of the river, the sailor of the ocean, or the scout of the forest, he has peculiar characteristics, both as regards manners and dialect. Constantly exposed to danger and hardship, he becomes reckless of the one and indifferent to the other. His whole life, from beginning to end, is a constant succession of perilous adventures; and so infatuated does he become with the excitement attendant upon these, that, confine him in a settlement, and he would literally pine to death for his free mountain air and liberty to roam as he lists.

There is no polish, no sickly, sentimental refinement in his manners and conversation—but, on the contrary, all is rude, rough, blunt, and to the point. When he says a thing, he means it; and, in general, has but little deceit. With death he becomes so familiar, that all fear of the dread king of mortality is lost. True, he clings to life with great tenacity—but then there is no whimpering and whining at his fate. When he finds his time has come to go, he stands up like a man, and takes the result with the stoicism of a martyr. He is frequently a great boaster, and, like the sailor, delights in narrating strange tales of his wonderful adventures and hairbreadth escapes. In his outward behavior, he is often sullen and morose; but, as a general thing, his heart is in the right place. He will kill and scalp an Indian foe, with the same indifference and delight that he would shoot a bear or deer—and yet you may trust your life and money in his hands with perfect safety. In fact, I may say, that his whole composition is a strange compound of odds and ends—of inexplicable incongruities—of good and evil.

Until within the last few days, I had never seen a trapper; and of course he was to me and my companions as great an object of curiosity, as would have been the aborigine himself. The four which we had joined, were genuine, bona fide specimens of the mountaineers. Each had seen much service, had been more or less upon trapping expeditions, and one had actually grown gray in the hardy life of the wilderness. Each had trapped on his own account and for others, and had scoured the country from the upper regions of Oregon to the Mexican latitude—from the States to the Pacific ocean. They were acquainted with the land in every direction—knew all the regularly organized fur companies—all the trading forts and stations—and consequently were just the men to initiate us into all the peculiarities of the wilderness, all the mysteries of the trapper's life, and excite our marvellous propensities by their startling and wonderful tales. They gloried in the *soubriquets* of Black George, Rash Will, Fiery Ned, and Daring Tom—appellations which had been bestowed on them for some peculiar look in their persons, or trait in their characters.

The first mentioned, Black George, was the eldest of the party, and had doubtless received his cognomen from his dingy complexion, which was but little removed from the sable son of Africa. Naturally dark, his skin had become almost black from long exposure to the weather. In hight he was fully six feet, gaunt and raw-boned, with great breadth of shoulders, ponderous limbs and powerful muscles, which gave him a very formidable appearance. Although approaching sixty, his vigor seemed not the least impaired by age. His coarse hair, once black, was now an iron gray. His face was thin and long, with high cheek bones, pointed nose, hollow cheeks, large mouth, and cold, gray eyes. The wonted expression of his countenance was harsh and repulsive, though occasionally lighted with a humorous, benevolent smile. He was generally liked and respected by the whites, but hated and feared by the Indians, of whom he was a mortal enemy, that seldom failed to take their "hair"* whenever opportunity presented.

The next in order, Rash Will, as he was denominated, was a stout, heavy built man, somewhat above the medium stature, and about forty years of age. He had a large Roman nose and mouth, thick lips, low forehead, and blue eyes. The general expression of his physiognomy was a blunt, straight-forwardness, without regard to consequences. He could do a good deed or an evil one; and if he could justify the latter to himself, he cared not a straw for the opinions of others. Headstrong and violent when excited by anger, he had been the author of some dark deeds among the savages, which fully entitled him to the appellation of Rash Will.

The third in order, Fiery Ned, was about thirty-five years of age, of a robust, handsome form, some five feet ten inches in hight, and fully developed in every part. His features were comely and prepossessing. The only marked points of his countenance were his eyes—which were small, black, restless, and piercing—and his forehead, which was high and ample. His temperament was ardent, passionate, and fiery. At times he was cool, frank and generous; but at others, especially in an Indian fight, he became wild, furious, and, in short, a perfect devil.

The last of the four, Daring Tom, was the youngest and the most to my liking of any. He was about thirty years of age, and of middling stature. Unlike his companions, his features were very fine, almost effeminate, with a mild, dignified expression, that instantly won the regard of all with whom he came in contact. He had a large, full, clear blue eye, which rarely varied in expression, be the circumstances what they might. Cool and collected at all times, he was never more so than when surrounded by imminent danger. There was no risk he would not run to serve a friend, and on no occasion had he ever been known to display the least sign of fear—hence was he called Daring Tom.

Such is an outline sketch of the trappers who had now become our companions; and probably, take us all together, there was not, in the whole broad West, another party of the same number, that could present a more formidable appearance, or perform greater feats in the heat of contest.

At the moment when I came up to the fire, each of the trappers was seated beside it on the ground, cross-legged, engaged in toasting slices of a fat buck, which one of them had killed and brought in not an hour before. They were talking away briskly all the while, telling some wonderful tale, or cracking some joke, to the great amusement of Teddy O'Lagherty, who, a little apart, was seated in a similar manner to themselves, and listening attentively, with mouth and eyes widely distended. A little distance from the fire, our hopled animals were quietly cropping the luxuriant herbage beneath them.

"So then, Charley," I said, after having taken a general survey, "I suppose we are to fatten on deer meat?"

"Deer meat and salt," he replied, with a laugh. "The fancy preparations of civilization will regale us no longer, and we may be thankful if we always get fare as good as this."

While saying this, Huntly had drawn nearer the fire, so that the last remark caught the ear of Black George, who was just on the point of enforcing some assertion with an oath, but who suddenly stopped

---
* Scalp.

short, and turned to him with a comical look.

"See heyar, young chap, didn't I hearn you say you was from Bosson, or some sich place in the States?"

"Doubtless," answered Huntly, "for that, I am proud to say, is my native city."

"O, it's a city, then. Big's St. Louey, hey?"

"Much larger."

"Do say. Why then it's some, I reckons."

"A very flourishing place."

"Hum! You was born to Bosson?"

"Ay, and bred there."

"Bread? O, that means you was foddered thar, spose?"

"Yes, brought up and educated there."

"Edicated—augh! Heyar's what never did that; never had no need on't; know how to shoot and trap, but can't make pot hooks; can't tell 'em when they is made; know they's some, though, and wouldn't mind I know'd 'em a few—but don't care much no how; couldn't live no longer for't; couldn't 'float my sticks'* no better, spect. Well, for a younker, you've had a right smart chance, and I spose know a heap.† Heyar's what's born way down to Arkansaw, on a swamp patch, that didn't yield nothin worth divin for. I's raised down thar, or bread, as you calls it, young Bosson, (spose you've got no objection to bein called arter your natyve city) though almighty poor bread I was, for I didn't git much on't for a spell—in fact till I'd nearly gone under‡—augh! Let's see, whar was I? O, you's saying sumthin 'bout bein thankful for sich fare's this. It tickled me a heap—it did—and I had to in'ardly hold on tight to my ribs, to keep from guffawing. Why, young Bossoners, (addressing both of us) ef you'd seen what I hev, a piece like that thar, (pointing to the meat on the end of his stick, which he was toasting at the fire,) would a bin a heaven on arth, and no mistake. Talk about bein thankful for sich fare's this! Wait till you've seen your hoss go under, and the last end o' the eatable part o' your possibles chawed up, and then talk."

Here the old man paused and chuckled heartily, and winked at his companions, who joined him in his merriment, to the utter consternation of poor Teddy, who, with mouth wide open, and eyes enlarged to their utmost capacity, simply exclaimed:

"Howly murther! what a baastly time on't yees had!"

"I suppose you have seen some very rough times?" I rejoined, anxious to draw the old man out in some of his wonderful tales of adventure.

"Well I has, hoss," was the quick response; "and ef you want to make folks stare in the States, you'd better jest jog down one I've a notion to tell."

"We shall all be eager listeners," I rejoined.

"Think you'd like to hear it, hey?"

"O, most certainly."

The old man smiled complacently, and stroked his beard of a day's growth, in a way to denote that he felt himself somewhat complimented.

"Got any bacca?"

I gave him a large piece.

"Well, plant yourselves down here in talking distance, and while this deer meat's sizzling, I'll tell you a trump, and an ace at that."

Huntly and myself at once seated ourselves upon the ground, as near the old man as possible, who, giving the weed a few extra turns in his mouth, began the tale which I give in the following chapter.

CHAPTER VI.

THE OLD TRAPPER'S TALE—ATTACK ON HIM BY THE INDIANS—HIS ESCAPE—THE DEAD PURSUER—SUFFERINGS—THE MYSTERIOUS PRAIRIE FLOWER, ETC.

"Ye see, strangers," said the old man, "or Bossoners, (though I spect it don't make no pertikelar dif'rence what I calls ye, so it don't hurt your feelins none,) as

---

* That is, couldn't get along any better. This is a common expression among the trappers, and its meaning depends altogether upon the sense in which it is used. It is derived from their occupation. A "stick" is attached to each trap by a string, and if the beaver runs away with the trap, the stick, floating on the surface of the water, indicates the whereabouts of the animal, and enables the trapper to recover his property.

† A western word, equivalent to "very much."

‡ Died—another expression peculiar to the trapper.

I sez afore, I was raised down to Arkansaw, or tharabouts, and it's nigh on to sixty year now sence I fust tuk a center-shot at daylight, and in course I've forgot all the feelins a fust sight gin me. Howsomever, that's nothin here nor tother. (I say Will, *ef* you've got that thar bottle about you, I doesn't mind a taste, jest to grease this here bacca—augh! Thankee, Will; you're some, *you* is.)

"Well, strangers, you needn't 'spect I'm agoin to gin ye my whole hist'ry, case I isn't, and don't know's I could ef I wanted to, case most on't's forgot. So now I'll jest jump over a cord o' time, and come down to 'bout four year ago come next Feberry, when it was so all-fired cold, it froze icykels on to the star rays, and stopped 'em comin down; and the sun froze so he couldn't shine; and the moon didn't git up at all, *she* didn't; and this here arth was as dark nor a stack o' chowdered niggers."

Here the Irishman, unable to stand it longer, roared out:

"Howly saints! ye're not spaking truth, now, Misther Black George?"

"Aint I, though?" answered the old trapper, gravely, slyly tipping the wink to one of his companions. "D'ye think I'd lie 'bout it? You remember the time, Will?"

"Well I does, hoss," replied Will, with a grin.

"In course ye does, and so does every body that know'd anything 'bout it. I may hev exaggerted a leetle 'bout the stars and them things, but I jest tell ye what was fact and no mistake; and I'll be dog-gone ef I doesn't stake my v'racity on it's being true's preachin!"

Here the old man made a pause.

"Well, well, go on!" cried I.

"Ay, ay!" echoed Huntly.

"Well," said Black George, "a leetle drap more o' that critter—jest a taste—case the truth makes me so infernal dry, you can't tell. Augh! thankee—(returning the bottle)—feel myself agin now. But let's see, whar was I?"

"You were speaking about the weather."

"So I was; that's a fact; I'll be dog-gone ef I wasn't! Well, as I's sayin, it got so cold that when you throwed water up in the air, it all froze afore it could git down, and acterly had to stay thar, case it froze right on to the atmospheric."

"On to what?"

"The atmospheric."

"What is that?"

"You doesn't know what atmospheric is? Well, I'll be dog-gone ef I'm goin to 'lighten nobody; much's I ken do to understand for myself. But I knows the water froze to that article, for that's what I hearn a schollard call it, and I reckon he knowed a heap any how."

"Well, well, the story," cried I.

"Yes, well, I haint got through tellin how cold it was yit. Not only the water froze to the atmospheric, but the animals as used to run o' nights all quit the business, and you could walk right up to one and pat him han'some; case why—his eye-sight was all froze right up tight to his head. Fact! I'll be dog-gone ef it wasn't!

"Well, I'd bin out a trappin, and had made a purty good lick at it, and was comin down to Bent's Fort, to make a lounge for the winter—leastwise for what was left on't—when jest as I crossed Cherry Creek, after having left the Sothe Platte, I wish I may be smashed, ef I didn't see 'bout a dozen cussed Rapahos (Arrapahoes) coming toward me on hosses, as ef old Nick himself was arter 'em. I looked around me, and darned o' a thing could I see but snow and ice—and the snow was froze so hard that the hosses' and muleys' feet didn't make no impression on't. I was all alone, hoss-back, with three good muleys, all packed han'some, for Jim Davis—him as traveled with me—and Andy Forsker, another chap that made our party—had gone round another way, jest for fear o' them same painted heathen as was now comin up. But ye see I'd bin bolder nor them, and now I was a-goin to pay for't, sartin; for I seed by thar looks, they was bound to 'raise my hair'* ef I didn't do somethin for my country quicker. I looked all around me, and thought I was a gone beaver fast enough. I had a purty good hoss under me, and I knowed he only *could* save me, and a mighty slim chance he'd have on't at that. Howsom-

---

* Take my scalp

ever. I reckoned it wasn't best to say die ef I could live, and I didnt' like the notion o' bein 'rubbed out'* by sich a dog-gone scrimptious lookin set o' half humans as them thar Rapahos. I cast around me, and seed that old Sweetlove, (rifle) and her pups, (pistols) and my butchers, (knife and tomahawk) was all about; and so I jest swore I'd set my traps and make one on 'em 'come,' ef I 'went a woltin' for it.

"I said thar was 'bout a dozen—maybe more—an 1 they was ticklin thar hosses' ribs mighty han'some, you'd better believe, and a-comin for me with a parfect looseness, every one on 'em carryin a bow, and every bow bent with an arrer in it. I knowed my muleys was gone, sartin, and all my traps and furs; but jest then I felt so all-fired mad, that I thought ef I could throw a couple, I wouldn't care a kick. So instead o' trying to run away, I hollered 'Whoa' to the animals, and waited for the redskins to come up.—(Jest a drap more o' that, Rash, ef you please; for this here hoss is as dry to-night as a dog-worried skunk.

"Well, on they comes, thunderin away like a newly invented arthquake, and I 'spected for sartin I was a gone beaver. Jest afore they got up so as they could let thar shafts riddle me, the infernal cowards, seein as how I didn't budge, had the oudaciousness to come to a halt, and stare at me as ef I was a kangaroo. I raised Sweetlove, and told her to tell 'em I's about, and 'some in a bar fight.' She answered right han'some, did Sweetlove, and down the for'ard one drapped right purty, he did. Well, this sot the rest on 'em in a rage, and afore I knowed it, they was all round me, yellin like the old Scratch. Half a dozen shafts come hissin through my buckskins, and two on 'em stuck right in my meat-bag, and made me feel all over in spots like a Guinea nigger. Instanter I pulled out Sweetlove's pups, and set 'em to barkin, and two more o' the humans drapped down to see how the snow felt. Knowin' it wasn't no use to be foolin my time, I jerked the ropes, and told Skinflint to travel afore my hair was raised, leavin the muleys to do what they liked.

"Seein me a-goin, the oudacious Rapahos thought they'd stop me; but I rid right through 'em purty, and got another arrer in m— back for it.

"Arter I'd got away, I looked round and seed two on 'em a-comin like all possessed, with their lariats doubled for a throw. I knowed ef they got near enough, I'd be snaked off like a dead nigger, and my hair raised afore I could say Jack Robinson. Maybe I didn't ax Skinflint to do his purtiest, and maybe he didn't, hey! Why he left a trail o' fire behind him, as he went over that frozen snow, that looked for all nater like a streak o' big lightnin. But it didn't seem to be o' no use; for the infernal scamps come thunderin on, jest about so fur behind, and I seed thar hosses was all o' the right stuff. The sun was about a two hour up, and thar he stayed, *he* did; for it was so almighty cold, as I said afore, he couldn't get down to hide.

"Well, on we run, and run, and run, till the hosses smoked and puffed like a Massassip steamer, and still we run. I made tracks as nigh as I could calculate for the mountains, in the direction of Pike's Peak, and on we went, as ef old Brimstone was arter us. I calculated my chasers 'ud git tired and gin in; but they was the real grit, and didn't seem to mind it. At last they begun to gain on me, and I knowed from the 'signs' o' Skinflint, that he'd have to go under, sure's guns, ef I didn't come to a rest purty soon. You'd better believe I felt queer jest then, and thought over all my sins, with the arrers sticking in my belly and back like all git out. I tried to pray; but I'd never larnt no prayers when a pup, and now I was too old a dog to ketch new tricks; besides, it was so all-fired cold, that my thoughts stuck in my head like they was pinned thar with icykels. I'd been chased afore by the Comanches and Blackfoot, by the Pawnees and Kickapoos, by the Crows and Chickasaws, but I'd never had sich feelins as now. The short on't is, boys, I was gittin the squaw into me, and I knowed it; but I'll be dog-gone ef I could help it, to save my hair, that stood up so stiff and straight as to raise my hat and let the atmospheric in about a feet. I was gittin outrageous cold, too, and could feel my heart pumpin up icykels by the sack full,

---

* Killed.

and I knowed death was about sartain as daylight.

"'Well,' sez I to myself, 'old hoss, you've got to go under and lose your top-knot, so what's the use a kickin?'

"'Howsomever,' I answered, 'sposin I has, I reckon's best to die game, ain't it?' and with this I pulled old Sweetlove round and commenced fodderin her as best I could. She knowed what was wanted, did Sweetlove, and looked right sassy, I'll be dog-gone ef she didn't.

"'You're a few, aint you?' sez I, as I rammed home an all-fired charge of powder, that made her grunt like forty.

"Well, I turned round, fetched her up to my face, and 'drawin a bead'* on to the nearest, pulled the trigger.

"Now you needn't believe it without ye take a notion, but I'll be rumfuzzled (stir that fire, Ned, or this here meat won't git toasted till midnight), ef she didn't hold shoot about a minnet, and I all the time squintin away too, afore the fire could melt the ice round the powder and let her off. That's a fact!—I'll be dog-gone ef it wasn't!

"Well, she went off at last, *she* did, with a whoosss-k cheeesss-cup cho-bang, and I hope I may be dogged for a possum, ef one o' my chasers didn't hev to pile himself on a level with his moccasin right han some. Now I thought as how this 'ud start the wind out o' t'other, and put him on the back'ard track. But it didn't. He did'nt seem to mind it no more'n's ef it was the commonest thing out.

"'Well,' thinks I to myself, 'maybe you'll ketch a few ef you keep foolin your time that-a-ways;' and so I set to work and foddered Sweetlove agin.

"By this time poor Skinflint, I seed, was gittin top-heavy right smart, and I knowed ef I done anything, it 'ud hev to be done afore the beginnin o' next month, or 'twouldn't be o' no use, not a darned bit. Well, I took squint agin, plum-center, and blazed away; but hang me up for bar's meat, ef it made the least diff'rence with the skunk of a Rapaho. I was parfect dumfouzled; complete used up; for I'd never missed a target o' that size afore, sence I was big enough to shoot pop-guns

---

*Taking close sight.

to flies. I felt sort o' chawed up. Never felt so all of a heap afore but once't, and that was when I axed Suke Harris to hev me, and she said 'No.'

"Now you'd better calculate I hadn't no great deal o' time to think, for thar he was—the cussed Injin—jest as plain as the nose on your face, and a-comin full split right at me, with his rope quirled in his hand, jest ready for a throw. Quicker as winkin, I foddered Sweetlove agin, and gin him another plum-center, which in course I spected would knock the hind-sights off him. Did it? Now you ken take my possibles, traps and muleys, ef it did. Did it? No! reckons it didn't. Thar he sot, straight up and down, a thunderin on, jest as ef the arth was made for his special purpose. I begun to git skeered in arnest, and thought maybe it was the devil deformed into a Injin; and I'd a notion to put in a silver bullet, only I didn't happen to have none 'bout me.

"On he come, the scamp, and I bolted—or tried to rayther—for Skinflint had got used up, and down he pitched, sending me right plum over his noddle on to my back, whar I lay sprawlin like a bottle o' spilt whisky.

"'It's all up now, and I'm a gone possum,' sez I, as I seed the Injin come tearin ahead; and I drawed the old butcher, and tried to feed one o' the pups, but my fingers was so numb I couldn't.

"Well up rides old Rapaho, lookin as savage nor a meat-axe, his black eyes shinin like two coals o' fire. Well now, what d'ye think he did? Did he shoot me? No! Did he rope (lassoo) me? No! Did he try to? No, I'll be dog-gone ef he did!"

"What did he do?" inquired I, quickly.

"Ay, ay, what did he do?" echoed Huntly.

"Howly Mary! if ye knows what he did, Misther George, spaak it, jist, and relave yer mind now," put in the Irishman.

The old trapper smiled.

"Rash," he said, "ef that thar bottle isn't empty, I'll jest take another pull."

"Taint all gone yit," answered Rash Will; "'spect 'twill be soon; but go it, old hoss, and gin us the rest o' that —— Rapahos affair."

The old man drank, smacked his lips, smiled, and remarked:

"How comfortable deer meat smells."

"But the Rapaho," cried I, "what did he do?"

"Do!" answered Black George, with a singular expression that I could not define: "Do! why he rid up to my hoss and stopped, he did; and didn't do nothin else, he didn't."

"How so?"

"Case he was done for."

"Dead?"

"As dog meat—augh!"

"Ah! you had killed him, then?" cried I.

"No I hadn't though."

"What then?"

"He'd died himself, he had."

"How, died?"

"Froze, young Bossons—froze as stiff nor a white oak."

"Froze!" echoed two or three voices, mine among the rest.

"Yes, blaze my old carcass and send me a wolfin, ef he hadn't! and I, like a ——fool, had been runnin away from a dead nigger. Maybe I did'nt swear some, and say a few that aint spoke in the pulpit. You'd jest better believe, strangers, I felt soft as a chowdered possum."

"But how had he followed you if he was dead?"

"He hadn't, not pertikerlarly; but his hoss had; for in course he didn't know his rider was rubbed out, and so he kept on arter mine, till the divin o' old Skinflint fetched him up a-standin."

"Of course you were rejoiced at your escape?"

"Why, sort o' so, and sort o' not; for I felt so all-fired mean, to think I'd bin runnin from and shootin to a dead Injin, that for a long spell I couldn't git wind enough to say nothin.

"At last I sez, sez I, 'This here's purty business now, aint it?' I reckons, old beaver, you've had little to do, to be foolin your time and burnin your powder this way;' and then I outs with old butcher, and swore I'd raise his hair.

"Well, I coaxed my way up to his old hoss, and got hold on himself; but it wasn't a darned bit o' use; he was froze tight to the saddle. I tried to cut into him, but I'll be dog-gone ef my knife ud enter more'n 'twould into a stone. Jest then I tuk a look round, and may I be rumboozled, ef the sun hadn't got thawed a leetle, and, arter strainin so hard, had gone down with a jump right behind a big ridge.

"'Well,' sez I, 'this nigger'd better be making tracks somewhar, or he'll spile, sure.'

"So wishin old Rapaho a pleasant time on't I tried Skinflint, but findin it wasn't no go, I gathered up sich things from my possibles as I couldn't do without, pulled the arrers out o' me, and off I sot for a ridge 'bout five mile away.

"When I got thar, it was so dark you couldn't tell a tree from a nigger; and the wind—phe-ew!—it blowed so one time that I had to hitch on to a rock to keep myself any whar. I tried to strike a fire, but my fingers was so cold I couldn't, and the snow had kivered up every thing, so that thar wasn't nothin to make it on.

"'It's a screecher,' I sez, to myself, 'and afore daylight I'll be rubbed out, sartin.'

"At last I begun to feel so queer, and so sleepy I couldn't hardly keep open my peepers. I knowed ef I laid down and slept, I was a gone beaver; and so stumblin about, I got hold o' a tree, and begun to climb; and when I got up high enough, I slid down agin; and you'd better believe this here operation felt good—ef it didn't I wouldn't tell ye so.

"The whole blessed night I worked in this way, and it blowin, and snowin, and freezin all the time like sixty. At last mornin come, but it was a darned long time about it, and arter I'd gin in that daylight wasn't no whar.

"Well, soon's I could see, off I sot, and traveled, and traveled, I didn't know which way nor whar, till night had come agin, and I hadn't seen nothin human—and besides, I'd eat up all my fodder. I tried to shoot somethin, but I'll be dogged ef thar was any varmints to shoot o' no kind—they was all froze up tighter nor darnation.

"That night went like tother, in rubbin a tree; and the next day I sot on agin, and traveled till night, without eatin a bit o' food. I had a leetle bacca, and that I chawed like all git out, until I'd chawed it all up, and begun to think I was chawed up myself. I'd got, though, whar I could find a few sticks, and I made a fire, and it'd a jest done ye good to seen the way I sot to it.

"The next mornin I put on agin, but I'd got so powerful weak, that I rolled round like I'd been spilin a quart. Night come agin, and I'd got worse tangled up nor ever, and didn't know the piht o' compass from a buffler's tail.

"'Well, it's all up with this here coon,' I sez; 'and so what's the use o' tryin? Might as well die now as when I've got more sins to count;' and so givin old Sweetlove a smack, and tellin her to be a good gal, I keeled over as nateral as shootin. I looked up'ard, and seed a bright star that 'ud just thawed its way down, and thinkin maybe I'd be thar soon, I gin in and shut my peepers, as I spected for the last time.

"How long I laid thar I never knowed, and never spect to; but when I seed daylight agin, I found this here hoss in a Injin lodge, somewhar about, and tickle me with a pitch pine-knot ef I ever knowed exactly whar—for I forgot to 'blaze'* the place, and couldn't never find it agin. At fust, in course, I thought I was in the other country folks tells about; and thinks I, I've bin stuck among the Injins, jest to punish me for raisin so much hair while on the arth. I begun to git skeered, I tell ye; but it wasn't long afore I seed a sight that made it seem like Heaven any how—leastwise I felt perfectly willin to be punished that way etarnally, I did. (I say, Bosson, got any more bacca? This here travels like a May frost.")

"Well, what did you see?" I inquired, as I hastily supplied him with the desired article.

"See, sposin you guess now. You're what they calls Yankee, and ort to guess any thing."

"O, I could not guess it, I am satisfied."

"I can now," said the Irishman.

"Well, Teddy, out with it."

"Why, he saan a bothel o' whisky, in course; what else should he sae to make him happy all of a sudden?"

A roar of laughter followed this witty

---

* To "blaze" a tree is to mark it with an axe, or in some way, so that it can be identified. A "blazed path" is one so marked throughout.

reply, in which Black George good humoredly joined.

"Well, you is some at guessin, you is," replied the old trapper; but you didn't quite hit it, hoss. I say, strangers, what's the purtiest sight you ever seed on the arth?"

"A beautiful female," I replied.

"Well, that's jest what I seen. I seed afore me a critter in the shape o' a gal, that was the most purty I ever drawed bead on."

"A beautiful girl!" I exclaimed.

"Well, stranger, she wasn't nothin else, *she* wasn't—I'll be dog-gone ef she was!"

"Describe her!"

"Jest describe a angel, and you've got her to a T—ef you haven't, why was beavers growed? that's all."

"Who was she?"

"Well now, hoss, you're gittin into the picters, and headin off this old coon right center. I never knowed who she was, unless she was a sperit—for I'll be dog-gone ef ever I seed any thing half as decent 'bout a Injin."

"Can you not describe her?"

"Describe thunder! Why she was the tallest specimen of a human as ever sp'ilt par-flesh of buffler, she was. She had long hair, black as a nigger in a thundercloud; and eyes black too; and so large and bright you could see to shave in 'em as easy as trappin. And then sich a face!—well that was a face, now, or I wouldn't tell ye so. It kept puttin me in mind o' summer weather and persimmons, it was so almighty warm and sweet lookin. O, sich a nose—sich lips—sich teeth—and, heavens *and* arth! sich a smile! (A drop more, Will, for this child's mouth's gittin watery a thinkin, and that meat looks like feedin time."

"Why, now, you have raised my curiosity to the highest point," I said, "and so I must have the rest of the story forthwith."

"Boys often git thar curiosity raised out here-aways, and thar hair too sometimes," replied the old hunter, coolly, taking his meat off the stick and commencing to eat.

"But you're going to finish your story George?" queried Huntly, quickly.

"Why, I spect I'll hev to; but I'l

make it short; for I never likes to talk much 'bout that gal; I al'ays feel so much all overish, I can't tell ye how."

"Perhaps you got in love with her," returned Huntly, jocosely.

The old trapper suddenly paused, with the meat half way to his mouth, and turned upon my friend with a frown and gleaming eyes.

"Look heyar, boy," he said, "you didn't mean to insult this child, I reckon?"

"Far from it," answered Huntly, quickly. "I only spoke in jest, and crave pardon if I offended."

"'Twon't do to jest about everything, young chap, case thar is spots as won't bear rubbin. Howsomever, I sees you didn't mean nothin, and so I'll not pack it. Talkin of love! Now I doesn't know much 'bout the article, though I've seed nigh sixty year, and never was spliced to no gal; but I'll tell you what 'tis, Bosson, ef I'd bin thirty year younger, ef I hadn't made tracks with that 'ar gal, and hitched, then call me a nigger and let me spile."

"How old was she?" I asked.

"Jest old enough to be purty, *she* was."

"But how had she found you so opportunely?"

"That's whar I'm fooled; for though I axed her, and she told me, I'll be dog-gone ef I wasn't thinkin how purty she looked when she talked, and let the whole on't slip me like tryin to throw a buffler with a greased rope. All I could ever ketch on't was, that she, or some other Injin, or somebody else, come across me, and tuk me in, did up my scratches, and fetched me sensible. She said she was purty much of a beaver among the Injins, and could do 'bout as she tuk a notion; but that ef I wanted my hair, I'd better be leavin right smartly, or maybe I'd be made meat of—ugh!

"Well, arter it come dark, she packed some fodder for me, and acterly went herself along and seed me through the camp—for it wasn't a reg'lar village of Injins no how.

"'What tribe's this?' I axed, arter I'd got ready to quit.

"'That you musn't know,' she sez. 'Ax no questions, but set your face that-a-ways, and keep your nose afore ye till daylight, and don't come heyar agin, or you're dead nigger.'

"'But ef you won't tell this child the Injins, tell me who you is!'

"'I'm called Leni-Leoti, or Perrarie-Flower,' sez she; and then afore I could say, 'O, you is hey!', she turned and put back like darnation.

"I'd a great notion to foller her, and I cussed myself arterwards case I didn't; but I spect I was feelin green then, and so I did jest as she told me—ef I didn't, I wish I may be dogged! When it come mornin, I looked all round, and concluded I was on tother side of the 'Divide.' So I tuk a new track, and arter many days' travel, fetched up in Brown's Hole, whar I found lots of trappers, and spent the winter—augh! Now don't ax no more, for you've got all this hoss is agoin to tell; for the whisky's out, the bacca's low, this coon's hungered, and the meat's a spilin."

Here, sure enough, the old trapper came to a pause; and although I felt a deep interest to know more about the singular being he had described, Prairie-Flower, I saw it would be useless to question him further. The conversation now turned upon trivial affairs, in which neither Huntly nor myself took much interest. We felt wearied and hungry; and so after regaling ourselves on toasted deer meat, without bread, and only a little salt, and having seen our animals driven in and picketed—that is, fastened to a stake in the ground, by a long lariat or rope of skin, so that they could feed in a circle—we threw ourselves upon the earth around the fire, and, with no covering but our garments and the broad canopy of heaven, brilliantly studded with thousands on thousands of stars, slept as sweetly and soundly as ever we did in a thick-peopled settlement.

———o———

CHAPTER VII

MORNING SCENE — CONVERSATION — BOTH IN LOVE — LUDICROUS MISTAKE — OLD FEELINGS TOUCHED — INTERRUPTION.

At the first tinge of day break on the following morning, I sprang to my feet, and rousing Huntly, we stole quietly from the circle of sleeping trappers, and took our way to the eminence from which I had viewed the farewell of day the evening previous. It was a splendid morning, and the air, clear, soft and balmy, was not stirred by a single zephyr. As we ascended the knoll and looked toward the east, we could barely perceive a faint blush indicating the rosy dawn of day, while a soft, gray light spread sweetly over the scene, and the stars, growing less and less bright, gradually began to disappear from our view. Presently the blush of morn took a deeper hue, and gently expanding on either hand, blended beautifully with the deepening blue. Then golden flashes shot upward, growing brighter and brighter, till it seemed as if the world were on fire; while night, slowly receding, gradually revealed the lovely prairie to our enchanted gaze. Brighter, more golden, more beautiful grew the east, and brighter the light around us, until the stars had all become hidden, and objects far and near could be distinctly traced, standing out in soft relief from the green earth and the blue and golden sky.

"Magnificent!" I exclaimed, turning toward my friend, who was standing with his face to the east, his gaze fixed on high, apparently lost in contemplation.

He did not reply, and repeating my exclamation, I lightly touched him on the arm. He started suddenly, and turned to me with an expression so absent, so vacant, that I felt a slight alarm, and instantly added:

"Huntly, are you ill?"

"Ill, Frank? No! no! not ill by any means," he replied. "Why do you ask?"

"You appeared so strangely."

"Indeed! Well, where think you were my thoughts?"

"How should I know?"

"True enough, and I will tell you. I was thinking of that fair being we rescued from the flames."

"And why of her now?"

"Not only now, Frank, but she fills my thoughts more than you are aware. Often do I see her in my dreams; and the mere resemblance of yonder sky to fire, vividly recalled to mind that never-to-be forgotten night when first I beheld her."

"Charley, you are in love."

"It may be," he answered with a sigh; "but, alas! if so, I love one whom I shall never behold again;" and he dropped his head upon his bosom in a musing mood.

"Nay, nay, old friend," I said gaily; "it will not do for you to be getting sentimentally love-sick, away out here upon the prairies. Who knows but some day she you are thinking of, may, in spite of your now doleful looks, become your wife!"

"Frank," said Huntly, in quick reply, with a look of reproach, "if you knew my feelings, you would not wound them, I am sure, by untimely jests."

"Good heavens! Charley," I exclaimed, in surprise, at once grasping his hand with a hearty pressure; "I wound your feelings? Why such a thought never entered my head. I spoke jestingly, it is true; but I was not aware that the affair had become so serious. I was thinking at the time that one ailing youth in our camp was sufficient."

"To whom do you allude?"

"Myself."

"How so? I was not aware that you were ailing, as you call it."

"Why, do you not know that I am in love, like yourself?"

"Heavens! not with her, Frank—not with her?" cried my friend, grasping my arm nervously, and peering into my face with a searching glance.

"Ay, Charles, and I thought you knew it. I acted wrongly, I know, and have deeply repented since."

"But then, you—you—love her still, Frank?"

"Devotedly, as God is my judge!"

Huntly released my arm with a groan, and turned away his head.

"What is the meaning of this, Charles?" I inquired, in a tone of alarm.

"Why did you not tell it me before?" he said, with a long, deep sigh.

"First, because it is a delicate subject, and I did not like to mention it. Secondly, because you have never before alluded to it yourself."

"True; but I did not dream it was so. O God! why, then, did you not let me perish in the flames?"

"Perish, Charles?—how strangely you talk! Why should I have let you perish?"

"To end my misery."

"Misery? You alarm me, Charles.

you are not well—you have bad news—or something has happened which you have kept from me?"

"You love her, you say—is not that enough? But go on! I will yield all to you. I will not stand in your way. No! sooner would I die than mar your happiness. But I regret I did not know of it before."

"Charles," I exclaimed, in real alarm, "what mean you by these strange words? *You* stand in my way? I do not understand you; you have some hidden meaning!"

"Have you, then, not divined that I love her?"

"Ay."

"And can two love the same, and both be happy?"

"Why not? I would not rob you of your love. True, I love her deeply, devotedly, I swear to you; and I know you love her also; but then our love is different. You love her as a brother—but I, as something more than brother."

"I see you are mistaken, Frank; and to show you how much I sacrifice to your happiness, I will say, once for all, I love her as deeply, as devotedly, as passionately as yourself; but not as a brother, my friend; O no, not as a brother."

"Indeed Charles!" I cried, with a terrible suspicion of something I dared not express: "Indeed, Charles!" and I grasped his arm, and sought his eye with mine: "Indeed, Huntly! No! no! gracious heavens! you cannot mean what you have said! Take it back, I beg of you, and avow you love her as a brother, and nothing more—for more would be criminal."

"I do not see the criminality you speak of," he answered coldly. "Is it not enough that I have offered to sacrifice my own happiness, without being charged with crime?"

"But Charles, my friend, consider!—you have no *right* to an attachment warmer than a brother's."

"*Right!*" echoed Huntly, turning pale with excitement: "*Right*, say you! By heavens! when it comes to that, I know not why my *right* to love her is not as good as yours."

"Shall I tell you?"

"Ay, do! Quote me the law that makes it criminal for me to love and not yourself," answered Charles, bitterly.

"The law of consanguinity?"

"Heavens! what do you mean?"

"Does not the same blood flow in the veins of both of you?"

"Good God! you chill my blood with horror! you do not mean this?" and my friend turned deadly pale, reeled like one intoxicated, and grasped my arm for support. "I was not aware of this, Frank."

I now became more alarmed than ever. Something had assuredly turned the brain of my friend, and he was now, (how I shuddered as I thought)—he was now a maniac!

"Why, Charley," I said, in a tone as soothing as I could command, "surely you know her to be your sister!"

"*Sister!*" he fairly shrieked.

"Ay, sister, Charley. Is not Lilian your sister?"

"Lilian!" he cried, with a start, and a rapid change of countenance that terrified me. "Lilian!—then *you* were speaking of my sister Lilian?"

"Assuredly! who else?"

Huntly looked at me a moment steadily, and then burst into an uncontrollable fit of laughter, that made my blood run cold.

"Great Heaven!" I cried, "his senses are indeed lost!" and I was on the point of hurrying to camp, to give the alarm and get assistance, when, seizing me by the arm with one hand, and giving me a hearty slap on the shoulder with the other, he exclaimed:

"Frank, if ever there were two fools, then you I and make four."

"Poor fellow!" I sighed, and my eyes filled with tears: "What a shock it will be to his family!"

"Why, Frank," he cried again, accompanying his words with another slap, "you are dreaming, man!—your senses are woolgathering."

"Exactly," I said; "he, of course thinks *me* insane, poor fellow!"

"Nonsense, Frank. It is all a mistake, my dear fellow, and a laughable one truly, as you must know. You were speaking of sister Lilian; while *I*, all the time, was alluding to the fair unknown."

"What!" cried I, comprehending all at a glance; "then it is no insanity with you—and we have both made fools of ourselves indeed?"

"Exactly; so give me your hand on it, my old chum!"

Instantly my hand was locked in that of my friend, and then such another shout of merriment as we both set up, at the ridiculousness of the whole affair, I venture to say was never heard in that part of the country before nor since.

"So, then," resumed I, "the secret is out, and we have both acknowledged to being deeply in love. Really, dear Charley, I feel under great obligations to you for that meditated sacrifice—more especially, as the lady in question is thousands of miles away, is entirely unknown to us, and will probably never be seen again by either Charles Huntly or Francis Leighton."

"Tut, tut, tut, Frank! 'No more of that, an' thou lovest me,'" returned my friend, good humoredly. "I admit that I have acted the simpleton; but, at the same time (and he gave me a comical look), I feel proud to say I have had most excellent company—Eh! my dear fellow?"

"I acknowledge the corn."

"But touching my sister, Frank."

"Well, what of her?" I cried quickly, while I felt the blood rush to my face in a warm current.

"Did you not act hastily—too hastily—in that matter, my friend?"

"I fear I did, and I have bitterly repented since. But I loved her so, Charley; and you knew my passionate nature could not brook a rival."

"A rival, Frank! I never knew you had a rival."

"What! not know the elegant Mr. Wharton?"

"Pah! you did not take him for a rival, I hope."

"Indeed I did. Does he not visit your house frequently?"

"Yes, and so do fifty others; but I assure you dear Lilian will not marry them all."

"But—but—I thought Wharton—a—a—"

"A fashionable gallant. So he is."

"No—a—a—special suitor to your sister's hand," I stammered, concluding the sentence my friend had interrupted.

"Pshaw! Frank. Why Lilian would not look at him—other than to treat him respectfully, as she would any visitor—much less *marry* him."

"Then you think she does not love him?"

"Love him!" echoed Huntly, with a smile of contempt, and an expressive shrug of his shoulders. "No! Lilian Huntly loves but one."

"And who is he?"

"One certain hot-headed youth, ycleped Frank Leighton."

"Are you sure of this, Charles?" and I caught the hand of my friend, and fastened my eye steadily upon his.

"I will stake my life on it; and had you been possessed of your usual good sense that night you must have seen it."

I released the hand I had clasped in mine, and staggered back as if struck a violent blow. My brain grew dizzy, my hands trembled, and it was with difficulty I could keep myself upon my feet. Instantly the arm of my friend encircled my waist, and he said, hurriedly:

"Good heavens! what have I done! Frank, Frank, take this not so hard—it will all be right in the end. Lilian and you were made for each other, I see; and this separation will only serve to knit more closely the tie of affection between you when again you meet."

I replied not; I could not; but I struck my head with my fist, and gave vent to a groan that seemed to issue from my very soul.

"Is it there ye is, your honors?" said the voice of Teddy, at this moment.—"Faith, now, I've bin lookin for yees wid my two eyes and ears this long while, to ax ye, would ye have your breakfast cooked, or be afther takin it raw?"

"Cooked, you fool!" cried Huntly, angrily.

"Thin all I have to say is, it's waitin, your honors, and done beauthifully, by the chief cook and buthler, Teddy O'Lagherty, barring that he's no cook at all, at all, worth mintion, and divil a bit o' a buthler is in him now. And what's more, I'm to till ye that the Misther Trappers is jist gitting ready to lave the whereabouts, and they sez be ye going wid them, they'll be axing yees to travel."

"Sure, enough," said Huntly, looking

down toward the camp, "they are preparing to leave in earnest. So come, Frank," and taking my arm in his, we descended the hill together in silence.

CHAPTER VIII.

OUR CAMP RAISED AND JOURNEY RESUMED—A HALT—COTTON'S CREEK—ORIGIN OF THE NAME—ALARM—PREPARATION FOR DEFENCE—CAMP, ETC.

By the time that we had joined the trappers, the sun was already risen, and streaming his golden light over the broad prairie with a beautiful effect. Hastily partaking of our breakfast, watering our animals at a small creek which ran bubbling round the base of the little knoll so often mentioned, we prepared to raise our camp, as packing up to leave is termed by the mountaineers. Placing our saddles, possibles, etc., on our horses and mules, we mounted and took a northern course over the prairie.

As we passed along, we saw a few deer away in the distance, and occasionally caught sight of a buffalo, while animals of various kinds and sizes appeared here and there, sporting in the glorious sunbeams and seeking their daily fare, both single and in numbers. However, as we had plenty of "meat" laid in for the present, we did not trouble them, but kept quietly along upon our course—Black George taking the lead as pilot, and the rest of us following in his track, Indian file.

A little past noon we came to a small creek which flows into the Blue Earth river, or "Big Blue," as I heard it called by the mountain men, and here we paused again to water our animals, and allow them a few minutes to crop the luxuriant grass beneath their feet.

"Thar's time enough, boys, I'm thinkin," said Black George; "so what's the use o' hurryin? Spect we wouldn't live no longer for't; and jest to tell the fact, I'm in no particular drive to quit this warm sunshine, for the clouds and snow and ice o' the mountains—Eh! Ned!—augh!"

"Don't know's the mountain 'll be any better for our waitin," grumbled Ned; "and as long's we've got to go, what's the use o' our throwin away time here?"

"Augh!" grunted the old trapper. "You're al'ays in a haste, boy, and some day you'll git rubbed out in a haste, or I'm no beaver. Come, what say you, Tom? you haint opened your face sence you bolted that meat—leastwise to my knowin."

"I don't care a chaw which—stay or go—suit yourselves," answered Daring Tom, sententiously.

"Well, boys," rejoined the old mountaineer, "we'll hold our wind here 'bout a quarter, and then travel."

Saying which, he dismounted his mule, drew his pipe from a little holder suspended round his neck, and squatting upon the ground, deliberately filled and ignited it, by means of punk, flint, and steel, and commenced puffing away, as indifferent to everything or person around him, as if he had been paid expressly to pass his life in this manner. Fiery Ned, however, was not pleased; and ripping out a few oaths, on what he termed the "d—d laziness of the other," he jerked up his mules and set forward, followed by Rash Will only—Daring Tom and ourselves remaining with Black George. The last mentioned puffed away quietly, until the foremost party had disappeared, when taking his pipe from his mouth, blowing out a large volume of smoke, and watching it as it curled round and round on its ascent, ere it disappeared, he turned to me with a comical look, and shrugging his shoulders and winking his eye, observed:

"They'll not live no longer for it, hoss, I'll be dog-gone ef they will!" Saying which, he drew his legs a little more under him, and resumed his pipe with the gravity of a Dutchman.

The spot where we were now halted was one of rare beauty. It was a little valley, nearly surrounded by hills in the shape of a horse-shoe, along the base of which, like a silver wire, wound the little murmuring rivulet, its waters sparkling in the sunshine, becoming glassy in the shade, and mirroring the steeps above it as it gaily took its way to unite with the larger waters of the Blue. Above us, on three sides, rose the horse-shoe ridge, partially bare with frowning rocks, and partially covered with a dwarfish growth of various kinds of wood. The valley or bottom was a rich alluvion, carpeted with fresh sweet grass—which our animals cropped eagerly—and with various kinds of wild flowers; while hundreds of gay-plumed birds were hovering over our heads, or skimming along the surface, and thus checkering and enlivening the scene with their presence, and filling the air and our ears with the melody of their voices. The point of the valley not belted with the hills, looked out upon a prairie, which stretched away to the west and south, its half-grown grass waving in the breeze and resembling the light ripples of some beautiful lake.

"What a lovely scene!" said Huntly, turning to me, as, dismounted, we both stood gazing upon it.

"A little Paradise that I have never seen surpassed," was my answer.

"Yes, but everything beautiful hereabouts gits sp'ilt to them as knows it a few," chimed in the old hunter, blowing the smoke deliberately from his mouth. "Now, I've no doubt this here place looks purty to you, but I've seen blood run hereaways—augh!"

"Indeed!" I exclaimed, advancing to the old trapper, as did each of the others, with the exception of Tom, who, having squatted himself some little distance off and lit his pipe, seemed wholly absorbed with thoughts of his own. "Then there has been fighting here in days gone by?" I pursued.

"Well, thar has, hoss," was the response. "Ye see that ar creek, don't ye?" pointing to it with the stem of his pipe.

"Ay."

"Well, it looks purty enough to one as don't know, but this coon's seen them waters red afore now."

"Tell us the tale," said Huntly.

"Why it's long, Bosson, and we haint got time to throw away—so I'll hev to let it slide, I'm thinkin. Howsomever, I'll gin ye the gist on't, and I spose that'll do as well. That creek you see yonder's bin called Cotton's Creek ever sence that time, and the reason on't is, case a powerful good chap called Jim Cotton, or "Snake-Eye," got rubbed out thar by the cussed Pawnees. Me and him, and Jake Strader, and Sigh Davis, had bin down to St. Louay, and sold our beavers to the Nor-Westers,* (and them was the days when they fetched somethin—five dollar a plew,† old or young uns, instead o' a dollar a pound—augh!) and coming out to Independence with the 'rocks' in our pockets, we got on a regular spree, and spent a few— but not all—and a infernal Greaser‡ somehow git tin wind on't, and findin out jest which way we's a-goin, put out ahead, and got some five or six Pawnees to jine him, and come down here to cache § for us.

"Well, in course we wasn't thinkin' o' nothin dangerous, case our bottles warn't all emptied, and we felt happy enough. Jest down here we stopped to water and rest like we're doin now, when all at once that ar bush you see yonder near the bank, let out seven bullets right among us. Jim Cotton was throwed cold, and never kicked arter, poor feller! Jake Strader got arm broke, Sigh Davis a ball through his shoulder, and me one right into my calf. Then thinkin they throwed the majority, the oudacious skunks come tearin and yellin like sin, old Greaser on the lead. A part broke for us, and the rest for our animals, so as ef they didn't 'count a coup' they could put us 'afoot.'

"'Heyars hair, and a chance for dry powder—gin 'em h—!' sez I; and I ups with old Sweetlove, and throwed old Greaser cold, right in his tracks—so cold he never knowed what made meat of him, Greaser didn't.

"Well, jest as mine went I heerd two more pops, and blow me for a liar ef two more of the —— rascals didn't drap purty! How they'd done it—specially Jake Strader with his broken arm—got me all of a heap; but done it they had, sartin as winkin; and thar the varmints lay, a-kickin like darnation. Now thar was only four left and grabbin Jim Cotton's rifle, afore they knowed what I was about, I laid another han'some. Now we was even, and I hollered to the skunks to come on and show fair fight, and I'd eyther lick the three or gin 'em my scalp. But they hadn't no notion o' tryin on't, the cowards! but turned and 'split' as ef the arth was agoin to swaller 'em.

---

* Hudson Bay Company is sometimes so called by the trappers.
† Pluie—a whole skin.
‡ Spaniard or Mexican.   § Hide—from cache.

"'Hurraw for us beavers!' I sez; 'and let us go hair-raisin;' and with that I takes my butcher and walks into the varmints; and them as wasn't dead I carved; and arter I'd done, me and Sigh — for Jake couldn't work well — we hove the meat into the water, christening it Cotton's Creek; then we dug a hole nigh 'bout whar you're standing, put in poor Jim, kivered him over, and jest as we was, all wounded, we mounted our critters and put out."

"And do ye think there is, maybe, iny of the likes of thim rid divils about here now, sure, Misther Trapper George?" inquired Teddy, with an uneasy look.

"Shouldn't wonder, hoss; for we're agoin right toward 'em."

"Faith, thin," said Teddy, turning slightly pale, "maybe it's the wrong road ye're going now?"

"O, ye needn't fear I'll miss the track," answered the old hunter, who put a literal construction on the Irishman's words. "I know the ground as well as you know your own daddy."

"Agh! and well ye may, Misther George, and have little to brag on the whiles, jist," rejoined the other quickly. "But what I maan is, it's maybe if we take anither way, we'll not rin among the divils, and git made maat of as ye calls it, now."

"Why, Teddy," said I, "you are not becoming alarmed at this stage of the journey I hope?"

"Och, no! it's not alar-r-med meself is gittin at all, at all, barring a little fright maybe I has for your honor's safety."

"O, never mind me, Teddy," I replied. "I assure you I am doing very well, and of course prepared myself to run all hazards before I came here."

"Well," observed Huntly, "I think we had better set forward again, and select our camp early."

"That's a fact," cried Black George, springing to his feet with the agility of a youth of twenty: "You is right, boy — right. Come, Tom, we's a-goin to put;" and he turned toward his saddle mule. "Hey! what!" he exclaimed suddenly, with a stress upon the words that instantly brought us all round him, eager to learn the cause.

But nothing could we discover, save that the old mule alluded to was snuffing the air, with her ears bent forward and pointing steadily in one direction. Two or three words, however, from the old trapper, sufficed to enlighten and alarm us at the same time.

"Injins, boys — rifles ready — Suke's no liar." Then turning to Tom, who had also started to his feet on hearing the first exclamation of Black George, he added: "Split for cover, Tom, and hunt for 'sign.'"

Scarcely was the sentence out of the old man's mouth, ere Tom was out of sight; for understanding all at a glance, he had turned at the first word, and, leaping across the stream, disappeared in a thicket on the other side.

I felt queer, I must own, for it was the first time that danger had become apparent to me; and this being concealed, I knew not what to expect, and of course magnified it considerably. Besides, the story I had just heard, together with the quick and decisive movements of the trappers, led me to anticipate a sudden onset from a large body of Indians. Determined to sell my life dearly, I grasped my rifle in one hand, and loosened my pistols and knife with the other. I cast a quick glance upon Huntly, and saw that he was also prepared for the worst. His features had paled a little, his brow was slightly wrinkled, and his lips compressed, showing a stern resolve. But the Irishman, in spite of my fears, amused me. Instead of bringing up his rifle ready for an aim, Teddy had griped it midway, and was whirling it over his head as he would a shelaleh, the while raising first one foot and then the other in great excitement, as if treading on live coals, his face flushed, his eyes fixed in one direction, his nostrils expanded, and his breast heaving with hard breathing.

"Quick!" exclaimed Black George; "fetch round the animals and make a breastwork to cover."

Instantly Huntly and I sprang to our horses, and the old trapper to his mules, while the Irishman, heeding nothing that was said, still continued his laborious gyrations. In less than a minute the animals were arranged in our front, and we were repriming our fire-weapons, and preparing to repel the attack manfully, should one be made. A minute of silence succeeded, when Black George cried out to Teddy:

"D'ye want to be made mea on, you thunderin fool! that you stand thar like a monkey target?"

But the Hibernian either did not hear, or, hearing, did not heed.

"Teddy," I shouted.

"Here, your honor!" answered Teddy, running up and crawling under my horse, he having been standing outside of our animal breast-work.

"What were you doing out there, Teddy?"

"Troth, I was gitting my hand in, jist."

"Yes, and you might hev got a bullet in your meat-bag," rejoined the old trapper, dryly.

"Ah!" said Teddy, dolefully, "if ye'll belave me now, it's that same doings that worries meself the most in this kind of fighting. Barring the shooting and the danger attinding it, it's me mother's son as wouldn't mind fighting at all, at all."

"There are a great many such heroes in the world," I rejoined, with a smile; "and most men are brave when there is no danger. But I'll exonerate you from being a coward, Teddy, for you once nobly saved my life; but at the same time I think I shall have to give you a few lessons when this affair is over, so that you will be able to act becomingly, under like circumstances, and know the proper use of your rifle."

"Hist!" said Black George at this moment.

All became a dead silence. Presently the faint cawing of a distant crow was heard in the woods nearest us.

"Injin sign—but no sudden dash," observed the old trapper again.

"Indeed!" I exclaimed, in surprise; "And pray how came you by your information?"

"Jest as easy as you ken look at pothooks and tell what they sez," answered the mountaineer. "You know how to read a heap in books; I know how to read the sign o' rater; and both is good in thar places. You heerd that crow, I'm thinkin?"

"I did."

"Well that was Darin Tom speakin to me, and tellin me what I told you."

Ere I had time to express my surprise, the person in question made his appearance, leaping nimbly across the little creek, and gliding up to us as silently as an Indian.

"What's the sign?" asked Black George.

"Pawnees," was the answer.

"How d' they number, and which way?"

"Twenty odd, and toward the sothe."

"Arter hair?"

"I reckon."

"Be apt to trouble us?"

"Think they passed with their eyes shut."

"Playin possum maybe. How long gone?"

"Less nor a quarter."

"Then Suke must have smelt 'em. She's a knowin one, is Suke, and don't fool her time. Spect we'd better put out and look for camp?"

"I reckon."

"Augh!"

Although this kind of dialogue was new to me, I nevertheless was able to understand that a body of Pawnees had passed us, and was either not aware of our proximity, or did not care to make an attack upon us in broad daylight. As the mountaineers concluded, they instantly mounted their mules and set forward; and springing upon our horses, we kept them company. As we left the little cove—if I may so term it—by way of the prairie, we were surprised to meet Fiery Ned and Rash Will on their return to join us.

"Well?" said Black George, interrogatively.

"Injins," returned Rash Will.

"Ahead or ahind?"

"Moccasins to the sothe."

"We've seed 'em—augh!"

No more was said; but wheeling their animals, the two mountaineers silently joined the cavallada, and we all moved forward together.

The country over which we were now passing, was exceeding beautiful and picturesque. Alternately well timbered bottom—steep, craggy, barren bluffs—open, rolling prairies—met our view; while sparkling little streams, winding around in every direction, appeared like silver threads fastening the whole together.

On our way hither, we had passed through Independence, one of the most important points in Missouri for obtaining an outfit, and taking much the same route as that now followed by Oregon emigrants, had crossed the Caw or Kansas river a day or two previous to our camp on the prairie, of which I have given a description. Although this, as I then said, was our first camp on the prairie, I wish the reader to distinctly understand it was not our first encampment beyond the boundaries of civilization. But as I did not care to trouble him with a tedious journey, which produced no important incident, I jumped over our progress to the time when I felt our adventures had really begun. I say this in explanation, lest having traveled the route himself, he might be puzzled to understand how, in so short a time from the raising of our camp, we could have become so far advanced.

It was now the middle of June, and the sun poured down his heat with great intensity, so that our animals perspired freely, and seemed far more inclined to linger in the shade when we passed a timbered spot, than to hurry forward in the open sunshine. Nevertheless we managed, before the sun sunk to rest, to put a good thirty miles between us and our camp of the previous evening. Reaching at last a smooth, pleasant spot — belted with hills, not unlike the one of our noonday halt, through which likewise murmured and sparkled a little rivulet — we paused and decided to camp at once. In a few minutes our animals were hoppled, and regaling themselves with great gusto upon the sweet, green blades which here grew exuberantly.

"Somebody'll hev to stand sentinel to-night," observed Black George, as we seated ourselves around the fire, which had been kindled for the purpose of toasting our meat, and keeping off the wild beasts. "Who's a-goin to claim the privilege?"

No one answered; but the other trappers all looked toward Huntly and myself, which I was not slow to understand.

"Do you think there is any danger to-night?" I inquired

"Thar's never a time in this part of the world when thar isn't, stranger," was the answer.

"But do you apprehend an attack from the savages to-night?"

"Maybe, and maybe not; but you know what happ'd to-day, and thar's sign about, clear as mud."

"Well, if you think I will answer the purpose, I am ready to volunteer my services."

The old trapper mused a moment, shook his head, and replied:

"I'm feared not. I'll keep guard myself; for you be young, and mightn't know a Injin from a tree; and it's like thar'll be powder burnt afore mornin."

Although these words portended danger, yet so fatigued was I from my day's travel, that in less than two hours from the time they were spoken, in common with the rest—Black George excepted, who, pipe in mouth, and rifle in hand, remained squatted before the fire—I was sound asleep.

CHAPTER IX.

A PAINFUL DREAM—ATTACK FROM THE PAWNEES—ALARM—TREEING—COWARDICE OF THE WESTERN INDIANS — COLD-BLOODED MUTILATION — COOLNESS AND VALOR OF THE MOUNTAINEERS.

I was once more in my native land Time had flown rapidly, years had rolled onward, thousands on thousands of miles had been gone over, and now I stood in the city of my nativity. Strange and powerful emotions stirred me. I was wending my way through the old and well-remembered streets to the home of one who had been daily and nightly in my thoughts during my long absence. I already pictured myself entering her abode, and the start and thrill of joyful surprise on her beholding me again. At length I reached the well known mansion. There it stood, just as I had left it. There were the same steps I had ascended, and the bell I had rung on the night when I had so abruptly and cruelly torn myself from her sweet presence. I felt a nervous tremor run through my whole system. I could scarcely stand. My heart seemed to shrink into nothing, my blood began to curdle in my veins, and my quaking limbs refused to do my bidding. There I stood, shaking like an aspen leaf, afraid to go forward, unwilling to retreat. At length, by a great effort, I grew more calm. With a fresh determination not to be conquered by myself, I rushed up the steps and rang the bell. A servant appeared. But he was not the one I had expected to behold; not the one that had answered my former summons; his face was new to me. This was a change, it is true, and produced some very unpleasant feelings; but this was a common one, and nothing to alarm me.

"Is Miss Huntly at home?" I inquired.

"Miss Huntly don't live here, sir."

"What!" cried I, gasping for breath, "not live here?"

"No, sir! this is Mr. Wharton's house."

"Wharton! Yes, well, he—he—is—married?"

"Yes, sir, he's married."

"Who did he marry?"

"Don't know, sir."

"Was it a—Lilian Huntly?"

"No indeed, I guess it wasn't. He wouldn't look at her, I know."

"Not look at her, villain! why not?" and, excited beyond reason, I seized my informant beyond the collar. "Why would he not look at her, wretch?" I repeated, hoarsely. "Tell me quickly, or I will dash your brains out at my feet!"

"Ca-cause she's poor," was the trembling reply.

"Poor!" I shouted.

"Ye-yes, sir."

"And where is she to be found?"

"Just round that alley yonder—first door on the left."

I followed with my eyes the direction indicated by the finger of my informant, and the next moment found the door slammed in my face. But for this I cared not. Lilian was in trouble. With one bound I cleared the steps, and darting down the street, turned the corner of the alley, and stood before a miserable wooden house.

"Great God!" I cried, mentally, "the home of Lilian, dear Lilian!" and the next moment, without pausing to knock, I burst open the door and entered a miserable apartment scantily furnished.

The first object that fixed my attention, was sweet Lilian herself; but oh! how altered! how pale! how wo-begone her look! Her dress and appearance bespoke poverty and suffering, and chilled my blood.

"Lilian!" I cried, rushing toward her, with outstretched arms.

She rose—stared at me—a frightful expression swept over her pale, grief-worn, but still lovely features—she struggled forward—gasped—and, uttering my name, with a terrible shriek, sunk senseless into my arms.

At this moment the door was burst rudely open, and Wharton, with eyes gleaming fire, pistol in hand, rushed into the apartment. Ere I had time for thought, the pistol flashed, the report rang in my ears, and the ball buried itself in the head of my beloved Lilian. With a shriek of horror, I dropped her lifeless body, and—*awoke.*

I looked up, and saw Huntly bending over me, and heard a confused noise, the discharge of firearms, and rising above all the din, the yells of savages.

"Awake, Frank!—up for God's sake! we are attacked!" cried Huntly.

Instantly I sprang to my feet, completely bewildered.

"Tree, tree, or you're dead nigger!" shouted a voice behind me.

I turned around, but was still too much confused to understand what was meant. The next moment Huntly seized me by the arm, and hurriedly dragging me to a neighboring tree, thrust me behind it on the side farthest from the fire. I had cause to be thankful for this; for as I moved from the spot where I had stood, a ball whizzed past me, which, had it been sped a second sooner, had doubtless proved fatal.

I now learned, from a few hurried words spoken by my friend, that the Indians—supposed to be Pawnees, and, in fact, the same party which had alarmed us at Cotton's Creek—had made a sudden dash at our animals, which were picketed within pistol-shot of the fire, and, with loud yells, had discharged their pieces and arrows into our camp, fortunately without doing us any injury. In a moment every one was on his feet, with the exception of myself, who, as the reader knows, was lost in the mazes of a troublesome dream, and had actually converted the screeches of the savages into cries from Lilian, and the report of fire-arms into the fatal shot from the pistol of one I had looked upon as a rival. Each of the trappers had hurriedly sought his tree, while the Irishman, though a good deal bewildered, had had presence of mind and good sense enough to imitate their example. Huntly of course could not leave me to perish, and had paused to rouse me in the manner shown.

By this time all had become silent as the grave. Our camp fire was still burning brightly, and by its light we could trace a large circle round it; but not an object, save our animals—some of which, particularly the mules, snuffed and snorted, and appeared very restless—was seen to stir. One would suppose, to have gazed around him in that warm, still night, that not a creature more dangerous than the fire-fly and musquito was at hand, to disturb the now seemingly deep and solemn solitude of the place. In this way some two or three minutes passed, during which you could have heard the fall of a leaf, when suddenly the stillness was broken by the report of a rifle within twenty feet of me, and was succeeded by a yell of agony some thirty paces distant in another direction, while an Indian, whom I had not before observed, staggered forward, and fell within the circle lighted by the fire.

Now it was, as if the whole wilderness were full of demons, that the most terrific yells resounded on all sides, and some fifteen or twenty savages, naked all but the breech-clout, hideously painted, were seen dodging among the scattering trees, making toward us, and discharging their muskets and bows at random. A bullet striking the stock of my rifle just above where my hand grasped it, splintering it, and sending some of the pieces into my face, maddened me not a little; and I vowed revenge upon the first savage I could lay eyes on.

"Give the skunks h——l!" shouted a voice; and ere the words were fairly uttered, some three or four rifles belched forth their deadly contents, and three more savages rolled howling in the dust.

At this moment I discovered a powerful Indian making toward me, not ten feet distant, his basilisk eyes fairly shining like two coals of fire; and raising my rifle quick as lightning to my face, without pausing even to sight it, I lodged the contents in his body. He staggered back, partly turned to fly, reeled, and then with a howl of rage fell to the earth a corpse.

The Indians of the Far West, of the present day, are not the Indians of former times, whose wigwams once rose where now stand our cities and hamlets, and whose daring in war, when led by a Phillip, a Pontiac, or a Tecumseh, could only be excelled by their cunning and ferocity. No! far from it. The present tribes have degenerated wonderfully. They are, take them as a whole, a dirty, cowardly, despicable set, without one noble trait, and not worth the powder it takes to kill them. They will attack you, it is true; but then they must treble you in numbers; and if they fail in killing or completely overpowering you at the onset, ten to one but they will beat a hasty retreat, and leave you master of the field.

Of such dastardly wretches was composed the party which had assailed us. Although vastly superior to us in numbers, they now seemed completely thunderstruck at the result of an attack, which, doubtless, they had counted on as certain victory. Five of their party had already bitten the dust, and yet not one of us had been touched. Notwithstanding this, even had they possessed one half the courage and daring of their eastern forefathers, they might to all appearance have annihilated us. But no! they *dared* not longer fight for victory. Like frightened poltroons, as they were, they wavered for a moment, and then, as their last hope, made a "break" for our animals, with the intention of seizing and making off with them, and thus leaving us to foot our long journey. But even in this they failed, through their own cowardice; for comprehending their intent, the trappers, with yells as savage as their own, sprang from their trees, and rushing toward them, they instantly abandoned their design, and again most ingloriously fled.

Two of our party, however, Fiery Ned and Rash Will, were far from being satisfied with even this victory. Maddened with rage, and a desire of farther revenge, they actually leaped onward after the fugitives, and quickly disappeared from our view. For a time we could hear them shouting and yelling; but gradually the sounds grew fainter and more faint, until at last nothing whatever could be heard.

"The infernal skunks!" said Black George, stepping out from behind his tree, and giving vent to a quiet, inward laugh, peculiar to men of his profession. "Reckon they'll stay put a few, and not trouble us agin in a hurry;" and again he laughed as before. "But what fools Ned and Will is? They're never content with a fair whip, but must al'ays be tryin to do a heap more; and some day they'll git thar hair raised, and go under with a vengeance. or I'm no sinner. But I say, Tom?"

"Well, hoss?"

"Didn't we throw 'em purty?"

"Well we did, old coon."

"I'll be dog-gone if we didn't. Come, let's lift thar hair—augh!"

With this, both trappers drew their knives, and taking from a little bag attached to their garments a small sandstone, commenced sharpening them with as much indifference as if they were about to slice a buffalo, instead of dipping them in the blood of human beings. When done, their whetstones were carefully replaced, and then turning to me, who with Huntly and Teddy had meantime gathered around the two, the old mountaineer said:

"Boy, you've done somethin for the fust time, and needn't be ashamed on't. Throwed him cold in his tracks, I'll be dog-gone ef you didn't!" and he nodded toward the Indian I had slain. "Well, he's your meat; and so at him and raise his top-knot afore he gits cold."

I shuddered at the bare thought of such barbarity, and involuntarily shrunk back.

"O, then you're a leetle squeamish, hey? Well, I've heern tell o' sich things afore: but it won't last long. Bosson, take my word for't. Ef you don't raise hair afore you're a thousand year older, jest call me a liar and stop off my bacca."

"No!" I replied, firmly: "I could never be brought to degrade myself by a custom which originated with, and, if it must still be practiced, should ever belong to, the savage. I may kill an Indian in my own defence, but I cannot mutilate him when dead. I was bred in a very different school."

"Bread, be ——!" returned Black George, not comprehending any meaning. "This here ain't bread—it's meat; and as to skule, as you calls it, why that ar belongs to the settlements; and haint got nothin to do out hereaways in the woods. Eh! Tom?"

"Well it haint."

"No, I'll be rumfuzzled ef it hev! And so, stranger, ef you want to show you're smart a heap, you'll jest lift that ar skunk's hair and say no more about it. Eh! Tom?"

"Fact!—augh!"

"No!" I rejoined in a decisive tone, "I will have nothing to do with it. If you choose to scalp the Indian, that is no business of mine; but I will not so degrade myself."

"Well, ef your mind's made up, in course it's no use o' talkin; and so, Tom, let's begin to slice."

At this moment we heard the report of a distant rifle, quickly followed by another.

"Them boys is eyther throwed now, or else some Injins have got rubbed out," observed Black George indifferently, "Come, Tom, let's lift."

Saying this, the old trapper and his companion set about their bloody work. The first Indian they came to was not dead; and running his knife into his heart, with a barbarous coolness that made me shudder, Black George observed:

"That's your meat, Tom."

He then passed on, leaving the latter to finish the bloody task. Bending over the now dead savage, and seizing him by the hair of the head—which, instead of a long lock or cue as worn by some tribes, was short and ridged, like the comb of a fowl. Daring Tom ran his knife round the skull bone with a scientific flourish, tore off the scalp, and knocking it on the ground to free it as much as possible from gouts of blood, coolly attached it to his girdle, and proceeded to the next.

"What a horrid custom!" I exclaimed, turning to Huntly.

"It is, truly," he replied. "But then you know, Frank, it is one that belongs to the Indian and mountaineer; and as we have come among them voluntarily, we have no right of course to quarrel with them for it."

"Be jabers!" cried Teddy, "is it murthering the Injins twice they is, now, your honors?"

"It would seem so," replied Huntly, with a smile.

"Faith, and your honor, and it's meself as thinks they naad it, sure, the blathering spalpeens, to be coming round us paceable citizens wid their nonsense, and cutting our troats. Och! if I'd a knowed how to let off this bothersome article, (holding up his rifle) I'd a killed a dozen o' the baastly crathurs, I would."

"Why, Teddy," I rejoined, "I thought you knew how to shoot a rifle? at least you told us so."

Teddy scratched his head, and put on a very comical look, as he replied:

"Yes, but ye sae, your honor, it was an Irish rifle I was spaking of, barring that it wasn't made in Ireland at all, at all, but in France, jist."

"But I thought they did not allow you to use rifles in Ireland, Teddy?"

"No more they don't; but thin, ye sae, it isn't sich murthering things as this now they uses."

"What then?"

"Why, I most forgit meself," returned the Irishman, with a perplexed look, again scratching his head. "Och! now I come to think on't, I belave it shot wid a long stick, and that it wasn't meself as shot it at all, at all, but me mother's father that knowed sich things—pace to his ashes."

"Teddy," I rejoined, assuming a serious tone which I was very far from feeling, "it is evident that this is the first rifle you ever laid hands on, and that the story you told us on the boat, about your exploits in shooting, was without the least foundation whatever."

"Ah! troth, it's like it may be," answered the Hibernian, penitently, with a sigh. "It's like it maybe, your honor; for divil a thing else can me make out of it. But ye sae, ye questioned me close now, and I's afeared that didn't I have the qualifications ye axed, I'd not be naaded; and as I saan ye was raal gintlemen, and no bluthers of spalpeens, it was going wid

yoursel's Teddy O'Lagherty was afther doing, if he told a story, jist—for which howly Mary forgive me!"

"Well, well, Teddy, never mind," I said, smiling. "I will show you the use of the rifle the first convenient opportunity; and so let what is past be forgotten."

"Ah!" cried the grateful Irishman, doffing his beaver and making a low bow "I knowed ye was gintlemen, your honors, every inch of yees, and wouldn t be hard upon a poor forlorner like meself."

"Ha!" exclaimed Huntly, "listen!" and at the moment we heard the gloomy howl of a pack of wolves.

"They already smell the feast prepared for them," I rejoined.

"Well, Frank, let us return to our camp fire; for I see the trappers have nearly completed their unenviable task."

Acting upon his suggestion, we set forward, and gaining the fire, were soon joined by Black George and Daring Tom, who came up with five bloody scalps dangling at their girdles—bringing with them also some two or three rifles, a fresh supply of powder and ball, and various other trifles which they had taken from the dead Indians.

"I think we can count a coup this heat," observed the old mountaineer, with his peculiar, quiet laugh: "Eh! Tom?"

"We can't do nothin else," was the satisfactory response.

"I say, Tom, them wolves smell blood."

"Well they does."

"Thar's plenty o' meat for 'em, any how; and ef they'll jest foller us, and them skunks of Pawnees want to try this here over agin, we'll make 'em fat. Eh! Tom?"

"Will so-o."

"Yes, I'll be dog-gone ef we don't! But I say, Tom, ain't it most time for Rash and Fire to be in?"

"I reckon."

"Hope they didn't git throwed. It 'ud be a pity to hev them go under jest now—and would spile all our sport."

"Well it would, hoss."

"Hark! thar goes a whistle! That's them, or I'm a nigger."

"'Taint nobody else," responded Daring Tom.

"All right. Augh! Let's smoke."

Squatting themselves upon the ground, cross-legged, the trappers filled their pipes, and commenced puffing away as though nothing had happened to disturb their equanimity. Such perfect recklessness of life, such indifference to danger, I had never seen displayed before; and though I abhorred some of their customs, I could not but admire their coolness and valor. Their sense of hearing I soon discovered was far more acute than mine; for when the old trapper spoke of the whistle of his comrades, I could not, for the life of me, detect a distant sound proceeding from human lips. But that he was right, was soon evident; for in less than five minutes after, Fiery Ned and Rash Will made their appearance, and quietly stealing up to the circle, threw themselves upon the ground without a remark. At the belt of each hung a fresh scalp, showing that two more of the enemy had been their victims.

For some time the two smoked away in silence, and then suggesting to the others the propriety of joining them, all four were soon in full blast. After a little, they began to talk over their exploits; and amusing themselves in this way for an hour or more, one after another straightened himself out on the earth, an example which Teddy soon imitated, and in five minutes all were lost in sleep.

As for Huntly and myself, slumber had fled our eyelids; and stirring the fire, we seated ourselves at a little distance and talked till daylight—I narrating my singular dream, and both commenting upon it. All night long we heard the howling of the ravenous wolves, as they tore the flesh from the bones of our dead foes, and occasionally caught a gleam of their fiery eye-balls, when they ventured nearer than usual to our camp.

———o———

CHAPTER X.

JOURNEY RESUMED—UNPLEASANT FEELINGS—CAMP—RESTLESSNESS—A HALF FORMED RESOLUTION—THE LONELY WATCH—TERRIFIC THUNDERSTORM—PAINFUL SEPARATION—JOYFUL MEETING—LOSS OF ANIMALS—SECOND CAMP.

At an early hour in the morning we resumed our journey. As we moved along, I beheld the bones of two of our late foes, basking white and ghastly in the sunlight, their clean-licked, shiny skulls, hollow sockets, and grinning teeth and jaws, fairly making my flesh to creep. And the more so, perhaps, as I took into consideration that only a few hours before, these same bones belonged to animated human beings; and that a mere turn of the wheel of fate might have placed me in their position, they in mine. Death is a solemn thing to contemplate at any time, and I was now in a mood to feel its terrors in more than their wonted force. My dream, although I tried to dispel it as only a dream, still made a deep impression upon my mind; and this, together with what occurred afterward, and the remembrance of the conversation I had held with my friend the morning previous, touching Lilian, all tended to depress my spirits and make me melancholy.

At length, to rouse me from my sinking stupor, I turned my eyes upon Huntly; but perceiving that he too was deep in thought, I did not disturb his revery; while my own mind, settling back into itself, if I may be permitted the expression, wandered far away to the past, recalled a thousand old scenes, and then leaped forward to the future, and became perplexed in conjectures regarding my final fate.

About noon we reached the banks of the Blue river, and, as on the preceding day, halted a few minutes to rest and refresh ourselves and animals. Here I noticed trees of oak, ash, walnut and hickory, with occasionally one of cottonwood and willow. The bottoms of this stream are often wide and fertile, on which the wild pea vine grows in abundance. The pea itself is somewhat smaller than that grown in the settlements, and can be used as vegetable, its flavor being agreeable.

As our meat was now running short, Daring Tom observed that he would "make somethin come;" and setting forth with his rifle, soon returned heavily laden with wild turkeys. Hastily dressing, we threw them into our possible sacks, and again set forward.

Traveling some fifteen miles through woodland and over prairie, we encamped at last in a beautiful little grove of ash and hickory, on the margin of a creek that flowed into the Blue. The day had been excessively hot and sultry, and all of us were much fatigued. Starting a fire as usual we cooked some of our turkey meat, and found it very delicious. As no Indian sign had been discovered through the day, it was thought unnecessary to set a guard, and accordingly we stretched ourselves upon the earth around the fire, and in a few minutes, with the exception of myself, all were sound asleep.

I could not rest. I tried to, but in vain. The air was filled with musquitoes, and various other insects, attracted hither by the fire-light, and they annoyed me exceedingly. This was not all. My mind, as in fact it had been throughout the day, was sorely depressed. A thousand thoughts, that I vainly strove to banish, obtruded themselves upon me. In spite of myself, I thought of my dream. Pshaw! why should that trouble me? It could not be true, I knew; and was only caused by the previous remarks of Huntly, my excited feelings, and surrounding circumstances. Still it came up in my mind, as startlingly as I had dreamed it; and, in spite of my scoffings, with every appearance of reality. I was not naturally superstitious, and did not believe in dreams—but this one haunted me as a foreboding of evil to her I loved; and as I lay and meditated, I half formed the resolution to set out in the morning upon my return, already sick of my undertaking.

It is one thing to read of adventures in others, and another to experience them ourself; and this I felt, oh! how keenly! To strengthen my resolution, I pictured the home of my parents, the sadness which I knew must be preying upon them on account of my absence, and the flash of joy that would light their faces and warm their hearts on beholding their only son once more seated at their fireside, never to depart again while he or they were blessed with life. I thought over all this, and grew stronger in my new resolve; and had it not been for the whimsical fear of ridicule—the idle jest of some coxcomb fool, for whose opinion or regard in any other way I cared not a straw—it is more than probable this narrative had not been written.

What a powerful engine is ridicule! It is the battering-ram of the mind, and will often destroy by a single blow the mightiest fabric of reason. It is used by fools and men whose minds are too imbecile to cope with the edifice of thought which towers above their limited grasp; and yet the very architect of such construction fears it, as does the poor red-man the annihilating artillery of the pale-face.

I lay and thought; and the more I thought, the more restless I became. I rolled to and fro in an agony of mind that at last became intolerable, and I arose. Stealing quietly from the sleeping circle, I proceeded to the creek, and having moistened my parched and feverish lips, and bathed my heated temples and brow, I took my way thence to a little bluff on the opposite side, whence I could overlook the valley for a considerable extent.

Seating myself upon a rock, I gazed around. Below was our camp fire, brightly burning, beside which I could trace, with a shadowy indistinctness, the outlines of the sleeper's dark forms. There they lay, all unconscious to the outer world, perhaps enjoying the pleasure of some delightful dream. How I envied them their sleep! Beyond them, by the same light, I could faintly perceive our animals—hoppled, but not picketed, the latter being thought unnecessary—quietly grazing.

It was a warm, still, starlight night. Above me the heavens were brilliantly studded with myriads of shining orbs whose light fell softly and sweetly upon the sleeping earth. Here, not a scud floated in the clear atmosphere; but in the west I could perceive huge black clouds, lifting their ill-shaped heads above the horizon, darting forth the red bolts of heaven, while a far-off rumbling sound came jarringly upon my ear.

Fixing my gaze at last in this direction, I sat and watched the rapid progress of an approaching storm. On it came like a mighty squadron, a few fleecy clouds as banners thrown out in advance, behind which flashed and thundered its dread artillery, making the very earth tremble beneath the sound.

From youth up, the rapid play of lightning had strongly affected my nervous system, and made me a coward; and now—lonely, sad and gloomy—I was in a proper condition to feel its effects more sensibly than ever. Half an hour past, and the rolling clouds had darkened the western heavens, while the almost incessant flashes of fire seemed to set the earth in a blaze, and as often vanishing, left it shrouded in a darkness almost impenetrable.

Dismal as was the scene, I sat with my eyes rivetted upon it, while a painful sense of awe made my limbs feel weak and my blood move sluggishly through my veins, or rush over me with flashes of feverish heat. Several times I arose with the intention of returning to camp, but as often resumed my former position, as if enchained to the spot by some powerful magic spell.

On came the storm with startling velocity, and presently I could see the tops of distant trees bending to the blast—the rain falling in broad, white sheets, as if about to deluge the earth—and hear the truly dismal roaring of the rushing winds. I would have returned to my companions now, but our camp afforded no protection, and I fancied myself as safe where I was.

At last it broke upon me in all its force; and such a storm I never witnessed before, and hope never to again. I feel myself incompetent to describe it. The rain fell in torrents; the wind blew a perfect hurricane; and tall, old trees, which had perhaps stood for centuries, were broken and uprooted; while others, together with surrounding rocks, were shattered by the fiery bolts, whose crashing reports fairly deafened me. How I maintained my position—why I was not hurled headlong down the cliff—is still a mystery to myself. Occasionally I caught a glimpse of my companions moving about below, evidently trying to secure their powder from the storm; while Huntly was running to and fro in search of his friend, and, to all appearance, surprised, alarmed and distressed. Our animals too had become frightened, and, rearing and plunging, they soon broke loose of their tethers, and dashed madly over the plain in every direction. I would have joined my companions now, but this had become impossible; for the rain had already swelled the little creek between me and them into a mighty stream, that rolled its dark, angry waters with fury below me, and added its sullen roar to the howlings of the storm. I shouted, but my voice was lost even to myself in the mightier ones of the furious elements.

Two hours—two long, never-to-be-forgotten hours—did the storm rage thus in fury; and in those two hours methought I lived a lifetime. Then to my joy it began to abate; and in half an hour more I again beheld the twinkling stars through rents in the driving clouds; while the flashing lightning and the roaring thunder gradually becoming less and less distinct to eye and ear, told me the devastating storm was fast speeding on toward the east.

I now descended to the creek to join my companions, but finding it too much swollen to attempt a passage with safety, I again ascended the cliff, and shouted to them to assure them of my safety. At first I could not make them hear; but after repeated trials, I had the satisfaction of receiving an answering shout from Huntly, who immediately set off in the direction whence he supposed my voice proceeded. After a minute's search, during which we both called to each other continually, Huntly, was enabled to make out my locality—but the creek prevented our meeting during the night.

At day-break I discovered him and Teddy standing on the opposite side; and as the flood had a little subsided, I plunged in and swam across—not, however, without much difficulty and danger, nor until the rushing waters had borne me some forty or fifty yards down the stream. No sooner was I safe on the bank, than Huntly threw his arms around my neck and wept like a child.

"Thank God! Frank, my friend," he exclaimed, "that I am able to clasp you once again! Oh! if you could but know my feelings of last night! I thought you were lost—lost to me forever!" and again he was forced to dash the tears from his eyes. "But tell me, Frank—how came you there?"

I proceeded to detail every particular.

"A horrible night to you, too, Frank," said Huntly, in reply. "But hereafter, my friend, you must not steal away from me in this way. If you have troubles, share them with me."

Teddy was greatly rejoiced to see me also; and he got me by the hand, and by the leg, and capered around me like delighted child—at the same time uttering various phrases in his peculiar style, which, in spite of all that had happened, did not fail to amuse and sometimes make me laugh aloud.

I found the trappers surly and grumbling at what they considered their ill-luck—being for the most part in the loss of a few pounds of powder, and their mules—all of which had escaped, as well as our horses.

"Augh!" grunted Black George as I came up. "Glad to see you, boy. Thought you'd gone under. It was a screecher of a night, wasn't it? Lost heaps of powder, and all the critters gone to the ——. Augh!"

My powder had fortunately been so packed that nearly all was safe; and as I had a great store on hand, I gave each of the mountaineers a pound, which served to put them in a better humor.

We now separated and set off in different directions to hunt our animals, with the understanding that this should be our rendezvous. We had a wearisome time of it, and it was late in the day before we all got together again. All, however, had been recovered; and mounting, we set forward once more rather briskly, and encamped some ten miles distant.

———o———

CHAPTER XI.

OUR COURSE ALONG THE PLATTE—KILLING AND DRESSING A BUFFALO—THEIR PATHS —THE PRAIRIE-DOG—THEIR TOWNS, APPEARANCE, HABITS, FOOD, ETC.—THE SOLITARY TOWER—CHIMNEY ROCK—SCOTT'S BLUFFS—ORIGIN OF THE NAME—FORT LARAMIE—ARRIVAL AT—ITS APPEARANCE, INMATES, ETC.—CURIOSITY.

The next morning we set forward again, and keeping a northwesterly course, mostly over a rolling prairie, encamped on the second night on the banks of the Nebraska or Platte river. This river is very shallow, and flows over a sandy bed. We found the bottom at this point some three or four miles wide, devoid of a tree, and covered with excellent grass, besprinkled with a salinous substance, which caused our animals to devour it greedily.

Setting our faces westward, we now followed the course of the Platte for several days, without a single incident occurring worth being recorded. The Platte bottoms we found to vary from two to four miles in breadth, and in some places our animals fared slimly. On the fourth day Fiery Ned shot a fat buffalo, which was the first I had ever seen close at hand. This animal dies very hard, even when mortally wounded; and an individual unacquainted with its nature—or, as the mountaineers would term him, a "green horn"—though never so good a marksman, would assuredly fail, using the hunters' phrase, "to throw him in his tracks." One would suppose that a shot about the head or central part of the body would prove fatal—but nothing is more erroneous. To kill a bull, the ball must either divide his spine, or enter his body behind the shoulder, a few inches above the brisket—this being the only point through which his heart and lungs are accessible. And even here, the vital part of all vitality, with a ball directly through his heart, I was informed by one of the hunters that he had known an old bull run half a mile before falling.

The buffalo killed was a fat cow; and turning her upon her back, the trappers proceeded to dress her in the real mountain style. Parting the skin from head to tail with a sharp knife, directly across the belly, they peeled down the hide on either side; and then taking from her the "hump rib," "tender loin," "fleece," "tongue," and "boudins," they left the remainder, with the exception of the skin, which was thrown across one of the mules, to the vigilant care of the wolves. The "boudin," a portion of the entrails, is considered by the mountaineers the titbit of all. Slightly browned over a fire, it is swallowed, yard after yard, without being separated, and, I may add, without resulting in the least inconvenience to the gormand.

Through this section of country I observed innumerable buffalo paths, running from the bluffs to the river, and crossing each other in every direction. These paths present a striking appearance to one unused to the sight, being more than a foot in width, some three or four inches in depth, and as smooth and even as if cut artificially.

But to Huntly and myself, the most

amusing and interesting sights of all we saw on the route, were the towns of the prairie-dog, which are to be found at different intervals along the whole course of the sandy Platte, and through several of which we passed. The first one we came to, so astonished and interested us, that Huntly, Teddy and myself dismounted to take a closer view, while the trappers, being of course familiar with such things, steadily pursued their way.

The prairie-dog is above the size of a large gray squirrel, somewhat longer than a Guinea-pig, of a brownish or sandy hue, with a head somewhat resembling a bull dog. Being of a social disposition, they collect together in large bodies, and build their towns on a gravelly plain, some of them being miles in extent, and with a population equalling the largest cities of America, or even Europe. Their earthen houses, which are from two to three feet in hight, are made in the form of a cone. They are entered by a hole in the top or apex, which descends vertically some three feet or more, and then takes an oblique course and connects with others in every direction. Their streets are laid out with something approaching regularity, and they evidently have a sort of police, and laws to govern them, not unlike those of superior and more enlightened beings. In some of the towns, a house larger than ordinary occupies a central position, which is tenanted by a sleek, fat dog, supposed to be the presiding functionary of the place, whose sole employment appears to be in sunning himself outside his domicil, and noting with patriarchal gravity the doings of his inferiors.

The town which myself and companions halted to examine, was one of the larger class, and covered an area, to the best of my judgment, of at least five hundred acres. On our approach, a certain portion of the little fellows ran to the mouth of their holes, and squatting down commenced a shrill barking, not unlike that made by a toy-dog—whereupon the pups and smaller sized animals betook themselves with the utmost despatch to their burrows. A nearer approach drove the more daring under cover, whence they took the liberty of peeping out to examine us, and occasionally of uttering a shrill bark, as a gentle hint that our company was anything but agreeable.

The food of these interesting little fellows consists, for the most part, of prairie grass and roots. They live a life of constant alarm—being watched and pounced upon continually by the wolf, the hawk, the eagle, &c. They are very hospitable to such animals as choose to come and live peaceably among them—and the screech owl and rattlesnake are their constant guests; and it is not unusual, I was told, to find all three burrowed together in one hole. They are sometimes eaten by the Indian and mountaineer.

Spending an hour or more in examining the town, we remounted our horses and soon overtook the trappers, Teddy observing as we quitted the village:

"Faith, your honors, but thim is queer bir-r-ds now, isn't they? Och! be me mother's hair! it's like they've bin down to St. Louey and got the notion in their heads and think they can baat the city, the spalpeens! I'd like 'em to go and sae Dublin, now—maybe that 'ud astonish 'em a wee bit, and give 'em some new idees respicting public idifices, jist. Ochone! Ireland's the place to taach 'em—the baastly serpints of bir-r-ds that they is."

The first natural object of curiosity I beheld after crossing the South Fork of the Platte, was the Solitary Tower, opposite which we encamped on the margin of a small stream called Little Creek. This tower, composed of sand and clay, resembles a stone edifice, and being some seven or eight hundred feet in hight, can be seen at a distance of fifteen or twenty miles. To the distant beholder it presents the appearance of some mighty structure of feudal days; but a near view dispels the illusion, and the spectator sees before him only a rough, unseemly, but stupendous pile —thus verifying the words of the poet, that

"Distance lends enchantment to the view."

I was informed by Black George, that this tower could be ascended, though at some risk to the adventurer; and that he and another trapper had made the trial some years before, and spent one cold winter's night in one of its damp crevices—escaping by this means a party of hostile savages on his trail. I did not attempt the ascent myself.

The following day, before noon, we reached Chimney Rock, another natural curiosity, which can be seen at a distance of thirty miles, and which afar off resembles a shot tower; but as you near it, it gradually assumes the appearance of a haystack, with a pole protruding from the apex. It is about two hundred feet in hight, and is composed of much the same substance as the Solitary Tower. The rains are gradually wearing it away, and in course of time it will cease to be an object of curiosity. Black George informed me that twenty years before, it was at least a hundred and fifty or two hundred feet above its present elevation.

Pursuing our journey, we encamped in the evening on Scott's Bluffs, where we found a good spring, and plenty of grass for our animals. As wood was abundant here, we started a fire, and while sitting around discussing our meat and smoking our pipes, the old trapper, who had not been loquacious for several days, observed:

"Strangers, heyar's what can't look round this spot without feelin badly—I'll be dog-gone ef I can!"

"And why so?" I asked.

"Case one o' the almightiest best fellers you ever seed, went under here. I knowed him like a trump; and he was one o' them chaps you could bear to talk about—real mountain grit, with a hand that u'd make your fingers ache when he squeezed 'em, and a fist that could knock a hole into your upper story and let in the atmospheric ef he didn't like ye. Yes, he was one o' the purtiest men that ever raised hair, throwed buffler, trapped beaver, swallered "boudins," or I'm a liar. But all wouldn't do. Death sot his trap and cotched him, and left jest a few floatin sticks in the shape o' bones to let us know he was a goner. He died right down thar, 'bout six paces from whar you're settin."

"Tell us the story."

"It's purty easy told. Him and a heap o' other fellers had bin up on a right smart trade with the Injins, and was comin down this way, going to the States, when a lot o' the cussed varmints jumped on to 'em and stole every blessed thing they had, even to thar guns, powder, meat, and be —— to 'em. Well, Jimmy Scott—him as I's tellin about—he hadn't bin well for a week, and gittin aground o' fodder fetched him right over the coals. He kicked mighty hard at first; but findin it wasn't no use, he gin in, and told them as was with him that his time was up, and he would hev to do the rest o' his trappin in another country, and that they'd best put out while they'd got meat enough on thar bones to make wolves foller 'em. They hated to leave him like darnation—but they had to do it; and so they sot him up agin a rock and vamosed. This was about a mile down on tother side thar; and arter they'd gone, Jimmy got up and paddled here, whar he laid down and went a wolfin. Nobody ever seed Jimmy Scott arterwards—but they found his floatin sticks here, and gin this the name o' Scott's Bluffs."

The next day, long before sundown, we came in sight of Fort Laramie, where it was the intention of Huntly and myself to spend a few days, to refresh ourselves and rest our animals, before attempting the perilous journey of the mountains. On our whole route, from the moment we crossed Kansas river, we had not been gladdened by the sight of a single white man but ourselves; and consequently my delight may be imagined, when I beheld the walls of this celebrated fortress appear in the distance, and felt that there at least I could rest in safety.

Fort Laramie stands upon slightly elevated ground, some two miles from the Platte, and on the west bank of Laramie Fork. It is a dirty and clumsy looking edifice, built of adobes,* after the Mexican style, with walls some two feet in thickness and fifteen in hight, in which are planted posts to support the roof, the whole being covered with a clay-like substance. Through this wall are two gateways, one at the north and the other at the south, and the top is surmounted by a wooden palisade. Over the main or front entrance is a square tower, built also of adobes; and at two angles, diagonally opposite each other, are large square bastions, so arranged as to sweep the four faces of the walls. The center of the fort is an open square, quadrangular in shape, along the

---

* Sun-burned bricks.

sides of which are dwellings, store-rooms, stables, carpenter shops, smith shops, offices, &c., all fronting upon the inner area.

This fort belongs to the North American Fur Company, and is a general rendezvous for traders, travelers, trappers, Indians, emigrants, &c., on their way to and from the different trading posts, Oregon and the United States. Here may be found representatives of all nations and colors, meeting on an equal footing, often drinking and gambling together, many of whom may be put down as implacable enemies, and who, at another time and place, would think nothing of cutting each others' throats. Here occasionally may be seen the Ponka, the Pawnee, the Crow, the Blackfoot, the Sioux and the Shoshone—intermingled with the Spaniard, the Frenchman, the Mexican, the Anglo-Saxon, the Dutchman and Negro. The trapper comes in at certain seasons loaded with furs, and receives in exchange for them powder, lead, tobacco, whisky, &c., at the most exorbitant prices. Then generally follow a few days of dissipation—in feasting, gambling, drunkenness, and sometimes riot—when he finds all his hard earnings gone, and he obliged to betake himself again to the mountains, to procure a new supply, to be squandered in the same reckless manner.

As we rode up to the fort, we noticed several Indians standing outside, carelessly leaning against the mud-covered walls, their persons bedecked with gew-gaws, and their faces bedaubed with paint, looking surly and ferocious, evidently under the excitement of liquor, and ready at any moment, did not their cowardice and fears restrain them, to take the life and scalp of the first white man that should come in their way. Standing among them, and addressing one who from his superiority of costume and equipments I judged to be a chief, was a man of small stature, mostly concealed under a large sarape and broad-brimmed sombrero.

"H—l!" exclaimed Black George, with an indignant scowl: "Ef thar aint one o' them infernal Greasers, I wish I may be dogged! Well, all I've got to say is, he'd better not come foolin round this child, or he'll find his hair lifted. Eh! Ned?"

"Won't nothin short."

Passing through the gateway, we soon had the satisfaction of seeing our cavallada well disposed of; and entering the common reception room, took a friendly drink together; after which, lighting our pipes, (Huntly and myself had already adopted this habit since leaving home,) we strolled around the fortress to gratify our curiosity, and while away the time till supper.

We found everything in perfect order, all the various compartments cleanly, and the fort well garrisoned by a dozen hardy fellows, each of whom had seen more or less service, and the commander of whom was at least a veteran in experience if not in years.

The fort was not crowded by any means —it not being the season of year for the traders and trappers to be "in"—but still the number of guests was quite respectable. There were a few families of emigrants on their way to Oregon and California, and one or two home-sick ones on their return to the United States, looking pale, sickly, and dejected. Some half a dozen Indians, two or three Mexicans, as many French *voyageurs*, four or five trappers and hunters—all of whom were recognized by our companions—a brace of Yankee speculators, another of *coureur des bois*,* together with the squaw-wives and children of the garrison—completed, as far as I could judge by a hasty glance, the present occupants of the station.

On the eastern side of the fort we found an additional wall to the one I have described, which connected with the main one at both extremities, and enclosed ground for stabling and *carrell*. A large gateway opened into this from the southern side, and a postern communicated with it from the main enclosure. Here were *carrelled* a few mules and cattle belonging to the emigrants, while in the stables our own horses were enjoying the best the country afforded, for which of course we expected to pay at least six prices. In view of this important item, and their incapacity to meet it, the mountaineers had taken care to put their mules on less expensive diet.

In the main enclosure or common, were

---

* Itinerant traders or peddlers.

several heavy Pittsburgh wagons, some of which were undergoing repairs at the hands of the various mechanics employed about the station. As we drew near them after leaving the carrell, we noticed that several had left their employment and collected in a group round some object which we could not make out from where we stood, while others had suspended their labors and were gazing in the same direction, evidently on the point of joining their comrades. As by this time Huntly and I were by ourselves, and our curiosity being excited, we eagerly sprang forward, and elbowing our way through the fast thickening crowd, to our surprise beheld what I shall proceed to describe in the following chapter.

CHAPTER XII.

THE CURIOUS INDIAN PONY—ALARMING RUMOR—POMPOSITY—THE RENOWNED MOUNTAINEER—THE AMUSING MISTAKE—THE MYSTERIOUS EQUESTRIENNE.

In the center of the ring stood an Indian pony of the largest class, and the most beautiful animal I had ever seen. His color was a jet black, and so glossy that it seemed to possess the power of reflection. Every point and limb was perfectly developed, with legs sleek and slim, and a beautifully arched neck, on which was a head that bore the look of conscious superiority and pride. His trappings were in perfect keeping with all the rest. A small, delicately formed Spanish saddle, designed for an equestrienne, surmounted his back, underneath which was a saddle blanket of wampum, most beautifully wrought with fine, shiny beads of all colors, into various birds and flowers, and which being long and hanging low, almost enveloped him in its ample folds. Even his bridle, martingales, reins, and belly-girth, were worked in the same beautiful manner, with beads of red, white and blue. He was walking to and fro, snuffing the air, pawing the ground, and occasionally turning his gaze upon the crowd with a proud look, as if conscious he was an object both of curiosity and admiration.

Various were the remarks of surprise and delight which were passed upon him by the excited spectators, some of whom ventured to pat his sleek neck and rub his head. At length one strapping fellow caught him by the bridle, and placed his hand upon the saddle as if with the intention of vaulting upon his back. But this, according to the pony's notion, was carrying familiarity a little too far; and with a loud neigh, a rear and plunge, he tore himself away, nor would he afterward permit a hand to touch him, although he still remained quietly in the ring.

"By heavens!" exclaimed Huntly, "saw you ever the like, Frank?—saw you any thing of the brute creation so beautiful?"

"Never in my life," I replied; "and I assure you I am anxious to behold his rider—for by the saddle it is a female."

"True; I did not think of that; and if she prove half as beautiful, i' faith I fear I shall find myself in love with her."

"Notwithstanding the lovely unknown —eh! Charley?"

"Come, come—no home thrusts now," answered Huntly, good humoredly. "Do not rub a part already too tender."

"Well, heyar's what's seed a good many sights in my time, but I'll be dog-gone ef ever I seed any thing o' the hoss kind as could hold a primin to this critter," said the voice of Black George, who had come up behind us.

"But who and where is the rider?" I asked, turning to him.

"Don't know whar, but spect it's some squaw or other—augh!"

"The rider is an Indian female, the most perfect I ever beheld," rejoined a stranger at my elbow, and whom I recognized as one of the speculators previously mentioned.

"Where is she? where is she?" cried several voices, before I had time to respond to my informant; and immediately the stranger became the center of observation

"She is now closetted with the commander of the garrison."

"Then perhaps she brings important news?" observed Huntly.

"Nothing more probable, sir," was the reply. "There is a good deal of dissatisfaction among the Indians, I understand."

"Indeed!" I replied. "And do yo

think the route westward particularly dangerous at this time?"

"I do; for rumors have reached us that the Crows, the Oglallahs, the Gros Ventres, the Cheyennes, and one or two other tribes, have vowed to take vengeance on all the whites that fall in their way; and it is said, I do not know with how much truth, that the Oglallahs are out on the Black Hill range and in the vicinity of the Red Buttes, while the Crows are skulking through the valley of the Sweetwater."

"Why this is alarming, truly," I rejoined; "and certainly discouraging to those who, like ourselves, are going merely for adventure and amusement."

"If adventure or *amusement* is your only object in crossing the Rocky mountains, take my advice, young men, and either turn back or remain where you are."

"And yet why should they turn back?" said a voice behind us. "All men ar born to die, and it's not probable any will go before thar time. Courage and resolution ar everything in this part of the world."

I turned round and beheld in the speaker a young man of small stature and robust frame, over whose clean-shaven face time had not drawn a wrinkle. His features were regular and prepossessing. The general expression of his intelligent countenance was so reserved and unobtrusive, that I readily felt surprised he should have hazarded the remarks just quoted, without first being called upon for his opinion. To all appearance he had not seen over twenty-five winters, though in reality he might have been much older, so difficult was it to determine by his countenance. He had light hair—a keen, restless, eagle-like gray eye—an ample forehead—and a skin which, but for exposure to all kinds of weather, had doubtless been as fair and as soft as a lady's. Though small in stature and small limbed, as I said before, I noticed there was in all a beautiful symmetry,—a perfect adaptation of one part to another. His limbs, though slender, were plump and wiry, with muscles of iron; and being something of a connoisseur in such matters, I at once put him down as an active, and, for his inches, a powerful man. He was costumed in the usual mountain style, and I judged had just entered the fort, as I did not remember having seen him before.

As he spoke, I noticed that several of the bystanders whispered to others, and that instantly all eyes became fixed upon him, with an air of curiosity which I could not account for—there being nothing particularly remarkable in his appearance, as I have shown by my description. The stranger to whom he had addressed his remarks, coolly examined him from head to foot, as one who felt a little nettled at his interference, and wished to assure himself of the exact importance that should be attached to his words before he ventured a reply. By a slight curl of the lip into something like a sneer, I saw at once he was not a judge of human nature, and had underrated the new comer not a little. He was himself a supercilious man, who delighted in giving advice with a patronizing air, and consequently did not care to have his wise counsel questioned by what he evidently considered an interloper. He therefore, after taking a complete and rather insolent survey of the other's person, replied rather pompously:

"Why should they turn back, say you? Because there is danger, great danger, to them if they advance farther, as any one who is at all acquainted with this part of the country must be aware. If you had traveled it as much as *I* have, sir, (there was an important stress on the pronoun,) you would, I fancy, understand the value of my advice; but young men (the speaker was about thirty) on their first hunt are apt to be very knowing and imprudent—and, sir, I may add, without wishing to be personal, a little *impudent* also."

Here the speaker straightened himself up with an air of importance, and glanced around upon the spectators, where he saw many a quiet smile, which he was fain to attribute to silent approvals of his own lofty and conclusive argument. The new comer also smiled slightly, as he quietly asked:

"May I inquire, sir, how much of the country you've traveled?"

"Thousands of miles, young man—thousands of miles, sir! Yes, sir!! I have been twice to Oregon, and once to California."

"Is that all?"

'That all, sir! Umph! that, let me tell you, is a good deal, sir, as you will find when *you* have gone over the half of it."

"I think I have already—at least that's my impression," was the somewhat nettling answer, which was rendered none the less so to the speculator, by a few half suppressed titters and one hearty laugh from the crowd.

"*Indeed!* young man. Pray be so good as to inform us *where* you have been?"

"It would be much easier to tell you whar I've *not* been," answered the other pleasantly. "But I may say, without fear of contradiction, that I've seen nearly every foot of ground from the Yellow Stone to the Spanish Peaks—from the Mississippi to the Pacific ocean."

"Your name, stranger?" said the other, a little crest-fallen.

"I'm called KIT CARSON."

At the quiet mention of that renowned name, better known on the mountains and over the broad West than that of any other living being, and which was as familiar to me as a household word, I involuntarily gave a start of surprise, while three deafening cheers went up from the crowd, mingled with boisterous shouts of laughter, to the no small chagrin and mortification of the pompous speculator, who muttered something which to me sounded very much like an oath.

Here, then, stood the famous Kit Carson! a being I had long had a secret desire to behold, but whom I had always pictured to myself as huge, rough, brawny and ferocious. Nor could I bring myself to realize that the person before me was that same incarnate devil in Indian fight I had heard him represented, and who had killed and scalped more savages in the same number of years than any two hunters west of the old Mississippi.

When the laugh and tumult had somewhat subsided, the stranger, anxious to escape ridicule, observed:

"Gentlemen, I acknowledge my verdancy, and feel myself indebted to you a treat. Kit Carson, your hand! and how will you have yours—mixed or clear?"

Another burst of merriment broke from the crowd, with three hearty cheers for the speculator and the prospect of a speedy "wet" all round. Suddenly the boisterous tumult subsided as if by magic, and not a man ventured a remark above a whisper, while the eyes of each became fixed upon some object on the opposite side of the square.

"Stand back! stand back! She comes! she comes!" I heard whispered on all sides of me.

"Look, Frank—look!" said Huntly, in a suppressed voice, clutching my arm nervously.

I did look; and what I beheld I feel myself incompetent to describe and do the subject justice. Before me, perfectly erect, her tiny feet scarce seeming to touch the ground she trod, was a being which required no great stretch of imagination to fancy just dropped from some celestial sphere. She was a little above medium in stature, as straight as an arrow, and with a form as symmetrical and faultless as a Venus. Twenty summers (I could not realize she had ever seen a winter) had molded her features into what I may term a classic beauty, as if chiselled from marble by the hand of a master. Her skin was dark, but not more so than a Creole's, and with nothing of the brownish or reddish hue of the native Indian. It was beautifully clear too, and apparently of a velvet-like softness. Her hair was a glossy black, and her hazel eyes were large and lustrous, fringed with long lashes, and arched by fine, pencilled brows. Her profile was straight from forehead to chin, and her full face oval, lighted with a soul of feeling, fire and intelligence. A well formed mouth, guarded by two plump lips, was adorned by a beautiful set of teeth, partially displayed when she spoke or smiled. A slightly aquiline nose gave an air of decision to the whole countenance, and rendered its otherwise almost too effeminate expression, noble, lofty and commanding.

Her costume was singular, and such as could not fail to attract universal attention. A scarlet waistcoat concealed a well developed bust, to which were attached short sleeves and skirts—the latter coming barely to the knees, something after the fashion of the short frock worn by the danseuse of the present day. These skirts were showily embroidered with wampum, and a wampum belt passed around her waist, in which glittered a silver-mounted Spanish dirk. From the frock downward, leggins and moccasins beautifully wrought into various figures with beads, enclosed the legs and feet. A tiara of many colored feathers, to which were attached little bells that tinkled as she walked, surmounted the head; and a bracelet of pearl on either well rounded arm, with a necklace of the same material, completed her costume and ornaments.

With a proud carriage, and an unabashed look from her dark, eloquent eye, she advanced a few paces, glanced loftily around upon the surprised and admiring spectators, and then struck the palms of her hands together in rapid succession. In a moment her Indian pony came prancing to her side. With a single bound she vaulted into the saddle, and gracefully waving us a silent adieu, instantly vanished through the open gateway.

Rushing out of the fort, the excited crowd barely caught one more glimpse of her beautiful form, ere it became completely lost in the neighboring forest.

"Who is she? who can she be?" cried a dozen persons at once.

"PERRARIE FLOWER, or I'm a nigger," shouted a well known voice in reply.

I turned and beheld Black George already working himself up to a great pitch of excitement.

---o---

CHAPTER XIII.

PRAIRIE FLOWER AND HER ALARMING INTELLIGENCE—SUPERSTITION—SPECULATION—
—THE DILEMMA—KIT KARSON'S SUGGESTION—THE DECISION—TEACHING TEDDY—
THE MARCH—THE SCOUTS—THE HALT AND PREPARATIONS FOR FIGHT.

THE news brought by Prairie Flower we learned in the course of the evening was of the utmost importance—being to the effect that a large band of warriors, composed chiefly of Oglallahs and Cheyennes, had taken up their position in the vicinity of Bitter Cottonwood—a place some twenty-five miles distant—and had vowed to cut off all the whites that came that way, either going to or coming from Oregon. The result of this information was to cause no little alarm in the station, particularly among the emigrants, who being for the greater part composed of women and children, were consequently in no fit condition to brave the assaults of a blood-thirsty body of savages.

But who was Prairie Flower—the mysterious messenger that belonged to the Indians, and yet came like a guardian angel to warn the whites of their danger? Who was she indeed! None could answer. To all save the commander of the garrison and Black George, (who now had to rehearse his remarkable story a dozen times, to gratify the curiosity of the excited inquirers, and who became a personage of no little importance in consequence,) she was an utter stranger; and for all any one knew to the contrary, might have dropped from the skies, a winged being of a fairer realm. The commander of the garrison, whom I shall term Captain Balcolm, had seen her once before, when she came to warn him of the Sioux, who were meditating a descent upon the fort, a surprise and general massacre of its inmates, and whose design by this timely notice was thwarted; but regarding who she was, how she gained her information, to what tribe she belonged; or why she was permitted to do these good acts and escape—he could give no satisfactory reply. On both occasions she had required a private audience with him; and on the former one had sent a request to him by an Indian half-breed, to meet her in a little grove some hundred yards distant from the walls of the fortress.

At first he had refused to go unattended, for fear of some stratagem to take his life or make him prisoner. The messenger had gone back evidently dissatisfied, but in a few minutes had returned with a skin parchment, on which the same request, as orally delivered, was written with a charred stick, with the additional statement that the writer was a female, and that the news she had to convey was of great moment. Ashamed to show further cowardice, he had armed himself to the teeth, and calling his garrison around him, had notified them to be in readiness to protect the fort if besieged, and avenge him on the half-breed, whom he left with them as hostage, in case he returned not within two hours—

merely stating, by way of explanation, that he was going to hold a private conference with a distinguished chief. The result of this conference, as before stated, had been to save the lives of all, and defeat a well laid scheme of their enemies.

Captain Balcolm furthermore stated, that Prairie Flower, as she called herself, spoke the English language well and fluently; and that to his inquiry regarding herself and tribe, she had answered with a smile, that she must ever remain a mysterious being to him and all of his race; that as to tribe, she found herself a welcome guest with all—came and went as she chose without question or hindrance—and that the language of each she understood and spoke as readily as her mother tongue.

"In conclusion," added the gallant captain, "I must say, that with all my experience, I have never seen so perfect, so mysterious, so incomprehensible a being as herself. Were I superstitious, I should unquestionably be tempted to doubt my senses, and believe her a supernatural visiter; but I have touched her, and *know* that she is flesh and blood."

Many there were in the fort, however, who had not so much faith in her identity with an earthly habitant as the captain; and I often heard confidential whispers to the effect, that she was a being from another realm, who had assumed the mortal shape for the time, merely to bring about some special design of the Great Spirit; and that when said design should be accomplished, she would never be seen again by living mortal.

The Indian, it is well known to all who know anything of his history, is the most superstitious creature on earth, and believes in the direct interference of spirits, in bodily shape or otherwise, on any and every momentous occasion; and as the trapper or hunter is but little removed from him by civilization, and not a whit by knowledge gained from letters, it is hardly reasonable to suppose that he would imbibe ideas at war with those among whom the most of his eventful life is spent. In his earliest venture, he learns and adopts the habits of his enemy, and in some cases it would seem his very nature also; and the result is, that he becomes at last neither more nor less than what I may venture to term a civilized savage. And here I may remark, *en passant*, that your real, bona fide mountaineer, rarely looks beyond the lodge of some favorite tribe for a partner to share his toils and rear his progeny; and to the truth of this assertion, even the garrison of Fort Laramie bore striking evidence; for scarcely a wife among them, but was a full-blooded squaw—nor a child, but bore the cross of the red man and white.

Various were the speculations that night regarding Prairie Flower and her alarming intelligence. The truthfulness of the latter none seemed to question, however much they might the identity of the former with the race called mortal. That the Indians were at Bitter Cottonwood in great force, was therefore a matter beyond dispute and the question was what should be done under the circumstances? To remain inactive, was only to act the part of cowards, doom a portion of their own race to certain destruction, augment the confidence of the wily foe in his own resources, and consequently raise his hopes with the flush of success, and increase his daring and audacity. While, on the other hand, to assail him in all his strength in his own stronghold, with only a handful of men, was like rushing unarmed into the lion's den and courting speedy annihilation. In this dilemma what was to be done? Something, all admitted, must be done, and that quickly—but what that something was, now became a matter of serious deliberation. Some proposed one thing, and some another, and the discussion waxed warm, and seemed likely to be protracted indefinitely, without resulting in the agreement of any two to the proposal of any other two.

At length Kit Carson, who had sat and listened attentively without venturing a remark, observed:

"Say what you will, comrades, thar is after all but one way of settling this affair, and that is to pitch into the —— varmints and lift their hair. I've had a little experience in my time, if I am young in years, and may safely say I've never knowed an Indian yet as wasn't a coward, when assailed in a vigorous manner by a determined pale-face. I've rode right among thar lodges before now, and alone, single-handed, raised a top-knot in full view of fifty able bodied warriors, and their squaws and pappooses. Now if I could do this myself, it argues favorably for an attack upon them in numbers."

"But what, then, do you propose?" I inquired.

"Why, sir, to arm and mount on good horses a dozen or fifteen of us, dash into them, and fight our way out."

As he said this, his brow wrinkled, his eyes flashed, and his whole countenance exhibited traces of that fiery, reckless daring, which, together with its opposite coolness and great presence of mind, had already rendered him so famous in the wilderness. I saw at once, that however mild and quiet he might appear when not excited, it only needed an occasion like the present to bring out his latent energies and make him a terrible foe to contend with.

"Well," I rejoined, "although I came merely for adventure, and beyond that have no object in pursuing my way further, yet I will readily volunteer my services in a case of such emergency."

"And I," responded Huntly quickly.

"Your hands, gentlemen!" said Carson. "I took you for men, and I see I was not mistaken. Who next?"

This rapid decision produced an electrical effect upon all, and in a moment a dozen affirmative answers responded to the challenge, while each, eager to get ahead of his neighbor, now pressed around the young, famous, and daring mountaineer.

In less than half an hour, all preliminaries were settled, and sixteen hardy, able-bodied men were mustered into the ranks. These included the four trappers who had been our companions, together with Huntly, Teddy and myself.

It was then agreed that Kit Carson should be our leader, and that on the following day we should mount ourselves on the best horses that could be procured, and taking a roundabout course, should approach the savages as near as possible without being discovered, and await the night to commence our attack. The matter settled, we retired to rest, some of us for the last time before taking that final sleep which knows no waking.

Rolling myself in a buffalo skin, I threw myself upon the ground—but it was a long time before I could close my eyes in slumber. Thoughts of what another night might bring forth, kept me awake. I might be lying cold and dead upon the earth, a prey to wild beasts—or what was more terrifying, be a living captive to a merciless foe, doomed to the awful tortures of the stake. I thought too of home—of Lilian—of the mysterious Prairie Flower—and in the confusion of all these, fell asleep, to find them strangely commingled in my dreams.

The morning broke bright and beautiful; and ere the sun had more than gilded the loftiest peak of the Rocky Mountains, we were all astir, preparing for our hazardous expedition. With the assistance of Captain Balcolm, we succeeded in mustering sixteen fine horses, including of course those we had brought with us. We then armed ourselves to the teeth, with rifles, pistols, knives and tomahawks, and partaking of a savory breakfast tendered us by the gallant commander of the garrison, prepared ourselves to sally forth.

Before we departed, however, I had a task, which proved far more amusing than desirable, in explaining to Teddy the proper method of using his rifle and pistols, and the manner in which he must conduct himself in the forthcoming fight. Having shown him how to load, prime and sight the former weapon, I discharged it at a target, and ordered him to imitate my example with all the despatch possible.

"Jabers!" shouted Teddy in great glee, scampering off to the target to make an examination of my shot.

In a moment he returned, bringing it with him; and pointing triumphantly to a bullet-hole which he found in its center, he said:

"Troth, your honor, but thim same shooters is beautiful things, now, for murthering the baastly blaggards of Injins, jist. Here, now, ye's boured a howle right cintral as asy as meself could do wid a gimlet, and yees a standing there too all the whiles! Be me sowl too! an' now I remimbers I didn't sae the ball at all, at all, though I looked mighty sharp at it all the time wid my two eyes. Howly murther! but Amirica is a great country now, barring the tieving baasts of savages that's in it."

Something like an hour was spent in making Teddy familiar with the rifle, at the end of which, I had the satisfaction of finding him fit for duty. By this time all save he and I were in their saddles; and hastily mounting, we joined the cavalcade—Carson in the van, and amid three hearty cheers from the regular garrison (most of whom remained to protect the station), and earnest prayers from all for our safety and success in the coming contest—we quitted the fort.

Shaping our course along the bank of the river, we advanced some ten or fifteen miles over the regular Oregon route, when we came to a place called Big Spring, which takes its name from a large spring of water gushing out at the base of a steep hill, some quarter of a mile below the traveled road. Here we halted and held a council of war regarding our further progress, which resulted in the decision to quit the road at this point, and, by striking off to the left, keeping ourselves covered as much as possible in the wood, endeavor to gain a safe lodgment near the Indian camp, and remain quiet till after nightfall, when we must be guided wholly by circumstances. It was also thought prudent to throw out a few scouts in advance, lest we unknowingly should enter an ambuscade and all be cut off. For this purpose Carson dismounted, and appointing me his lieutenant, gave me private instructions regarding the route, and at what point, provided he had not joined us meantime, I was to halt and await him. Then ordering two Canadian-French voyageurs to dismount also, he said a few words to them in a jargon I did not understand, and in another moment all three had separated, and were buried in the surrounding wood at so many different points of compass.

Leading the unridden horses of the scouts, we slowly picked our way over rough and sometimes dangerous ground, keeping a sharp lookout on every side for fear of surprise, until the sun had reached within an hour and a half of the horizon, when we came to a beautiful little open plat, covered with rich green grass and blooming wild flowers, in the center of which bubbled up a cool crystal spring, forming a sparkling little rivulet, and the whole of which was surrounded by a dense thicket, not more than a hundred yards distant at any point. This beautiful spot to me seemed the oasis of the desert; and being to the best of my judgment the one described by Kit, where I was to await him, I accordingly ordered a halt. Dismounting and refreshing ourselves at the spring, we watered our animals and allowed them to graze around us, holding fast to the bridle reins the while, prepared to remount at a moment's notice or the first sign of danger.

Half an hour passed in this way, and some of the mountaineers were becoming impatient, when, to our great delight, we beheld the welcome visage of Carson, as he glided noiselessly into the open plat and rejoined us. And, singular enough! almost at the same moment the two voyageurs made their appearance at different points, not one of the three having seen either of the others since their parting from us in the morning.

"Well, boys," said Carson, thar'll have to be some warm doings to a certainty; and those of you who aint prepared to lose your scalps, had better be backing out or getting ready as soon as convenient."

"Have you seen the Indians?" asked Huntley.

"Well I have, and know Prairie Flower didn't lie either. Thar ar three distinct lodges of them—composed of Sioux, Cheyennes and Blackfeet—at least to the best of my judgment, for I didn't like venturing too close. They are camped in a little hollow just below Bitter Cottonwood, not more than three miles distant, and evidently have no suspicion of our being near them."

"Well, what is now to be done?" I asked.

"Wait till I've had a talk with these Canadians."

With this Kit called the scouts aside, and after a few minutes' conversation, returned to me and said:

"La Fanche and Grenois both report, they've seen no Indian signs to alarm, from which I argue, that thinking themselves secure where they ar, the savages haven't taken thar usual precaution to send out scouts. Regarding the plan of attack, I think we'd better let our horses feed here till dark, and then ride through the forest for a couple of miles or so, *cache* them, and take it afoot. I've got the plan fixed in my head, and will tell you more then. And now let's feed and smoke while we've got time."

We had provided ourselves with a good supply of jerk, and as none of us had eaten a morsel since leaving the fort, we proceeded to satisfy the demands of nature. This done, we lighted our pipes and smoked and talked till the shades of night warned us to be again on the move. Guided by Kit, we entered the thicket and advanced slowly, cautiously, and silently, for the better part of an hour, when we came to a dense cover of cottonwood.

"Halt and rope," said Kit, in a low tone.

In a moment each man was on the ground, and engaged in attaching his horse securely to a tree, though so dark was it here that everything had to be done by the sense of touch.

"See that all your arms ar about you, and ready, and then follow me, Indian file," said Carson again; and in less than three minutes, with stealthy tread, sixteen determined men, one after another, glided from the thicket into an open wood, like so many specters stalking from the tombs of the dead.

CHAPTER XIV.

THE EVENING'S CAMP—OUR STEPS RETRACED—OUR SECOND ADVANCE—TERRIBLE AMBUSCADE—THE BLOODY CONTEST—KIT CARSON'S WONDERFUL FEATS—REINFORCEMENT OF THE ENEMY—IMMENSE SLAUGHTER—MY HORSE KILLED—A FOOT ENCOUNTER—DESPAIR—KIT'S EFFORT TO SAVE ME—UNCONSCIOUSNESS

SOME three-fourths of a mile brought us to the brow of a hill, whence we could overlook the stronghold of the enemy. Immediately below us were several lodges made of skins, around which we could faintly perceive numerous dark figures moving to and fro, and evidently, as we thought, preparing to turn in for the night. A little beyond this was another encampment, or cluster of lodges, and still beyond another—the three taken together numbering not less than a hundred and fifty or two hundred warriors. And here stood we, a little band of sixteen men, about to assail, at the least calculation, ten times our own force. What rashness! what a fool-hardy undertaking!

"Charles," whispered I to my friend, "it is well that you and I are single men."

"Why so, Frank?"

"Because neither wife nor child will be left to mourn our loss."

"That is true," answered he with a sigh. "But do you then think our doom certain?"

"If we attack I do; or least, that we have ten chances against us to one in our favor."

"It won't do," whispered Carson at this moment, retreating a few paces, and motioning us to follow him. Then he added in a low tone:

"We're too soon, and it will never do to try it afoot. I must stick to my first calculation. Our only chance of escape from certain death must be by our horses. We'll return to them and await the midwatch of night. Then we must dash among them, raise all the hair we can, and split for cover, or we shall be rubbed out before we know it. I thought when I reconnoitered, it would do better to steal in among them and work silently—but I see now our only hope is by storm."

Accordingly we retraced our steps, and having gained the cover where our animals were concealed, squatted down upon the earth. As it was yet too early for our meditated attack, we once more replenished our pipes, and enjoyed the refreshing fragrance of some prime tobacco.

"I say, Kit," observed Black George, "what d'ye think o' that thar Injin gal, hey?"

"Think she's a mysterious one."

"Ever seed her afore?"

"Never."

"I have—augh! Think she's a speret, hey?"

"No! think she's a human."

"Well, I'll be dog-gone ef I do! I jest believe she's got wings and ken fly—ef I don't, call me a nigger and put me among the cotton plants—augh!"

"Faith, thin, Misther Black George, yees and mesilf is thinking much alike now," interposed Teddy. "I thought all the whiles she was a bir-r-d, barring the feathers which is all beads on her."

"Augh!—put out for a greenhorn now," returned the old trapper sarcastically. "She's no bir-rer-rerd as you sez. She's a angel, she is—ef she isn't, heyars what don't know 'fat cow from poor bull.'"

Talking of Prairie Flower, our present design, together with various other matters, we whiled away some two or three hours, when Carson notified us it was time to be on the move. Mounting once more our horses, we set forward, and bearing to the left, descended immediately into the valley in which the foe was camped, instead of keeping along the brow of the ridge as before. We were now compelled to use the utmost caution, as the least sound might betray us and thwart our plans.

At length we again made a halt in full view of the dark lodges, which were faintly perceptible in the dim light of the stars, and one or two smouldering fires near the center of the encampment. All was still as the grave, and, from anything we could discover to the contrary, as devoid of living thing. Not a word, not even a whisper, was heard from one of our party. Each sat erect upon his horse, motionless as a statue, his eyes fixed upon some object before him, and his mind it may be upon death and the great hereafter. At least so was mine; and though I rarely knew fear, yet from some unaccountable cause I now felt my heart die within me, as if something dreadful were about to befall me. Our pause was but momentary; but in that short space of time, methought I lived a year.

"Forward!" whispered Carson, solemnly. "Each man for himself, and God for us all!"

Scarcely had the sentence passed his lips, when, to our astonishment and dismay, a tremendous volley rang on all sides of us, and a shower of bullets and arrows came whizzing through the air, accompanied by yells that made my blood run cold; while on every hand we beheld a legion of dark figures suddenly spring from the earth, their murderous knives and tomahawks faintly gleaming in the dim light, as, flourishing them over their heads, and yelling their appalling war-whoops, they bore down upon us in overwhelming numbers. To add to our consternation, we heard the thundering tramp of a body of horse, in front and rear, rushing up to join our enemies and hem us in completely.

Instead of surprising the enemy as expected, we now found ourselves surprised in turn, and drawn into a terrible ambuscade, from which there seemed no chance of escape. Our design had doubtless been betrayed—but by whom I had no time for conjecture; for what between the yells of savages—groans and curses from our own little band—many of whom were wounded and some seriously—the rearing and plunging of the horses, and my desire to do the best I could for myself and friends—I had no time for speculation. Two of the enemy's balls had passed through my hat—one of them within an inch of my skull—and another through the sleeves of my frock, slightly grazing my arm; but fortunately none had injured myself nor horse.

"Riddle them—tear out thar hearts—scalp and send them to h—l!" shouted Carson, in a voice that rose distinctly above the din of conflict; and wheeling his charger, he dashed into the thickest of the fray, with that utter disregard to personal safety, which Napoleon once displayed at the far-famed bridge of Lodi.

Determined to share the fate of Kit, whatever it might be, I called to Huntly to join me, and rushed my horse alongside of his. Now it was that I had an opportunity of witnessing that coolness and intrepidity, those almost superhuman resources and exertions, which, together with other matters, have rendered the name of Kit Carson immortal.

Discharging his rifle and pistols at the first he came to, Carson raised himself in his stirrups, and swinging the former weapon over his head, with as much apparent ease as if a mere whisp, he brought it down upon the skulls of the dusky horde around him with fatal effect. Not less than a dozen in the space of twice as many seconds bit the dust beneath its weight, while his horse, madly rearing and plunging, trod down some four or five more. Still they thickened around us, (for Huntly and myself were alongside, imitating to the best of our ability his noble example,) and still that weapon, already reeking with blood, was hurled upon them with the same astonishing rapidity and the same wonderful success.

On every hand we were hemmed in, and every man among us was fighting valiantly for his own life and vengeance. There was no opportunity for cowardice—no chance for flight—retreat was cut off—we must fight or die. All seemed to understand this, and used superhuman exertions to overcome the foe, who fell before us as grass before the scythe of the mower; but alas for us! only to have their places supplied by others equally as blood-thirsty and equally as determined on our annihilation.

On all sides resounded hideous yells, and curses, and groans, and shouts—mingled with the reports of firearms, and the clash of deadly weapons. Fear we knew not—at least I judge by myself—for under the intoxicating excitement of the time, I experienced no passion but uncontrollable rage, and a desire to vent it upon our swarthy foe. Success so far had been with us, and numbers of the enemy had fallen to rise no more, while all but two of our own party were in their saddles, though some of them badly wounded. Above the tumult and din, I could now distinguish the voices of Carson, the trappers and Teddy, showing that each was doing his duty.

"Down, old paint-face!" cried one.

"Take that, and keep them company as has gone under afore ye!" shouted another.

"H–ll's full o' sich imps as you!" roared a third.

"To the divil wid ye now, ye bloody nagers! for attacking honest, dacent white paples—ye murthering tieves of Sathan, yees!" yelled the excited Irishman, as, in all the glory of making a shelaleh of his rifle, he laid about him right worthily.

At this moment, when the foot began to waver—when victory was almost ours—up thundered some thirty horsemen to reinforce our foes, revive their courage, and render our case terribly desperate, if not hopeless.

"At 'em, boys!" shouted Carson, apparently not the least disheartened; and driving his spurs into his horse, dropping his bridle rein upon the saddle bow, hurling his already broken and useless rifle at the heads of the nearest Indians, and drawing his knife and tomahawk, he charged upon the new comers, seemingly with as much confidence in his success as if backed by a whole battalion.

No wonder Kit Carson was famous—for he seemed a whole army of himself. A bare glimpse of one of his feats astonished me, and for the moment almost made me doubt my senses. Two powerful Indians, hard abreast, weapons in hand, and well mounted, rushed upon him at once, and involuntarily I uttered a cry of horror, for I thought him lost. But no! With an intrepidity equalled only by his activity, a weapon in either hand, he rushed his horse between the two, and dodging by some unaccountable means the blows aimed at his life, buried his knife in the breast of one, and at the same moment his tomahawk in the brain of the other. One frightful yell of rage and despair, and two riderless steeds went dashing on.

Side by side with Huntly, I fought with the desperation of a madman, and performed feats which astonished even myself. Thrice did I find my bridle rein seized by no less than three or four stalwart savages, and thought that all was over; but as often by some inexplicable means, my path was cleared, and not a scratch upon my person.

For ten minutes did the carnage rage thus, during which time no less than forty of our foes had been killed or disabled, and six of our own gallant band had gone from among the living. Still the savages pressed around us, and I now found my situation growing more and more desperate. From over exertion, I began to feel weak; and my gallant steed, having been less fortunate than I, was already staggering under his wounds. A few more painful efforts to bear down upon his foes, and he reeled, dropped upon his knees, tried to recover, failed, and at last rolled over upon his side and expired.

As he went down, I leaped from his back to the ground, and instantly found myself surrounded by savages. Striking right and left with renewed activity, I shouted to Huntly; and in a moment he charged to my rescue, and by our combined exertions, we managed for a moment or two to keep the foe at bay. But the strength of both of us was failing rapidly, and already I found myself bleeding from numerous flesh wounds. A few stabs and one musket shot killed the horse of my friend, who was by this means brought to the same desperate strait as myself.

"It is all over, Frank," he groaned, as a blow on the head staggered him back against me.

"Never say die," I shouted, as with my remaining strength I sprang forward and plunged my knife into the breast of the aggressor, whose hatchet was already raised for a final and fatal stroke.

Partly recovering from my lunge, a blow on the back of my neck brought me to my knees; and before I could regain my feet, I saw another aimed at my head by a powerful Indian, who was standing over me. At this moment, when I thought my time had come, and "God have mercy on my soul!" was trembling on my lips, Kit Carson, like an imbodied spirit of battle, thundered past me on his powerful charger, and bending forward in his saddle, with a motion quick as lightning itself, seized the scalp lock of my antagonist in one hand, and with the other completely severed his head from his body, which he bore triumphantly away. I now sprang to my feet, only to see my friend struck down, and be felled senseless to the earth myself.

CHAPTER XV.

CONSCIOUSNESS— PAINFUL SURMISES — THE MYSTERIOUS OLD INDIAN—APPEARANCE OF PRAIRIE FLOWER—HER DEVOTION—OUR SINGULAR CONVERSATION REGARDING HERSELF AND TRIBE, THE FIGHT, MY FRIENDS, AND MANY OTHER IMPORTANT MATTERS.

When consciousness was again restored, I found myself lying on a pallet of skins, in a small, rude cabin, curiously constructed of sticks, leaves, earth and a few hides of buffalo.

The first sensation was one of painful confusion. I felt much as one does on awaking from a troubled dream, without being able to recall a single event connected with it, and yet feeling the effects of all combined. I was aware that either something terrible had happened, or I had dreamed it; but what that something was, I had not the remotest idea. The most I could bring to mind, was a painful sensation of death. Perhaps I was dead? Horrible thought! I tried to rise, but could not—could not even lift my head from its rude pillow. By great exertion I raised one hand a little—but the effort exhausted all my strength, and it fell back heavily, causing me the most excruciating pain.

What did all this mean? Surely I was not dead!—for dead people, I thought to myself, feel no suffering. But where was I, and how came I here, and what was my ailment? And then—strange thought —*who* was I? Laugh if you will, reader —but I had actually forgotten my own name, and for a moment could not recall a single event of my existence. I had a confused idea of having lived before—of having been somebody—of having experienced sensations both of pleasure and pain; but beyond these, all was blank and dark as a rayless night.

Suddenly one remembrance after another began to flash upon me. First my youth—my school-boy days—my collegiate course; and then, the train once fired, years and events were passed with the velocity of thought itself; and in one brief moment, everything, up to the time of my fall in the fight, rose fresh in my memory.

But still the mystery was as dark as ever, and my curiosity as much unsatisfied. How had the battle gone? Were my friends the victors? But no! that were impossible, or I should not be here. Had they all been killed or taken prisoners? And Huntly—my friend! Great Heaven! the very thought of him made me shudder with dread. Alas! he was dead. I knew it—I felt it. I had seen him fall, and of course he could not have escaped. Poor, poor Charles Huntly — my bosom companion—friend of my happier days! The very thought of his untimely fate—cut off in the prime of life—made me groan with anguish.

But where was I, and how came I here? Why had I been saved and not my friend? But it might be that he was dead; while

I, by showing signs of existence, had been brought hither and restored to life, only to be the victim of some oblation of thanksgiving to the imaginary deity who had vouchsafed the victory to my foes. Ay, this was the true, but horrible solution of the mystery! My friends were dead—my foes had triumphed—and for this (horrible thought!) I was about to be the sacrifice of rejoicing on a heathen shrine.

Was I alone? I listened, but could hear no sound indicating the presence of another. Not satisfied with this, I turned my head slightly, as much as my strength would permit, and in the center of the lodge, squatted on the ground, over a small fire, with a long pipe in his mouth, I beheld a little, old, dried up man, whom, but for now and then a slight motion, I might have taken for a heap of clay or a crumbled up Egyptian mummy—so much did the skins worn around his body, and his own shrivelled and livid flesh resemble either.

Drawing in the smoke a couple of times, and puffing it out to the right and left, he arose and shuffled toward me. Curious to learn the object of such a visit, I thought it best to feign unconsciousness. Accordingly shutting my eyes, but not so as to prevent my seeing him, I lay and watched his motions.

He was a miserable and loathsome looking being, the very sight of whom sickened and disgusted me, particularly as I fancied him my surgeon and jailor, who would heal my wounds, only to pass me over to the executioner. In hight he could not have exceeded five feet even in his palmiest days, and this was now much reduced by age and debility. He was thin and skinny, and his small, puckered-up visage bore the complicated autograph of a century. His head was bald, save a few white hairs on the crown, where had once been his scalp lock; his nose and chin almost met over his toothless gums; and, to complete, his trembling limbs and tottering frame exhibited a striking resemblance to the bony picture of death. Only one feature about him gave evidence of his being more than a mere walking automaton; and that was his keen, eagle eye, whose luster, apparently undimmed by years, still flashed forth the unconsumed fires of what had once been a mighty soul, either for good or evil.

As he approached, he fastened his sharp eyes upon me with such intensity, that involuntarily I let mine drop to the ground, lest he should detect the feint. When I raised them again, I found him occupied with some mysterious ceremony, probably an incantation to lay the wrath or solicit the aid of some imaginary spirit.

Taking his pipe from his mouth, he blew a volume of smoke in a certain direction, toward which he pointed the stem of his pipe. This was done to the four cardinal points of compass, and then a volume was blown upward and another downward, after which he bent over me and went through a series of mysterious signs. Then taking one of my hands in his, he felt my pulse, during which operation I could perceive his face brighten with an expression of internal satisfaction. Then his bony fingers were pressed upon my forehead and temples, and a single "Onhchi," which I interpreted from his manner to mean "Good," escaped his livid lips.

Thinking longer deception unnecessary, I opened wide my eyes and said:

"Who are you?"

"Cha-cha-chee-kee-hob'ah," was the answer.

Then straightening himself as much as age would permit, he placed his pipe again in his mouth, and turning his face toward the door of the hut, struck the palms of his hands three times together, and uttered in a cracked voice the single word:

"Leni!"

Wondering what all this meant, I turned my eyes in the same direction, and the next moment, to my astonishment, beheld the beautiful form of the mysterious Prairie Flower enter from without.

With a light, quick tread, her face flushed with animation and joy, she glided up to the decrepid old Indian, and in a silvery voice, such as one might expect from so lovely a creature, said a few words and received a reply in a language to me wholly unintelligible. Then springing to me, she kneeled at my side, and turning her eyes upward, her sweet lips seemed moving to an earnest prayer from a guileless heart.

I no longer had fears for my safety—

for in such a presence and with such an act of devotion, I knew myself safe. I was only afraid to speak or move, lest I should wake to find it all a delusive dream.

But my desire to be assured of its reality would not long let me remain silent, and at last I said:

"Sweet being, tell me the meaning of all I see."

"Friend, you must not talk," she replied in good English; "it will do you harm."

"Nevertheless, fair creature, you must answer my question. My curiosity is wonderfully excited, and silence will harm me more than conversation."

She turned and addressed a few words to the old man, who now approached her side and gazed down upon me with a mild look. His reply was apparently satisfactory; for looking full upon me again, she said:

"You may be right, and I will answer. You were badly wounded in the fight."

"I am aware of that."

"You were left upon the ground for dead."

"Ha! indeed! But the battle—who won?"

"Your friends were victorious."

"Surprising! What lucky chance of fortune gave them the victory?"

"A reinforcement."

"Indeed! from where?"

"Fort John."

This fort, now demolished, stood at the time of which I write about a mile below Fort Laramie, and was well garrisoned. From a mistaken confidence in our own abilities to win the day, we had neglected calling there for volunteers to augment our numbers and render our success more certain.

"And what brought them to our aid so opportunely?" I inquired.

"Certain timely information."

"By whom conveyed?"

"A friend to your race."

"By the same messenger that brought intelligence of the enemy to Fort Laramie?"

"It matters not by whom. Let the result suffice."

"How shall I thank you, sweet Prairie Flower?"

"For what?"

"For all that you have done."

"I need no thanks."

"O say not thus."

"Then thank me by your silence."

"I will; and by my prayers for your safety and happiness."

"Bless you!" she exclaimed, fervently "The only boon I would have asked, save one."

"And what is that?"

"That you will not seek to know more of me and my history than I may choose to tell; and that whatever you may see and hear that seems mysterious, you will reveal to none without my permission."

"To please sweet Prairie Flower," I answered, "I will strive not to be a meddler nor a babbler; though she must bear in mind where so much interest is excited, the task she has imposed is a hard one."

"Then by adhering to it, you will confer upon her the deeper obligation."

"Yet I cannot forbear one question."

"Well?"

"Is Prairie Flower not of my race?"

"The judgment of the querist must answer him."

"Will not you?"

"Not now—perhaps never."

"I regret your decision, yet will not press the point. But to return to the battle."

"What would you know?"

"How it was won—how I came to be neglected—and why I am here."

"A reinforcement charging suddenly upon the enemy, alarmed and put him to flight. The victors pressed upon his rear, and left their killed and wounded upon the gory field. Before they returned, a few who beheld, but did not join the fight, found you and another in whom life was not yet extinct, and bore you both away."

"And — and — that other?" I gasped.

"Was — was it — my friend?"

"None other."

"And he—he—is—alive?"

"Ay, and doing well."

"Thank God! thank God! A weight of grief is lifted from my heart. But where—O, tell me quickly—where is he now?"

"Not far hence."

"And all is owing to you?"

"Nay; I said not that."

"God bless you for an angel of mercy! I must thank you—my heart is bursting with gratitude!"

"Nay, spare your thanks to mortal! Thank God—not me—for I am only an humble instrument in his hands."

"Mysterious being, who art thou?"

"Remember your promise and question not."

"But you seem more of Heaven than earth."

"It is only seeming then. But I must remind you that you have now talked full long."

"Nay, but tell me where I am?"

"In the lodge of Cha-cha-chee-kee-hobah, or Old-Man-of-the-Mountains."

"Is it he that stands beside you?"

"The same. He is 'Great Medicine,' and has cured you."

"And how long have I been here?"

"Four days."

"Good heavens! you astonish me!—Surely not four days?"

"Prairie Flower would not tell you wrong," said my informant, with a reproachful look.

"I know it, sweet being. I will not doubt you—and only intended to express surprise. Then I have been four days unconscious."

"Ay, a week."

"A week?" I exclaimed, looking her earnestly in the face: "A week, say you? And was the battle fought a week ago?"

"It was—a week ago last night."

"And pray in what part of the country am I now?"

"On the Black Hills."

"Indeed! And how far from Fort Laramie?"

"Not less than sixty miles."

"And how was I borne here?"

"On a litter."

"By whom?"

"My friends."

"White men or red?"

"The latter."

"And for what purpose?"

"To restore you to health."

"And what object could you or they have in bestowing such kindness on strangers?"

"To do good."

"For which of course you expect a recompense?"

Prairie Flower looked at me earnestly a moment, with a sweet, sad, reproachful expression, and then said with a sigh:

"Like the rest of the world, you misconstrue our motives."

"Forgive me!" I exclaimed, almost passionately — for her appearance and words touched my very soul: "Forgive me, sweet being! I was wrong, I see. On your part it was solely charity that prompted this noble act. But it is so rare that even a good action is done in this world without a selfish motive, that, in the thoughtlessness of the moment, I even imputed the latter to you."

"That is why I suppose so few understand us?" she said, sadly.

"You must be a very singular people," I rejoined, looking her full in the eye. "Will you not tell me the name of your tribe?"

She shook her head.

"I told you before," she answered, "you must not question me touching my history or tribe. Let it suffice that we are known as the Mysterious or Great Medicine Nation; that to us all roads are free, and with us all nations are at peace. We war upon none and none upon us."

"And yet do you not excite others to deeds you seem to abhor?"

"What mean you?" she asked quickly, a flush of surprise giving a beautiful glow to her noble features.

"Forgive me if I speak too plainly. But was not your message to Fort Laramie the cause of a bloody battle between the whites and Indians at Bitter Cottonwood?"

"The immediate cause of warrior meeting warrior in the game of death, most undoubtedly," she answered, with a proud look and sparkling eyes. "But do you not overlook the fact, that it was done to save the innocent and defenceless? Were not the Indians gathered there in mighty force to prey upon the weak? and was it not the duty of those who sought to do right to warn the few against the many—the unwary of their hidden foe? Could Prairie Flower stand idly by and see defenceless women and children drawn into a fatal snare, and made a bloody sacrifice to a heartless enemy? Had the pale-face so laid in wait for the red-man, Prairie

Flower, if in her power, had so warned the latter. Prairie Flower did not call the redman there; she regretted to see him there; but being there, she could do no less than warn and put the pale-face on his guard."

This was said with such a proud look of conscious rectitude—an expression so sublime, and an eloquence so pathetic—that I could hardly realize I was gazing upon and listening to an earthly habitant. I felt ashamed of my ungallant and unjust insinuation, and hastened to reply:

"Forgive me, sweet Prairie Flower, for having again wronged you—for having again done you injustice! But, as before, I overlooked the motive in the act. I will strive not to offend again and wound your sensitive feelings by doubting your generous intentions. Are there many more like you, sweet Prairie Flower?"

"Our tribe numbers between sixty and seventy souls."

"Is this your fixed abiding place?"

"Only for a time. Our home is everywhere between the rising and the setting sun. We go wherever we think ourselves the most beneficial in effecting good."

"Perhaps you are Christian missionaries?"

"We believe in the holy religion of Jesus Christ, and endeavor to inculcate its doctrines."

"Why then did this old man use mysterious signs?"

"He is of another race and generation, was once a great medicine in his tribe, and cannot divest himself of old habits."

"You seem rightly named the Mysterious Tribe; and of you in particular I have heard before."

"Indeed! When and how?"

I proceeded to detail briefly the story of the old trapper.

She mused a moment and replied:

"I remember such a person now, methinks. He was found, as you say, with life nearly extinct. By careful nursing he was restored to health. But he seemed inquisitive, and I employed the ruse of telling him his life was in danger to hurry his departure, lest he might prove troublesome. I trust there was nothing wrong in that. But come, come, I have forgotten my own caution, and talked too long by far. You need repose and silence."

"But one thing more! My friend?"

"You shall see him soon—perhaps to morrow."

"O, no! say to-day!"

"I cannot. To-morrow is the earliest. And so adieu! Seek repose and forgetfulness in sleep."

With this she turned, and glided out of the apartment in the same noiseless manner she had entered it. The old man looked at me a moment—shook his head and trembling hands—turned—shuffled away to his fire—and I was left alone to reflect on what I had seen and heard and my present condition.

---o---

CHAPTER XIV.

SICK-BED REFLECTIONS—GREAT MEDICINE—REAPPEARANCE OF PRAIRIE FLOWER—OUR CONVERSATION—GRATITUDE—MY WOUNDS—HER SUDDEN EMBARRASSMENT—DEPARTURE, ETC.

IT is a painful thing to one who has never known sickness, to be confined day after day to his bed, racked with torture, debarred even the liberty of enjoying for a moment the bright sunshine and clear air of heaven, unable perhaps to lift his head from his pillow, and yet beholding others, flushed with health and happiness, coming and going as they please, and seeming to prize lightly all which he most covets. It is only on a bed of sickness and pain, that we are taught to value as we should that greatest of all blessings, good health—a blessing without which all others are robbed of their pleasures: for what are fortune and friends and all their concomitants, to one who is borne down by a weight of bodily suffering? True, these may in a measure minister to his comforts—for without money and friends, the sick bed is only a pallet of the most abject misery—yet all the joys arising therefrom in connection with health, are lost to the invalid; and he lays, and sighs, and groans, and envies the veriest strolling mendicant on earth the enjoyment of his strength and liberty.

Such were my thoughts, as hour after hour, from the disappearance of Prairie Flower, I lay and mused upon all the events of my chequered life, up to the present time. Born to wealth, blessed with health, kind friends, and a college education, I might have passed my whole life in luxurious ease, but for the restless desire of travel and adventure. Not a discomfort had I ever known ere my departure from the paternal roof; and when I remembered, that now I was thousands of miles away, in an Indian camp of the wilderness, wounded nigh unto death, unable to rise from my pallet, solely dependent upon strangers of a savage race for my existence and the few favors I received, perhaps rendered a cripple or an invalid for life, and reflected on how much I had sacrificed for this—my feelings may be better imagined than described.

To what extent I was wounded I knew not—for I had neglected to question Prairie Flower on the subject—and I was now too weak to make the examination myself. My head, one of my arms, and both of my lower limbs were bandaged in a rude way, and my weakness had doubtless been caused by excessive hemorrhage. From the manner of Prairie Flower and the old Indian, I was led to infer that the crisis of danger was past; but how long it would take me to recover, I had no means of ascertaining, or whether I should be again blessed with the use of my limbs. Perhaps I might here be confined for months, and then only regain my wonted strength to find myself a cripple for life.

These thoughts pained and alarmed me, and I looked eagerly for the return of Prairie Flower, to gain the desired information. But she came not; and through sheer exhaustion, I was at last forced to drop the subject, while I strove to resign myself to such fate as He, who had preserved my existence as it were by a miracle, should, in his wise dispensation, see proper to decree.

Then my thoughts turned upon Prairie Flower. What mystery was shrouding this singular and angelic being, that she feared to be questioned regarding her history and tribe? Was she of the Indian race? I could not believe it. She seemed too fair and lovely, and without the lineaments which distinguish this people from those nations entitled to the name of pale-face. Might she not be a missionary, who, blessed with great self-denial and a desire to render herself useful while on earth, and yet too modest to avow it, had, at a tender age, gone boldly among the savages and labored zealously in her noble calling, to enlighten their dark minds and teach them the sacred truths of Christianity? She had admitted that all believed in the doctrines preached by the Saviour; and though she had not openly acknowledged, she certainly had not denied, my imputation regarding the calling of herself and friends. This, then, was the best solution of the mystery I could invent. But even admitting this to be true—that she was in reality of the Anglo-American race, and a pious instructor who found her enjoyments in what to others would have been a source of misery—still it was a matter for curious research, how one of her age should have become so familiar with the language and habits of all the various tribes of the Far West—and why, if she had friends, she had been permitted to venture among them alone and at the risk of her life. View the matter as I would, I found it ever shrouded with a vail of mystery and romance, beyond which all my speculations were unable to penetrate.

Thus I lay and pondered for several hours, during which time I saw not a living soul—the old Indian excepted—who, having finished his pipe, sat doubled up on the ground by his smouldering fire, as motionless and apparently as inanimate as so much lead. Once, and only once, he raised his head, peered curiously around him for a moment, and then settled down into the previous position. Fixing my gaze upon him, and wondering what secrets of the past and his own eventful life might perchance be locked in his aged breast, I at last felt my eyes grow heavy, the old man grew less and less distinct, and seemed to nod and swim before my vision, sometimes single and sometimes double, and then all became confused, and I went off into a gentle sleep.

How long I slept I am unable to say; but an acute sense of pain awoke me; when, to my surprise, I found it already dark, and the old man bending over me, engaged in dressing my wounds, and applying a kind of whitish liniment of a soothing and healing nature, prepared by himself and kept on hand for such and similar purposes.

Some half an hour was he occupied in this proceeding, during which I suffered more or less pain from the removal of the bandages, which, having become dry and stiff, adhered rather too closely to the affected parts.

Thinking it useless to question him, I made no remark, but passively suffered him to do as he pleased—which he did, without appearing to notice me any more than if I were dead, and he performing the last office of sepulture.

At length, the bandages being replaced, and my condition rendered as comfortable as circumstances would permit, he tendered me some light food and water—both of which I partook sparingly—and with the single word "Onh-chi," and a nod of his head, turned away and left me to my meditations. In ten minutes I was again asleep.

When I next awoke, the sun was streaming through the open doorway and crevices of the old cabin, and, to my surprise, I found Prairie Flower again kneeling by my side. Her eyes were turned upward as before, and her lips moved, but not a sound issued from them. She was evidently making a silent appeal to Heaven in my behalf; and as I lay and gazed upon her sweet, placid countenance, and felt that all this was for me, methought I had never beheld a being so lovely; and she seemed rather an immortal seraph, bent at the Throne of Grace, than a mortal tenant of this mundane sphere.

At length she arose, and with a charming smile upon her features, and in the sweetest tone imaginable, said:

"And how fare you this morning, my friend?"

"I feel much refreshed," I answered, "by a night of calm repose—and my strength is evidently improving."

"I am glad to hear it—for you have been nigh unto death."

"I am aware of it, and know not how to express to you my deep obligations for my recovery."

"As I told you before, no thanks are due me. I did but my duty, and my own conscience has already rewarded me tenfold. Those who labor to effect all the good they can, need no thanks expressed in words—for words are superfluous."

"And yet had I done for you what you have done for me, would you not have thanked me?"

"Doubtless I should."

"And will you not allow me the privilege you would have claimed yourself! Would it have pleased you to find me ungrateful?"

"I cannot say it would," she replied, musingly; "for, like others, I am only mortal; and perhaps vain—too vain—of having what little I do appreciated. I should not have such feelings, I am well aware; but they are engrafted in my nature, and I cannot help it."

"Then even oral thanks cannot be displeasing to sweet Prairie Flower?"

"Understand me, friend! There is a vast difference between expressing thanks by word of mouth, and being ungrateful. That you are not ungrateful, your look and actions tell—therefore are words superfluous."

"Well, then, I will say no more—but trust that time will give me an opportunity of proving by *acts*, what at best could be but feebly spoken. I agree with you, that words in a case like mine are of little importance. They are in fact 'trifles light as air,' and as often proceed from the lips merely, as from the heart. But now a word of myself. Tell me, fair being, and do not fear to speak plainly regarding my present condition. Can I ever recover?"

"Great Medicine has pronounced you out of danger."

"Shall I ever regain the full use of all my limbs?"

"I know nothing to the contrary."

"And my wounds—what are they?"

"You were found with your head frightfully gashed, and your skull slightly fractured. Your left arm was broken, and the flesh around it badly bruised, apparently by the tread of a horse. Various other flesh wounds were found upon your person—made, seemingly, by some sharp instrument—from which you bled profusely. These, together with loss of blood, produced a delirious fever, from which kind Providence has restored you, as it were by a miracle. For a week, life and death contended equally as it seemed for the victory. Many a time have I stood by your side, and thought every breath you drew your last I can only compare your critical condition to a person suspended by a mere cord over a terrible abyss, with a strain upon it so equal to its strength that another pound would divide it and render death certain, and there hanging seven days and nights, ere a safe footing could be effected on the solid earth above."

"You draw a fearful picture, Prairie Flower. But my friend — did he know of this?"

"Not fully. He knew you were badly wounded — but we gave him all the hope we could, lest, with his own wounds, the excitement should prove fatal to him also. As it was, he was often delirious, and raved of you, and accused himself of dragging you hither and being the cause of your misery, perhaps death. Had we informed him you were dead, I do not think he would have survived an hour."

"God bless him for a noble fellow — a true friend!" I cried, while tears of affection flooded my eyes.

As I spoke, I noticed the countenance of Prairie Flower become suddenly crimson, and then white as marble, while she averted her head and seemed uncommonly affected. What all this meant, I was at a loss to conjecture. In fact I did not give it much thought, for my mind was filled with the image of Charles Huntly, and I quickly added:

"Is he not a noble friend, sweet Prairie Flower?"

"He is indeed!" she exclaimed, looking at me earnestly a moment, as if to detect a hidden meaning in my words, and then dropping her eyes modestly to the ground.

"But his wounds?"

"Like yourself, he received two very severe contusions on the head, which rendered him senseless for several hours."

"And how is he now?"

"He has so far recovered that he leaves his lodge, and occasionally takes a short stroll."

"And has he not been to see me?"

"No! we would not permit him."

"And how did a refusal affect him?"

"Quite seriously. But we told him that your life, in a great measure, depended on your being kept perfectly quiet, and that as soon as he could do so with safety, he should be admitted to your presence. He seemed to grieve very much, but uttered no complaints."

"But you must let me see him now, Prairie Flower!"

"I do not know," she answered: "I will consult Great Medicine."

"But, Prairie Flower!" I called as she turned away.

"Well?"

"Remember, I *must* see him!"

"But surely you would not endanger your life and his?"

"Certainly not. But do you think such would be the effect of our meeting?"

"I am unable to say, and that is why I wish to consult Cha-cha-chee-kee-hobah —or, as we often term him, Great Medicine."

"Go, then, and Heaven send I get a favorable answer."

Prairie Flower turned away, and approaching the Old-Man-of-the-Mountains, held with him a short consultation. Then returning to me, she said:

"Great Medicine thinks it imprudent; but if you insist on it, he says you may meet; but at the same time he bids me warn you both to be cautious and not become too much excited, or the worst of consequences may follow."

"I will endeavor to be calm, and see no cause why I should be more than ordinarily excited."

"You perhaps overlook, my friend, that a great change has taken place in the appearance of each of you since last you met; and your system being in a feeble state, a sight of your friend may affect you more than you are now aware of. The greatest change, however, is in yourself; and I must prepare your friend to behold in you a far different person than he beheld on the night of the battle. I charge you beforehand, to brace your nerves and meet him calmly!"

Saying this, she turned and quitted the hovel.

CHAPTER XVII.

VISIT OF MY FRIEND—HIS CHANGED APPEARANCE — SINGULAR MANNER OF PRAIRIE FLOWER—HER ABRUPT DEPARTURE—HER RESEMBLANCE TO ANOTHER—OUR SURMISES REGARDING HER — MY FRIEND IN LOVE, ETC.

HALF an hour of the most anxious suspense followed the disappearance of Prairie Flower, during which, in spite of myself, I suffered the most intense mental excitement, and my hands shook like the quaking aspen, and I felt both sick and faint. At the end of the time mentioned, Prairie Flower appeared and announced that my friend would shortly be with me.

"But you seem agitated," she added, with an expression of alarm.

"O, no—mere nothing, I assure you," I quickly replied, fearful she would alter her arrangement and put off our meeting to another day. "My hand shakes a little perhaps—but you see, Prairie Flower, I am quite composed—quite collected, indeed."

She shook her head doubtingly, and was about to reply, when Huntly made his appearance, and approached me with a feeble step.

Heavens! what a change in sooth! A wild exclamation of alarm and surprise was already trembling on my lips, when, remembering the injunction of Prairie Flower, I, by a great effort suppressed it.

Could this feeble, tottering form approaching me, indeed be the gay, dashing, enthusiastic Charles Huntly, whom I had known from boyhood? His face was pale and thin—his lips bloodless—his eyes had lost much of their luster, and moved somewhat nervously in their sunken sockets—his cheek bones protruded, and his robust figure was wonderfully emaciated—while the wonted expression of fire and soul in his intelligent countenance, had given place to sedateness and melancholy. To complete, his head was rudely bandaged, and his habiliments exhibited marks of the recent conflict. If such was his appearance, what, judging from the remarks of Prairie Flower, must have been mine! I shuddered at the thought.

As he came up, so that his eye could rest upon me, he suddenly started back, with a look of horror, threw up both hands and exclaimed:

"Merciful God! can this be Francis Leighton?" and staggering to my side, he dropped down upon the ground and burst into tears.

"Beware!—beware!" cried Prairie Flower earnestly, her features turning deadly pale. "Remember, Charles Huntly—remember my warning! or you will do what can never be undone, and all our efforts to save you both will have been made in vain."

"Charles," gasped I: "Charles—Huntley—my friend—compose yourself, or you will destroy us both!"

"Oh, Frank, Frank!" he rejoined somewhat wildly, "I never thought to see you thus, when in an evil moment I urged you to leave home. Oh! why did I do it! Forgive me my friend—forgive me, for God's sake! or I shall go distracted."

"For Heaven's sake, my friend, do not blame yourself! I left home by my own desire and free will. You are not to blame, any more than I. Of course, we could not foretell what fate had in store for us. Rather thank God, dear Charles, that we are both alive and likely to recover!"

"And you think, dear Frank, I am not to blame?"

"Not in the least."

"God bless you for a generous soul! Oh! if you could but know what I have suffered! Tortures of mind beyond the strength of reason to bear."

"I have heard so from the lips of our sweet benefactor."

"Ay, sweet benefactor, indeed! God bless you, lovely Prairie Flower!" he added, passionately, suddenly turning his eyes upon her. "If you are not rewarded in this world, I am sure you will be in the next."

At the first sentence, the face of the maiden flushed, and then changed quickly to an ashen hue, while her breast heaved with some powerful emotion, like to the billowy sea. She strove to reply, but words failed her, and turning suddenly away, she rushed from the lodge, leaving us alone.

"Angelic creature!" pursued Huntly, gazing after her retreating form with an expression of sincere admiration. "A lily too fair to bloom in a region so desolate as this. But why did she leave us so abruptly, Frank?"

"I cannot say, unless it was her dislike of praise."

"I could adore her, Frank, for her goodness. Where would we be now, think you, but for her timely aid?"

"In another world, most probably," I answered solemnly.

"Ay, truly in another world," rejoined Huntly with a sigh. "And you, Frank, if one may judge by your looks, are not far from there now. Great God!" he continued, gazing steadily on me, while his eyes became filled with tears—"what a change—what a change! I cannot realize even now, that I am speaking to Francis Leighton. And this the work of one short week! Oh! how have I longed to see you, Frank! How on my knees have I cried, begged and implored to be permitted to see you! But I was denied—unresistingly denied—and now I am thankful for it; for had I seen you in that unconscious state described to me by Prairie Flower, I fear I should have lost my reason forever, and the sods of the valley would soon have been green above my mortal remains."

This was said with an air and tone so mournfully, touchingly sad, that in spite of myself I found my eyes swimming in tears.

"Well," I answered, "let us forget the past, and look forward with hope to the future; and return to Him—who has thus far watched over us with His all-seeing eye, and raised us up friends where we least expected them, in our moments of affliction—the spontaneous thanks of grateful hearts!"

In this and like manner we conversed some half an hour without interruption. As my friend had been struck down at the same moment with myself, he was of course unable to give me any information regarding what happened afterward. Whether any of our friends were killed or not, we had no means of ascertaining, and could only speculate upon the probability of this thing or that. What had become of Teddy? Had he survived?—and if so, what must have been his feelings when he found we came not to his call, and appeared not to his search!

This train of conversation again brought us back to Prairie Flower, and each had to rehearse the little he had gleaned, and the much he had surmised concerning herself and the tribe; and in many points we found our conjectures to correspond exactly.

"By-the-by," I observed at length, "it strikes me I have seen some face like hers—but where and when I cannot tell—perhaps in my dreams."

"Indeed!" replied Huntly, quickly; "and so have I—but thought it might be fancy merely—at least that you would think so—and therefore kept it to myself."

"Who, then, is the person?"

"You have no idea?"

"None in the least."

"And if I tell you, and you see no likeness, you will not ridicule my fancy?"

"Ridicule, Charles? No! certainly not. But why such a question?"

"You will understand that full soon."

"Well, then, the lady?"

"Have you forgotten the fair unknown?"

"Good heavens! how like!" I exclaimed. You are right, my friend—there is indeed a wonderful likeness. Perhaps——But no! the idea is too chimerical."

"Speak it, Frank—perhaps what?"

"I was about to add, perhaps they are related—but that could not be."

"And why not?" asked Huntly. "Such a thing is not impossible."

"Very true—but most highly improbable, as you will admit. The beautiful unknown we saw in New York—the beautiful mysterious, if I may so term her, in the Far West: the former, perhaps, a daughter of fashion in the gay and polished circles of civilization—the latter among barbarians, a prominent member of a roving tribe of savages."

"But you overlook that she could not be bred among savages."

"And why not?"

"Because her English education, manners and accomplishments, all belie such a supposition. I admit with you, that the suggestion advanced by yourself looks highly improbable—at the same time I contend, as before, it is not impossible."

"Well, at all events, Charles, you must

admit it utterly useless to argue a point founded solely upon speculation on both sides. We have not even the history of Prairie Flower to go upon, setting aside entirely that of the other party, and consequently must come out exactly where we started, neither of us the wiser for the discussion."

"Nothing more true," answered my friend, musingly. "I would to Heaven I could learn the history of Prairie Flower! Can she be an Indian?"

"I think not."

"What a perfect creature! and with a name as beautiful as her own fair self. Do you know, Frank, I——"

"Well, speak out!"

"You will not ridicule me?"

"No."

"I am half in love."

"With whom?"

"Prairie Flower."

"Indeed! Well, that is nothing strange for you. I feel grateful enough to love her myself. But, Charley, you did not allow her to perceive any symptoms of your passion?"

"Not that I am aware of. But why do you ask?"

"Because it would offend her."

"Do you think so?"

"I am sure of it."

"And wherefore, Frank?" asked my friend, rather anxiously.

"Wherefore, Charley? Why, I believe you are in love in earnest."

"Have I not admitted it?"

"Only partially."

"Then I acknowledge it fully."

"But how about the unknown?"

"I am in love with her too."

"Ay, and with every pretty face you meet. But surely you are not serious in this matter?"

"I fear I am," sighed Huntly.

"But you cannot love either much, when you acknowledge to loving both."

"You forget the resemblance between the two. I could love any being methinks, in the absence of the unknown, who bore her likeness."

"But, for heaven's sake, Charley, do not let Prairie Flower know of this!—for it would only be to make her avoid us and perhaps result in unpleasant consequences."

"And yet, Frank, at the risk of being thought egotistical, I must own I have reasons for thinking my passion returned."

"Returned, say you? Why, are you dreaming?"

"No, in my sober senses."

"And what reasons, I pray?"

"Her manner toward me whenever we meet, and whenever I speak to her. Surely you must have noticed her embarrassment and change of countenance when I addressed her last, ere her hasty departure."

"I did—but attributed it, as I told you then, to a dislike of flattery or praise to the face."

"I formed a different opinion."

"Why then did you ask me the cause of her leaving so abruptly?"

"Merely to see if you suspicioned the same as I—that, if so, my own fancies might have the surer foundation. Often when she thought herself unnoticed, have I, by turning suddenly upon her, caught her soft, dark eye fixed earnestly upon me, with an expression of deep, quiet, melancholy tenderness, which I could not account for, other than an affectionate regard for myself; and the more so, that when my eye caught hers, she ever turned her gaze away, blushed, and seemed much confused. It was this which first divided my thoughts between herself and you, and awakened in my breast a feeling of sympathy and affection for her in return."

"You may be right," I answered, as I recalled her strange manner of the day previous, when I spoke to her of my friend —and I proceeded to detail it to Huntly. "But I am truly sorry it is so," I added, in conclusion.

"Why so, Frank?"

"Because it will only render her unhappy for life."

"What! if I——"

"Well, say on! If you what, Charley?"

"I was going to add—a—marry her," he replied in some confusion.

"Marry her? Are you mad, Huntly?"

"Only a little deranged."

"Not a little, either, if one may judge by such a remark. Why, my friend, you talk of marrying as if it were the most trifling thing in the world. You cannot be in earnest, surely! and it is a bad matter for a jest."

"I am not jesting, at all events," he replied. "But why not marry her, if we both love? Is there anything so remarkable in marriage?"

I looked at him earnestly, to detect, if possible, some sly curl of the lip, some little sign which I could construe into a quizical meaning; but no! the expression of his countenance was uncommonly serious, if anything, rather melancholy. He was sincere beyond a doubt, and the very thought kept me dumb with surprise.

"You do not answer," he said at length. "Perhaps you do not believe in my sincerity?"

"Ay, too truly I do," I rejoined; "and the very knowledge made me speechless. Why, my dear friend, what are you thinking of? You, the young, wealthy, aristocratic Charles Huntly, prating seriously to me of marriage, and that to a nameless Indian girl of whose history you know nothing, and whose acquaintance you have made within a week! What! can this be the same wild, reckless school-mate of mine, whose mind six months ago rarely harbored an idea beyond uttering a jest or playing a prank upon some unsuspecting individual? Surely you are not in your sober senses, Charley! or this is a land of miracles, indeed."

"I am not what I was," sighed my friend, "though, I believe, not the less in my senses for that. That I was a gay, wild youth once, is no evidence I should always remain one. To me there appears nothing remarkable, that one whose life has been a scene of folly, should become changed by the near approach of death. I have suffered too much within the past week, both in body and mind, not to have had very serious reflections. As regards Prairie Flower, I acknowledge, as before, I am totally ignorant of her history; that, as you say, I have known her barely a week; but I cannot forget that I am her debtor, both for my own life and yours. That she is a rare being, too good almost to grace a world so cold and uncharitable as this, none who have seen and conversed with her as much as I, can doubt for a moment. Regarding marriage, I am very far from thinking it a trifling affair—on the contrary, one of the most serious of a man's life. It is an event to make or mar his happiness; and for that reason should be considered with all due solemnity, and everything pertaining to it duly weighed, that none may afterward be found wanting. Had I proposed to you to unite myself with a lady of fine accomplishments and fortune, would you have asked the question if both loved—if she was one to make me happy? Probably not; for her wealth would prove the 'silver vail,' to conceal all her defects. Should a man take the solemn vows of marriage to please himself or friends? Should he do so merely to make a display in public, and render his heart in private the seat of misery? Of what value is gold, if it add nothing to a man's happiness? Riches are unstable, and often, as the proverb has it, 'take to themselves wings and fly away.' And then, to him who has made these his god—who has wedded them and not the *woman*—what is the result? A few days of misery and an unhappy end. Do not conclude from this, my dear Frank, that I have resolved to marry Prairie Flower; for until it was suggested by your own remarks, such a thought never entered my head; and even now such a result is highly improbable. I merely hinted at the possibility of the thing, to ascertain what effect it would have upon you."

"Well, I am happy in knowing the matter is not so serious as I was at first led to suppose. Take my word, Charley, it is only a mere whim of the moment, which will pass away with a return of health and strength. When the body becomes diseased, it is not uncommon for the mind to be affected also; and though the idea you have suggested may seem plausible now—mark me! you will yet live to think it preposterous, and laugh at your present folly."

"Then, Frank, you think my mind unsound?"

"Not in a healthy state, certainly—or, with your quick sense of perception, you would have become aware ere this, that, no matter how deep her love, Prairie Flower is one to reject even Charles Huntly."

"Reject me, Frank, say you?—reject me?" cried Huntly, quickly, with a look of surprise.

"Ay, reject you—even you—the rich, educated, and polished Charles Huntly."

"And why, Frank?"

"First, because her proud, retiring nature would rebel at the thought of an alliance with one whom the world might consider her superior. Secondly, because her sense of duty would not allow her to depart from her tribe, to which she belongs either by birth or adoption. Thirdly, and conclusively, because she is one who has evidently resolved to remain single through life. She is a girl possessed of a remarkable mind, which once fixed upon a point, remains unchangeable forever. That she loves you, I now believe; that you return the passion, in a measure, you have acknowledged; but that she would consent to leave her tribe and pledge herself to you for life, I believe a thing impossible."

"You perhaps have reasons for thinking thus?" observed Huntly, eyeing me sharply.

"Nothing more than what I have gathered from noting her closely, during the brief period of our acquaintance. I may be wrong, but time will show. At all events, my friend, I warn you, if you feel an increasing passion or affection for this girl, to suppress it at once, and leave the vicinity as soon as the health of both of us will permit."

"I will think of it my dear friend; and in the mean time, do you watch Prairie Flower closely—as I will myself—to learn if your surmises be correct; and should a convenient opportunity offer, fail not to use it to find out the true state of her feelings regarding myself. I —— But enough— she comes."

As he spoke, Prairie Flower entered the lodge to put an end to our conversation, lest harm might be done me by too much excitement. I now observed her narrowly, and saw their was a constraint in her manner, which she only the more exposed by trying to conceal and appear perfectly natural. She gently reminded Huntly it was time for him to withdraw; and though he strove hard to catch the soft glance of her dark beaming eye, yet all his efforts proved fruitless; and pressing my hand, with a hearty "God bless you!" and a deep, earnest prayer for my speedy recovery, he quitted the apartment.

Asking me one or two questions regarding the effect produced upon me by my friend's visit, and finding instead of injury it had resulted to my benefit, Prairie Flower bade me seek instant repose in sleep; and promising that Huntly should see me again on the following day, she turned, and in a musing mood, with her head dropped upon her bosom, and slow steps, disappeared.

There was no mistaking it; Prairie Flower was in love with my friend; and I sighed at the thought, that the hour of her friendship to us, might prove the data of her own unhappiness.

———o———

CHAPTER XVIII.

CONVALESCENCE—THE MYSTERIOUS OR GREAT MEDICINE TRIBE—THEIR MANNERS—THEIR DAILY MODE OF WORSHIP—THEIR MORNING, NOON, AND EVENING SONGS—A WEDDING— A FUNERAL, ETC.

TIME rolled on slowly, each day adding something to my convalescence, and the expiration of a month found me so far recovered as to venture on a short stroll in the open air. During this long period of confinement, (to me it seemed a year,) Prairie Flower and Huntly visited me every day, though rarely together; and toward the last, my friend became an almost constant companion.

Never shall I forget the emotions of gratitude and joy which I experienced on beholding once more the green leaves and blades, the bright flowers and glorious sunshine, feeling again the soft, balmy breeze of heaven upon my emaciated frame, and hearing the artless songs of the forest warblers. Earth, which for a time had seemed cold and dreary, now appeared changed to a heavenly paradise, and I could not realize I had ever seen it look so enchantly beautiful before. In this I was doubtless correct; for never before had I been absent from it so long; and the contrast between the grim, rude walls of my late abode, and all I now beheld, was enough to have put in ecstacies a far less excitable and enthusiastic individual than myself.

The village of the Mysterious or Great Medicine Tribe, I found to consist of some fifteen or twenty lodges, situated on the side of the mountain so as to overlook a beautiful valley some quarter of a mile below, through which flowed a murmuring stream that formed one of the tributaries of the Platte. The cabins, though only temporarily erected, were very comfortable, and placed so as to form a complete circle, in the center of which stood the Great Medicine lodge of Cha-cha-chee-keehobah, where I had been confined, and by which, as I now learned, I had been highly honored, inasmuch as not a soul besides its owner and Prairie Flower, unless by special permit, was ever allowed to cross its threshold. This then accounted for my not having seen any of the tribe during my confinement in bed. The Great Medicine lodge, and one other, were distinguished from the rest by their whitish appearance, done probably by a limish composition found on the mountains. This other alluded to, was the residence of Prairie Flower, and two young, dark-skinned, black-haired, bright-eyed, pretty-faced Indian girls, whose countenances and costumes bespoke intelligence and superiority.

Among this tribe were some twenty females and as many children, and the balance males, all of whom were decently clad, and clean and tidy in their appearance. Save Prairie Flower, but very few of them wore any kind of ornaments, and their dark, clear skins were not in the least bedaubed with paint. Most of them spoke the English language, and some quite fluently; and I observed many an old well-thumbed book—generally a bible—lying about their wigwams. In their intercourse with myself and friend, they displayed a dignified courtesy, and not one of all the children did I ever observe to behave in a rude or unbecoming manner.

They were, take them all in all, a remarkable people, and rightly named the Mysterious Tribe; and, as far as I could judge, very zealous in the cause of Christianity. Three times a day did they collect for public devotion to the Great Spirit; and their ceremony, though simple, was one of the most impressive I ever witnessed. It was in the following manner:

At sunrise, noon, and sunset, Prairie Flower and her two Indian companions would come forth from their lodge, arrayed in neat and simple attire, each bearing in her hand a kind of drum, or tamborine without the bells, and approaching the Great Medicine Lodge, would arrange themselves in its front. Then bowing to the east and west, the north and south, they would beat the tamborines with their fingers—whereupon the whole village—men, women and children—would hastily quit whatever occupation they might be at, and assemble around them, their faces expressive of the importance and solemnity which they attached to the occasion. The tamborines would continue to beat until all were gathered together, when a deep and impressive silence would ensue, during which each face would be turned upward, as if to solicit the Great Guardian of all to be with them in their devotions. Then the maidens would strike out into a clear, silvery song, and at the end of each stanza would be joined in the chorus by all of both sexes, young and old, during which each would kneel upon the earth, and continue there until the commencement of the next, when all would again rise to their feet.

These songs, of which there were three, were translated to me by Prairie Flower, at my request, and I herewith give them—if not in language, at least in spirit and sentiment—commencing with the

MORNING SONG.

The day is up, the sun appears,
That sun of many thousand years,
And morning smiles through evening's tears:
    Thanks! thanks! thanks!
To Thee who made the earth and sky,
The hosts that go revolving by,
And all that live and all that die—
    God! God! God!

CHORUS.

Kneel! Kneel! Kneel!
  O, bless us, Spirit,
    That doth inherit
      The earth and air,
      And everywhere,
    And save us, Thou,
  To whom we bow,
All humbly now,
Our Great and Heavenly Father!

The day is up, and through our sleep
We've felt no visitations deep,
And nothing wherefore we should weep
    Thanks! thanks! thanks!
Preserve us still throughout the day,
Teach us to seek the better way,

And never let us go astray—
    God! God! God!
        CHORUS.
    Kneel! kneel! kneel!
    O, bless us, Spirit,
    That doth inherit
      The earth and air,
        And everywhere!
    And save us, Thou,
      To whom we bow,
        All humbly now,
Our Great and Heavenly Father!

NOON-DAY SONG.

The day moves on and all goes well,
More blessings now than we can tell,
With gratitude our hearts do swell:
    Thanks! thanks! thanks!
Bless and preserve us still, we pray,
With food and raiment line our way,
And keep us to the close of day—
    God! God! God!
        CHORUS.
    Kneel! kneel! kneel!
      Father of Heaven,
      To Thee be given
        Unbounded praise,
    Through endless days!
    And like the sun,
      In Heaven above,
    Pour on us now
      Thy warmth of love!
    And may our feet
      Forever press
    The virtuous paths
      Which Thou doth bless!
To Thee all praise, Lord, God, our Father!

The noon-day breezes now go by,
The forest gives a welcome sigh,
The murmuring streamlets sweet reply:
    Thanks! thanks! thanks!
The birds carol, the insects sing,
And joy beams out in everything,
For which all praise to Thee we bring—
    God! God! God!
        CHORUS.
    Kneel! kneel! kneel!
      Father of Heaven,
      To thee be given
        Unbounded praise,
    Through endless days!
    And like the sun,
      In heaven above,
    Pour on us now
      Thy warmth of love!
    And may our feet
      Forever press,
    The virtuous paths
      Which Thou dost bless!
To thee all praise, Lord, God, our Father!

EVENING SONG.

The day is dying, wood and wold
Are growing dim, as we behold,
And night will soon us all enfold:
    Thanks! thanks! thanks!
That Thou the day hath kept us through,
Taught each his duty right to do.

And made us all so happy too—
    God! God! God!
        CHORUS.
    Kneel! kneel! kneel!
All heaven, and earth, and sea, and sky,
Are marked by His all-seeing eye,
Which will look deep into the night,
To note if each one doeth right,
And watch us in our dreams of sleep,
On all our thoughts and actions keep:
So may each thought, each deed we do,
Be one that will bear looking through!
    And bless us, Thou,
      To whom we bow,
        All humbly now,
Most great Lord, God, Almighty!

The sun hath set in yonder west,
The beasts and birds are seeking rest,
All nature is in sable dressed:
    Thanks! thanks! thanks!
Preserve us, Thou, till morning light
Doth lift the sable vail of night!
May holy angels guard us right,
Our sleep be sweet, our dreams be bright,
And not a thing our souls affright—
    God! God! God!
        CHORUS.
    Kneel! kneel! kneel!
All heaven, and earth, and sea, and sky,
Are marked by His all-seeing eye,
Which will look deep into the night,
To note if each one doeth right,
And watch us in our dreams of sleep,
On all our thoughts and actions keep:
So may each thought, each deed we do,
Be one that will bear looking through!
    And bless us, Thou,
      To whom we bow,
        All humbly now,
Most great Lord, God, Almighty!

It is impossible for me to convey the sweet and plaintive melody which accompanied each song, and which, before I knew a word that was uttered, produced upon my mind, and that of my friend, the most pleasing and solemn effect—particularly as we noted that each was accompanied with an earnestness and sincerity of manner, such as I had rarely witnessed in Christian churches within the borders of civilization. At the end of each of these songs, and while the assemblage remained in the kneeling posture of the chorus, the Old-Man-of-the-Mountains would suddenly make his appearance, and hooping his arms before him and bowing, after the Turkish fashion, would utter a few words as a sort of benediction—whereupon all would rise, and each depart quietly to his ledge, or his previous occupation.

The devotional scenes just mentioned

were of every day occurrence, when nothing of importance had transpired to elate the actors with joy, or depress them with grief—in either of which events, the songs and manner of worship was changed to suit the occasion.

With this people, a wedding or a funeral was a very important affair; and as I sojourned some two months or more among them, ere my strength permitted me to depart, I had an opportunity of witnessing both. As the former was the first in order of occurrence, I shall proceed to describe it first.

The bride was an interesting Indian maiden, some seventeen years of age, and the groom a tall, athletic Indian, her senior by at least five more. Both were becomingly decked with wampum belts, figured moccasins, and various ornaments worn around the neck and arms; those of the maiden being bare above the elbow, and displaying her rich, dark skin to good advantage. Around the head of each was bound a wreath of ivy, diversified with a few sprigs of cedar, emblematical, as I was informed, of their love, which must ever remain green and unfading.

The nuptial ceremony took place in the lodge of the bride, and was as follows: On the announcement that all was ready, a deputation of maidens, consisting for the most part of Prairie Flower and her companions, surrounded the bride, and placing their hand on her head, asked her several questions pertaining to herself and lover, the most important of which were, if she truly loved him she was about to take forever, and thought that marriage would increase her happiness. Receiving replies in the affirmative, they commenced singing in a low, melodious tone, the subjoined

BRIDAL SONG.

Blooming maiden,
Heavy laden
With new hopes, and joys, and fears—
Sad with gladness,
Glad with sadness,
Thou art going, young in years,
To another,
More than brother,
Father, mother,
Or aught other
Which among thy race appears.

We have bound thee,
As we found thee,
With unfading green wreathed thee—
Emblem fitting,
Unremitting
Must thy love forever be;
That thou ever
Must endeavor
Not to sever,
Now, nor never,
Bonds of time, eternity.

Now go, maiden,
Sweetly laden
With all blessings we've in store—
Take him to thee,
Who did woo thee,
Deeper love him than before:
God be sending
His defending,
Joy portending,
Never ending
Blessings on thee, evermore!

On the conclusion of this song, each of the singers laid her right hand upon the head of the bride, and commenced dancing around her in a circle. This lasted some ten minutes, during which time a deputation of Indian youths—or what in any other tribe would have been termed braves—led forward the groom to within a few feet of his intended, and commenced a similar dance around him, accompanying it with a song, the same in sentiment, if not in language, as the one just given. This dance over, the youths and maidens fell back in two rows, facing each other, while the groom and bride modestly advanced, unattended, and took hold of hands.

In this manner all quitted the lodge for the open air, where the villagers were drawn up to receive them, and who immediately formed a dense circle around them. Then, amid a deep silence, all kneeled upon the earth, and rising, pointed their right fore-fingers to the sky, and bowed to the four great points of compass. Then all, save the bride and groom, united in the following

BRIDAL CHORUS

Joined in heart, and joined in hand,
By great Heaven's wise decree,
Ye must ever so endeavor,
That you ne'er may parted be—
Never! never!
So, forever,
May Almighty Power bless ye
In your prime,
And through all time,
And on through all eternity!

As the chorus concluded, the ring opened.

and the Old-Man-of-the-Mountains made his appearance, bearing in one hand a long staff, and in the other a horn cup of smoking incense, which he waved to and fro. Approaching the bride and groom, he held it between them, and laying his staff on their heads, and bidding them again join hands, he proceeded to chant, in a feeble, cracked voice, the

CLOSING MARRIAGE STRAIN.

As this incense to Heaven,
So your vows here are given,
And written by angels above,
On the ponderous pages,
Of the great Book of Ages,
And stamped with His great seal of Love.

By earth and by air,
By water and fire,
By everything under the sun—
By your own plighted faith,
To be true unto death,
In God's name I pronounce you twain one.

Waving his stick once more above their heads, and uttering his usual word "Onhchi," Great Medicine retraced his steps to his lodge. On his departure, the friends of the newly married pair stepped forward in the order of relation, and greeted both with a hearty shaking of hands, and invocations of blessings from the Great Spirit. Then followed a feast prepared for the occasion, consisting principally of buffalo, bear and deer meat, together with that of various wild fowls. This was eaten seated upon buffalo skins, and was served to the larger party by four waiters, two of both sexes. After this came one or two more songs, in which all joined, and a general dance closed the festivities of the day.

The funeral which I witnessed, was that of a young man greatly beloved by his tribe. The day succeeding his death, was the one appointed for the solemn ceremony of sepulture. Meantime the body remained in the lodge where the vital spark had been extinguished, and, locked up with it from all intrusion, remained also the near relatives of the deceased, fasting and employing their moments in prayer.

When the time for the funeral service ad arrived, four Indian youths who had been companions of the deceased, entered the lodge, and wrapping the body in a buffalo-hide, bore it to that of Great Medicine, and deposited it on the ground, outside. Hither followed the relatives, their heads bound with withered flowers, and leaves, emblematical of the decay of every thing earthly, however fair and beautiful. Forming a narrow circle round the body, they knelt upon the earth, and placing their right hands upon the breast of the departed, and their left upon their hearts, uttered low and plaintive moans—the signal that all was ready for the mournful rite. Next appeared Prairie Flower, with three other maidens, and approaching the youths, all clasped hands and formed a ring outside the circle of kneeling and weeping relatives. Then they commenced walking round the living and dead, and as they passed the head of the latter, each uttered a short prayer that his noble spirit might find eternal rest beyond the grave. When this was concluded, Great Medicine appeared, holding in his hand a drum, which he beat rapidly a few times, whereupon the remainder of the villagers came forth from their lodges, and formed a third circle outside of all. The second circle now fell back to the largest, leaving a wide space between it and the mourners, who still remained kneeling as before. A short silence followed, when the leader of the corpse bearers stepped forward and set forth, in a clear, musical tone, the many virtues of the dead, and pronounced a eloquent eulogy over his remains.

On the conclusion of this, the speaker took his place among the rest, when all broke forth in the following

FUNERAL DIRGE.

Gone! gone! gone!
From earth gone forever:
No more here we'll meet him,
No more here we'll greet him,
No more, nevermore—
All is o'er, evermore—
Forever! forever!
He's gone from the mortal—
He's passed Death's great portal—
And now will his spirit
Forever inherit,
In regions of bliss,
What it could not in this.
Passed from all sorrow,
Vexation and care,
Gone to the regions
That bright angels share,
In yon golden Heaven
His spirit will rest,
With joys the most holy
Forever be blessed.

Weep! weep! weep!
But weep not in sorrow:
  With tears bend above him,
  With tears show you love him—
  But weep for relief,
  Rather than grief—
  For to-morrow—to-morrow—
Ye may join him in glory,
To tell the bright story,
  Of earthly denials,
  Losses and trials,
  Of unwavering faith,
  Of your joy to meet death,
That your spirit in freedom
  Forever might roam,
O'er the sweet vales of Eden,
  Your last lovely home—
To join there in singing,
  As bright angels do,
The songs of Great Spirit,
  Eternity through

That the dead,
  Before ye lying,
Made a happy
  Change in dying
And ye dead,
  Here rest in quiet,
Till ye hear
  The final fiat,
That in voice,
  More loud than thunder,
Shall command
  Your tomb asunder!
To earth we consign thee!
To God we resign thee!

CHORUS.

Sleep! sleep! sleep!
The birds shall carol o'er thy head,
The stream shall murmur o'er its bed,
The breeze shall make the forest sigh,
And flowers above thee bloom and die—
But birds, and stream, and breeze, and flowers,
Shall joy no more thy sleeping hours.
  To earth we consign thee!
  To God we resign thee!
    Farewell!

This was sung to a mournful tune, and when the last strain had died away upon the air, all simultaneously dropped upon their knees, and bowed their heads to the earth in token of submission to the Divine will. Then they rose to their feet; mourners and all, and forming themselves into two long lines, the four bearers proceeded to raise the corpse slowly and in silence; and preceded by Great Medicine, and followed by the maidens, the relatives and the rest, two by two, all moved solemnly forward to the last earthly resting place of the dead—a rude grave scooped out in the side of the mountain, some forty rods distant from the village.

Depositing the body in the ground with all due reverence, the bearers threw upon it a handful of loose earth, and moved aside for the others to do the same. This concluded, the villagers formed a large ring around the open grave, when Great Medicine stepped forward to the center and chanted

THE LAST DIRGE.

Formed of dust
  The spirit spurneth,
Back to dust
  The body turneth—
But the spirit,
  Passed death's-portal,
Doth become
  A thing immortal.

Ye who mourn him,
  Be unshaken,
That Who gave,
  Again hath taken—

The chorus was sung by all with impressive solemnity, and on its conclusion, the four corpse bearers advanced, and with wooden spades buried the dead for ever from the sight of the living. Two by two, in the same order they had come hither, the whole party returned to the village, and the day was spent in fasting and devotional exercises.

The food of the Great Medicine Nation consisted, for the most part, of meat of various wild animals, which they generally killed with rifles, together with a few fish, for which they angled in the streams. Sometimes they planted and raised a small patch of corn, as was the case in the present instance; but their roving life, as a general thing, led them to depend upon such vegetable food as chanced in their way. Among them they owned some fifteen horses, as many tame goats, which they milked daily, and twice the number of mules. They also owned a few traps, and when in a beaver country, did not fail using them to procure pelts; which, together with buffalo and bear skins, they traded with the whites for such extras as they considered useful. With them, all property, with the exception of bodily raiment, was in common; and each labored, not for himself alone, but for his neighbor also. During the day their animals fed around the encampment, and in the valley at the base of the mountain—but at night all were driven in and carrelled, or yarded, within the village.

Never before had I seen a people appear so wholly content with whatever Providence might give them, and so perfectly happy among themselves; and the time I spent with them, however singular the statement may seem to others, I must account one of the most pleasant periods of my life

―――o―――

CHAPTER XIX.

RESOLVE TO RESUME OUR JOURNEY—ANNOUNCEMENT TO PRAIRIE FLOWER—HER SURPRISE AND REGRET—DANGERS ENUMERATED—A CARELESS QUESTION—ABRUPT ANSWER—ALARMING AGITATION OF PRAIRIE FLOWER—OUR JOURNEY POSTPONED FOR THREE DAYS—HASTY DEPARTURE OF PRAIRIE FLOWER.

It was about the beginning of September, that I found my wounds so far healed and my strength so much recovered, as to think seriously of taking my departure. The air, too, on the mountains was becoming cool and frosty; and as my friend and I had decided on crossing to Oregon or California before the snow-storms of winter should entirely bar our progress, we thought best to be on the move as soon as possible.

During my stay in the village, I had seen and conversed more or less with Prairie Flower every day, and noted with regret that her features gradually grew more and more pale, her eye more languid and less bright, her step less elastic and buoyant, and that she moved slowly and heavily over the ground, with her head bent forward in a mood of deep abstraction. The cause of this I was at no loss to conjecture, particularly as I saw a studied effort on her part to avoid my friend on all occasions, and that, when they did meet, she ever exhibited toward him a coldness totally foreign to her warm, frank, open, generous nature. Huntly noticed her seeming aversion to him, with less philosophy than I had expected to see him display. In fact he became exceedingly troubled about it, and often told me with a sigh, that he must have been mistaken—that she did not love him—but that it was me on whom her affections were placed. I contradicted him only so far as to say, that she cared no more for me than for him; but did not care to tell him the real cause of her coldness—for I saw it would only serve to inflame his passion, and, from what I could judge, render both the more unhappy.

That Prairie Flower loved my friend, and that too against her will, was to me as clear as daylight; and the anguish it must have cost her gentle heart to avoid and appear cold and indifferent toward him, I could better imagine than realize. Several times had I been tempted to broach to her the subject, that I might learn from her lips the true state of her heart; but the slightest allusion to my friend, always produced such visible, painful embarrassment, that I instantly abandoned the idea, and adroitly changed the conversation to something as foreign as possible. Of one thing I became satisfied; and that was, that the sooner we took our departure, the better it would be for all parties; for both Prairie Flower and Huntly were becoming touched with a melancholy that I feared might lead to something more serious.

Accordingly, as soon as I fancied my strength sufficient to encounter the fatigue of a perilous journey, I announced my intention to Huntly, and wrung from him a reluctant consent to depart forthwith. My next move was to see Prairie Flower, and announce the same to her. As chance would have it, I shortly discovered her just outside the village, taking a stroll by herself—a habit which had now become with her of daily occurrence. Bidding my friend remain in the village, I hastened after, and presently overtook her; but so deep was she buried in meditation, that my steps, close behind, failed to rouse her from her reverie.

"You seem lost in communion with your own thoughts, sweet Prairie Flower," I said, in a cheerful tone; "and were I bent on surprising you, I might have done so to good advantage."

She started, a slight flush suffused her pale features, and turning her lovely countenance upon me, with an expression of deep surprise, she rallied herself for a reply.

"Really, I must crave pardon. M

Leighton—but I was so engaged in reflecting on—a—various matters, that I failed to catch the sound of your footsteps."

"I saw you were deeply abstracted, and would not have intruded on your privacy, only that I have a matter of some little moment to communicate."

"Indeed!" she rejoined, turning deadly pale and trembling nervously: "I trust nothing has happened to—to—any one?"

"Give yourself no uneasiness, dear Prairie Flower. I have only come to thank you, and through you your friends, for the kindness and unbounded hospitality of all to myself and Huntly, and inform you that we are on the point of taking our departure."

For a moment after I spoke, Prairie Flower stood staring upon me with an expression of intense anguish, her breast heaving tumultuously, and apparently without the power to utter a syllable in reply. At length, placing her hand to her throat, as if she felt a choking sensation, she fairly gasped forth:

"Not—not—going—surely?"

"I fear we must, dear Prairie Flower," I answered sadly—for I felt touched to the very soul at this unusual display of feeling and sorrowful regret at our departure—coming too from one to whom both Huntly and I were under such deep obligations for the preservation of our lives, and the many kindnesses we had received. "We have intruded upon your hospitality too long already," I continued, "and have at last decided to depart immediately."

"But—but—your wounds?"

"Are nearly healed."

"And your—your—strength?"

"Sufficient for the journey, I think."

"And whither go you?"

"Over the mountains—to Oregon, or California, as the case may be."

"But have you considered the dangers?"

"Everything."

"But the Indians may be in your path?"

"We must take our chance, then, as before. We have decided on taking a new route, however, and consequently will avoid all ambuscades."

"Still there are ten thousand dangers or a new route. You may get lost, get buried in the snows of the mountains, fall over some precipice—or, escaping all these, get captured by some roving tribe and put to the tortures."

"There are many dangers, sweet Prairie Flower, as you say; but had we feared to encounter them, we should never have been here."

"But you have no horses."

"We can purchase them at Fort Laramie, together with what other things we may need."

"You have no companions!"

"We may find some there, also—if not, we can venture alone."

"But—but——. You will go, then?"

"I fear we must—loth as we are to part from you and your people, with whom (I wish not to flatter when I say it) some of the happiest moments of my life have been spent."

For some time Prairie Flower did not reply, during which her eyes were cast upon the ground, and a look of deep sorrow settled over her lovely features, and her bosom heaved with internal emotions. Raising her soft, dark eyes again to mine, I was pained to behold them slightly dimmed with tears, which she had striven in vain to repress.

"I did not think," she said, with a deep sigh, "that you would leave us so soon."

"Soon? dear Prairie Flower! God bless your noble soul! Soon, say you? Why, have we not been here two long months and more?"

"True," she answered, as I fancied a little reproachfully, "I had forgotten that the time must have seemed long to you."

"Nay, sweet Prairie Flower, I meant not that. You are too sensitive—you misconstrue me. I only meant, it was long for utter strangers to share your hospitality, and trouble you with their presence."

"You would not trouble us if you staid forever," she rejoined, with an air of such sweet simplicity, that in spite of all my assumed stoicism, I felt a tear trembling in my eye.

Prairie Flower saw it, and quickly added, with an earnest, tender expression, which could only be realized by being seen:

"Oh sir! I fear I have wounded your feelings!"

No wonder Huntly was in love, if he had ever seen anything like this—for with all my philosophy and sober reasoning, I felt myself in a fair way of becoming his rival.

"God bless you, Prairie Flower!" I exclaimed from my very heart. "If Heaven holds many like you, no wonder it is a paradise beyond mortal conception."

"O, do not compare me with those who dwell in that bright realm," she quickly rejoined; "for I at best am only a poor sinful mortal."

"Then God help me!" I ejaculated—"if *you* are considered a sinner."

"But your—your—friend?" she said, hesitatingly. "Is—he—anxious to leave us?"

She strove to assume an indifference as she said this, but the effort to do so only the more exposed her feelings, of which becoming aware, she blushed deeply, and on the conclusion hung her head in real embarrassment.

"No, dear Prairie Flower," I said, appearing not to notice her confusion; "my friend is not anxious to leave; on the contrary, it was with much difficulty I could convince him of the necessity of our immediate departure, and gain his consent to set forth."

"And wherefore, do you think, is he loth to go?" she asked, carelessly turning her head aside, and stooping to pick a beautiful flower that was growing at her feet.

"Because sweet Prairie Flower goes not with him," I answered, rather abruptly, curious to see what effect such information would produce.

The next moment I regretted I had not hinted, rather than spoken, this important truth. As I pronounced the sentence, the hand of Prairie Flower, which already clasped the stem of the flower in the act of breaking it, became violently agitated and relaxed its hold; while its owner, raising her face, as pale as death, staggered back, and, but for my support, would have fallen to the ground.

"Good Heavens! Prairie Flower," I exclaimed, throwing an arm around her slender waist, and feigning ignorance of the cause of her agitation; "what has happened? Are you bit, or stung?—Speak! quick! tell me!"

"A-a-little weakness—a-a-sudden weakness—a-a-kind of faintness," she stammered, endeavoring to recover her composure, and evidently relieved that I had not imputed her agitation to the right cause. "I don't know that I ever was so affected before," she continued, smiling faintly. "But I think it will soon pass away. I feel much relieved now. There, there—thank you! that will do. Quite sudden, was it not?"

"Quite, indeed!" I replied, adding mentally, "Poor, poor girl! how I pity thee!—thy peace of mind is gone forever."

"But you spoke of leaving immediately," she resumed. "What day have you set for your departure?"

"This."

"Not to-day, surely!" she exclaimed, in surprise.

"So had we determined."

"But you must not go to-day!"

"And why not?"

"O, it is not right to leave us so abruptly; and besides, I have reasons for wishing you to delay three days at least!"

"What reasons?"

"I cannot tell you now; but remain, and you shall know."

"Anything to please you, sweet Prairie Flower."

"Then I have your promise?"

"You have."

"Thank you! thank you!—you will not regret it. But come, let us return to the village, for I see the sun is three good hours above the hills, and I have a long journey before me."

"What! are you going to leave, then?"

"I must! I have important business. But ask me no questions, and do not depart till I return."

Half an hour later, Prairie Flower mounted on her beautiful Indian pony, as I had first beheld her at Fort Laramie, rode swiftly out of the village, unattended, and disappeared down the mountain.

CHAPTER XX.

PRAIRIE FLOWER STILL ABSENT — RESOLVE TO DEPART—BID OUR FRIENDS ADIEU—SET FORWARD WITH OUR GUIDE—UNEXPECTED MEETING WITH PRAIRIE FLOWER—RETURN TO THE VILLAGE — A SPLENDID PRESENT—OUR ROUTE CHANGED—SECOND ADIEU—PRAIRIE FLOWER AS GUIDE—OUR LAST PAINFUL PARTING WITH OUR SWEET BENEFACTRESS.

THREE days dragged on wearily—for without Prairie Flower, the Indian village seemed gloomy and insipid both to Humtly and myself—and the fourth morning had come, and yet our fair benefactress had not made her appearance. Where had she gone, and wherefore did she not return? We questioned several of the villagers; but all shook their heads and replied, some in good and some in broken English, that they did not know, that she was frequently absent a month at a time, and that she rarely told on leaving where she was going or when she would return. Perhaps, then, her journey was merely taken to avoid a farewell scene, thinking we should depart in her absence; and this I mentioned to Huntly, whose surmises I found corresponded with mine.

"She has done it," he said, somewhat bitterly, "to put a slight upon us, or rather upon me, whose presence lately seems most offensive to her; and for myself I am going to leave — you can do as you like."

In this I knew my friend was wrong altogether; but I did not contradict him—for under the circumstances, I preferred he should think as he did, rather than be made aware of what, as I imagined, was the true cause of her actions. I therefore replied:

"Let us away, then, as soon as possible."

"Agreed."

Upon this we hastened to bid our Indian friends a long adieu, who seemed greatly surprised and expressed astonishment that we should leave so suddenly, without having given them a previous notice. Having gone the entire rounds, shook the dusky hands of each, young and old—Great Medicine not excepted, who enlarged his small, dark eyes to their utmost tension, but merely grunted a farewell—and thanked each and all heartily for their hospitality and kindness to us as strangers, we prepared to set out at once for Fort Laramie. As the direct route was unknown to us, we inquired the way particularly—whereupon a stout, rather good-looking, intelligent Indian youth volunteered his services to act as guide—a proposition which we readily and gratefully accepted, with a promised reward when we should arrive safely at our destination.

It was a bright, clear, frosty morning, and the sun, just rising above the mountains, poured down his radiant light, gladdening the forest and our hearts with his presence; and this, together with the bracing air, the freedom we fancied we were about to experience after our long confinement, in being once more upon our journey in good health, produced feelings of buoyancy and independence, such as we had not known for many a long day.

Our guide had left us, as he said, to make preparations for our journey, and we were already becoming impatient at what we considered his tardiness, when, to our surprise, he reappeared, mounted on one, and leading two horses, which he significantly intimated were at our service. This was a kindness we could fully appreciate, and of course felt no desire to chide him for his delay. Thanking him in unmeasured terms for his happy foresight in thus insuring us speed and safety against fatigue, we vaulted into the saddles with as much agility as if we had never known a mishap.

Waving a silent adieu to the villagers, who came forth in a body to see us depart, we turned our horses' heads down the hill, and setting forward, soon reached the valley, crossed the stream, and burying ourselves in the forest, shut the Indian village completely from our view.

"Well, Frank," exclaimed Huntly, gayly, as with a spirited gallop we buried ourselves deeper and deeper in the forest of the valley, "this seems like old times—eh! my dear fellow?"

"It does, indeed!" I replied in the same joyous manner, as I felt the warm blood of active excitement again coursing through all my veins.

Scarcely had the words passed my lips, when our guide, who was riding in advance, suddenly drew rein, brought his horse to a halt, and exclaimed:

"She comes!"

Ere we had time to inquire who, we beheld, much to our surprise, the beautiful Prairie Flower dashing up the valley we were descending, directly in our front. Of course there was no means of avoiding her, had we designed doing so, and accordingly we rode slowly forward to meet her. As we advanced, I could perceive that her pale features looked unusually care-worn, and that her lips were compressed, as by some inward struggle to appear entirely at her ease. As we met, she said, half in jest and half in earnest, while a slight flush tinted her cheeks and made her sweet countenance look lovely beyond description:

"Good morning, my friends. Not running away, surely?"

"Why," I answered, in some confusion, "we have bidden our friends of the village a last adieu, and are, as you see, already on our journey."

"Indeed! you surprise me! And could you not have deferred your departure till my return?"

"Why, the fact is—we—that is I—we waited three days—the time mentioned by you—and as we thought—that—as you had not made your appearance—that——"

"I would not return at all," she rejoined, completing the sentence which my embarrassment forced me to leave unfinished. "I truly grieve, my friends," she continued, with a look of sorrowful reproach, "that, having known me so long, you should be led to doubt my word. Did I ever deceive you, that you thought I might again?"

"Never! never!" cried both Huntly and I in the same breath, while the conscience of each accused him of having done wrong. "But as the three days had expired," I added, by way of justification, "and as none of the villagers knew whither you had gone, we feared to tarry longer, lest the coming storms of winter should catch us on the mountains."

"Perhaps, then, you were right after all," she said with a sigh. "True, I did not return so soon as I expected, on account of an unforseen delay; and though I did request you not to depart till I came back, and though I fondly relied on seeing you again, still I must admit that your promise has been faithfully kept, and that you had a perfect right to go, and I none to think you would stay to your own inconvenience."

This was said in a tone so sad, with such modest simplicity, that, knowing the true state of her heart, and remembering that to her generous nature and untiring watchfulness and care we both owed our lives, every word sunk like burning lava into my heart, and I felt condemned beyond the power of self-defence. For a moment I knew not what nor how to reply, while Prairie Flower dropped her eyes to the ground and seemed hurt to the very soul.

"Forgive us, sweet Prairie Flower!" I at length exclaimed, to the promptings of my better nature. "Forgive us both, for having done you wrong! I cannot exonerate myself, whatever my friend may do. I had *no* right to doubt you—no right to wound your feelings by leaving in a manner so cold, so contrary to the dictates of friendship and gratitude. But still, dear Prairie Flower, if you knew all my motives, you would, perhaps, blame me less."

She looked up at the last words, caught the expression of my eye, and seemed to comprehend my meaning at a glance; for she colored deeply, turned aside her head, and quickly answered:

"I do not blame you. Let it pass. But whither are you bound?"

"To Fort Laramie."

"I trust, then, I have saved you that journey."

"Indeed!" I exclaimed in surprise, as a new idea suddenly flashed across my mind. "You have been there, then?"

"I have."

"And all for us?"

"But for you, I do not think I should have gone at present."

"God bless your noble, generous soul!" I cried, feeling more condemned than ever. "How fortunate that we have met you, that we can at least make the slight reparation of apology and regret for having misconstrued your motives! What must have been your feelings, had you returned your heart bounding with delight at having done us a service, and found we had repaid you by leaving in your absence, without even so much as thanks for your kindness!"

"I should have felt hurt and grieved, I must own," she answered, quietly.

"It is my fault, Prairie Flower," said Huntly, riding up to her side. "Blame me for all, and not my friend! To speak plainly, I fancied my presence was hateful to you, and that you had gone away, merely to put a slight upon me, by avoiding even to the last, as you had avoided me all along."

"You—you think this?" cried Prairie Flower, turning upon him a look of anguish I shall never forget, and becoming so agitated she could scarcely sit her horse. "You think this? O, no, no, no! you did not, could not, think I intended to insult you!" and she buried her face in her hands and shook violently.

"Great Heaven! what have I done!" cried Huntly in alarm. "Look up, sweet Prairie Flower—look up and forgive me! If I thought so then, I do not think so now, and God pardon me for harboring such a thought at all! But I could not understand why you avoided me, unless it was through dislike — in which case my absence would be little likely to cause a regret. I see my mistake now, and am satisfied that, whatever your motive might have been, it was one which you at least felt to be right and pure."

"Indeed it was!" returned Prairie Flower, raising her sweet, sad face, and her soft, dark eyes to his, and then modestly dropping her gaze to the ground.

Huntly seemed about to reply, but paused and gazed silently upon Prairie Flower, who, again raising her eyes, and meeting a peculiar glance from him, blushed and turned her head quickly away. It was evident that both were getting embarrassed, and I hastened to relieve them by saying:

"And what news from Fort Laramie, Prairie Flower? What of our friends?"

"I could learn nothing definite, save that eight only, of the sixteen with whom you went into battle, returned, and that the rest, including yourselves, were supposed to have been killed or taken prisoners.— One of the former, I think they called him an Irishman, made great lamentations over you, declaring that the Indians or wild beasts had destroyed you."

"Poor Teddy!" I sighed; "he did indeed love us. But what became of him?"

"He left a few days after, with a party of trappers."

"Then it may be a long time before we meet again, if ever. But do you think we can procure a regular outfit at the fort?"

"What do you require?"

"Two good horses, a brace of rifles, plenty of ammunition, and three or four buffalo skins. By the way, this reminds me that we left our possibles at the fort, stuffed with clothes, which will now be of valuable service."

"Come with me to the village," rejoined Prairie Flower, "and we will talk the matter over."

"Why, as we are so far on the way, it will only cause us unnecessary delay; besides, we have spoken our farewells to all, and turning back, when once started on a journey, is said to give bad luck."

"Yet I have but one observation to make to all your objections," returned Prairie Flower, peremptorily; "and that is, you *must* come with me."

"If you insist on it, certainly."

"I do."

On this we turned, without more ado, and took our way back, wondering what new mystery or surprise would greet us next. The Indians appeared more rejoiced than astonished at seeing us again, and crowded around us, and shook our hands, with as much apparent delight as if we had been absent a month.

"What is the utmost limit of your stay with us, my friends?" inquired Prairie Flower.

"An hour is the extreme," I replied.

Upon this she turned and addressed a few words to the young Indian who had volunteered to act as our guide, and then bidding us dismount and follow her, she led the way into the lodge of Great Medicine. Making some excuse, she went out, and shortly returned, bringing with her our rifles and plenty of powder and ball.

"Now that you are going," she said, "I will restore you your arms, with a sincere prayer that, with the aid of Heaven, they may prove sufficient to preserve your lives from your natural enemies, the savages and wild beasts."

Here was another unexpected kindness, and both Huntly and myself were profuse in our thanks. Prairie Flower then inquired the route we intended to take; and being answered that this would depend much upon circumstances, she advised us to cross the Black Hills some ten miles south of our present location, and hold our course westward over Laramie plains, Medicine Bow Mountains, and the North Fork of Platte, to Brown's Hole on Green River, where doubtless we should find many trappers, and perhaps some of our old acquaintances—giving as a reason for directing us thus, that there would be less danger from the Indians, who, notwithstanding our signal victory at Bitter Cottonwood, still continued in parties along the regular Oregon route, killing the whites whenever they could do so without too much risk to themselves.

Thanking Prairie Flower for her advice, I replied that, having reached Fort Laramie, it would be doubtful if we returned this way—that in all probability we should join some party of emigrants—or, failing in this, take a middle course and run our risks.

"But I see no necessity for your going to Fort Laramie," she rejoined.

"You forget, Prairie Flower, that we have no horses, and it would be foolish at least to attempt such a journey on foot."

To this she made no direct reply, but went on suggesting various things for our convenience and safety, with as much apparent concern for our welfare, as if her own life and fortunes were bound up in ours.

At length the conversation slacked, and thinking it a good opportunity, I declared that our time had expired, and that we must start forthwith.

"Well, I will not detain you longer," replied Prairie Flower, leading the way out of the cabin.

To our surprise, we found at the door two beautiful steeds, (not the ones we had just ridden,) richly adorned with Spanish saddles, bridles, and apishamores,* with two sacks of jerked meat hanging to the horns, and four large buffalo skins strapped on behind, while along side stood the handsome pony of our fair benefactress, each and all ready for a start.

"What mean these?" I inquired, turning to Prairie Flower.

"Simply," she answered, with the utmost *naïvete*, "that you must accept from me these horses and trappings, without a word, and allow me to be your guide to the point where you will turn off to cross the mountains."

"But, Prairie Flower——"

"Not a word—not a single word—such are the conditions."

"But we have money, and——"

"Surely you would not insult me," she interrupted, "by offering to *pay?*"

I saw by her manner that to say more would only be to offend; and seizing her hand, I pressed it, with a hearty "God bless you!" while my eyes, in spite of me, became dimmed with tears. Huntly was too deeply affected to speak at all, and therefore only pressed her hand in silence, during which the features of Prairie Flower grew very pale, and she was forced to turn aside her head to conceal her emotion. We now comprehended all—why she had gone to Fort Laramie, and had insisted on our return with her to the village—and as we recalled her former kindness and generosity, and our own base suspicions of her intention to slight us, the result was to make both Huntly and myself very sad. She had her revenge, we felt, and a noble one it was too.

Mounting our horses, we again bade a silent adieu to the Mysterious Tribe, and, in company with Prairie Flower, quitted the village the second time, with more regret than the first, and took our way southward, in a direction almost opposite our previous one.

As we rode on, I noticed that our fair guide became exceedingly abstracted, and when she fancied herself unobserved, that she frequently sighed. Poor girl! she was laboring to suppress feelings, which, like the pent up fires of a volcano, were preparing to rend the tenement which confined them; and the very thought clouded my path with melancholy. Huntly, too, was abstracted and silent, so that little was said

---

* Saddle blankets of buffalo calf-skin, dressed soft.

on the way; and though everything above, around and beneath, seemed conspiring to make us cheerful, yet our thoughts only rendered our hearts the more gloomy by contrast.

A ride of less than three hours brought us to a spot of the mountain that seemed of easy ascent, when Prairie Flower drew in rein, and said with a sigh:

"Your route lies yonder. Keep a little to the south of west, and avoid traveling after dark, or you may plunge over some precipice and be dashed to pieces."

Huntly now appeared too agitated to reply, and it was with difficulty I could myself summon words to my aid.

"And so, dear Prairie Flower," I at length articulated, "we are to part here?"

"I fear we must."

"Shall we ever meet again?"

"God only knows," she answered, trembling nervously, and dropping her eyes to the ground."

"To attempt to express our gratitude to you," I rejoined, "would be worse than vain; words could not speak it; the heart alone can, and that you cannot see, only through external expressions. Of one thing, fair being, rest assured: that in the secret chambers of the souls of Francis Leighton and Charles Huntly, is engraved a name that will never be erased—that of the noble and generous Prairie Flower."

"Say no more—I—I—beg of you!" she gasped, waving her hand, and then placing it to her heart, as if to still its wild throbbings.

"Prairie Flower," said Huntly, in a tremulous voice, "if I part without a word, you may think me ungrateful. It is not so. Do not think so. I—— Could you know this heart——"

"No more—no more!" cried the other. "I see—I know—I understand all. Too much—too much. Go! go! I—— Go, and God's blessing attend you both! I ——"

She paused, and grasped the mane of her beast to save herself from falling.

"Then farewell," rejoined Huntly, riding up to her side and extending his hand. "You will never be forgotten by me; and should we meet not again—then —farewell—for-ever."

Prairie Flower clasped his hand, but her own trembled violently, and her lips refused a reply. The next moment, fearing doubtless the effect of a longer trial of her feelings and nerves, she turned her pony, and signing me an adieu with her hand, dashed rapidly away, and soon disappeared from our view in the deep forest.

Huntly sighed, but made no remark, and silently and slowly we began our ascent of the mountain.

That night we slept on the brow of the Black Hills, at a point overlooking a large extent of the Laramie Plains.

———o———

CHAPTER XXI.

IN SIGHT OF BROWN'S HOLE—A DASH DOWN THE MOUNTAIN — APPEARANCE OF THE PLACE—THE OLD TRAPPER—DISAPPOINTMENT—EXORBITANT PRICES—A GAMBLING QUARREL—A MOUNTAINEER DUEL—HORRIBLE RESULT.

IT was a beautiful morning, not far from the middle of September, that, ascending a hill at the base of which we had encamped the night previous, we overlooked a charming green valley, completely shut in by hills, through the very center of which, like a long line of molten silver, we beheld a bright stream taking its devious course. Not the least agreeable and enchanting to to us, was the sight of a few shanties, erected along the margin of the river, and the moving to and fro of several white human beings. And not the less pleasant the sight, that we had been some two weeks on a fatiguing journey of more than two hundred miles, over mountains, plains, and rivers, without having seen a solitary individual but ourselves.

The valley we now beheld was the point of our present destination, a rendezvous for the trappers, hunters, and traders of this part of the country, and known as Brown's Hole. I have not described our journey hither, after parting with Prairie Flower, as but little of interest to the general reader occurred on the route, beyond fatigue of travel, an occasional escape from a fatal plunge over some precipice, and one violent storm on the Medicine Bow, which proved far more disagreeable than dangerous

Here, then, we were at last, in full view of what seemed to us a paradise; and a simultaneous shout of delight, not only told our feelings, but that our lungs were still in good order.

"Well, Frank," exclaimed Huntly, with great animation, "we are now in a fair way of coming in contact with somebody besides Indians, and so let us down the mountain with all the haste possible."

"Here goes, then, for a race," I cried; and urging my noble animal forward, I dashed down the declivity, to the imminent danger of myself and horse, followed by Huntly in the same reckless manner, both shouting and wild with excitement.

Reaching the base of the mountain, we galloped swiftly over the valley, and brought up at last in the center of the encampment, where curiosity soon surrounded us with a medley of various nations and complexions, all eager to learn who we were and what our business. Here we beheld Indians of different tribes, Spaniards, Mexicans, Englishmen, Frenchmen, Creoles, Canadians, together with Anglo-Americans from all parts of the United States. Some of these were trappers, hunters, traders, *coureur des bois*, and speculators in general—all congregated here to carry on the traffic of buying and selling—this one to make money, and that one to squander his hard earnings in gambling and dissipation. Already had the trade of the season opened, although the greater part of the trappers were not yet "in" from the mountains with their furs, pelts, and robes.

Outside the shanties, of which there were some half a dozen—belonging, the principal one to the agent of the Hudson Bay company, and the others to different traders—were built fires, around which groups of bronzed mountaineers were squatted, lost to all consciousness of the outer world, in the exciting games of "euchre," "poker," "seven up," &c., &c. In one place was meat in the process of jerking, in another skins stretched over hoops for drying, while here and there was a rude block of graining, together with various other implements used in the fur trade.

All these I noted with a hasty glance as I drew in rein, and while the medley crowd, before spoken of, was gathering around us. I looked keenly at each as he came up, but failed to recognize a single face, much to my disappointment, as I had been rather sanguine of here finding some of my old acquaintances.

"Whar from?" asked a tall, dark, athletic mountaineer—eyeing us, as I fancied, a little suspiciously.

"Over the mountains," I answered.

"Whar's your traps and beavers?"

"We have none."

"Injins raise 'em?"

"We never carried any."

"Traders, hey?"

"No."

"What then?"

"Adventurers."

"That's a new callin, spose?"

"That is ours, at all events."

"Fine hosses you got thar."

"Very good, I believe."

"Going to stop?"

"Think we shall."

"Well, ground yourselves, put your hosses to feed, and let's see how you look."

Upon this we dismounted, and while doing so, Huntly observed:

"I say, friend, do you know most of the trappers?"

"Know a heap—all I ever seed."

"Did you ever see one, then, called Black George?"

"D'ye ever see your own mother, stranger? Didn't I used to trap with him fifteen years ago?—and hain't I fit him out of many a Injin snap? Ef that ain't knowin him, jest tell me what is."

"That is knowing him certainly," returned Huntly, smiling. "But have you seen him of late?"

"Not sence two year come calf time. B'lieve he went over to the States, or some sich outlandish place or other."

"Then I have seen him since you."

"Whar d'ye leave him?" inquired the other with interest.

"In an Indian fight at Bitter Cottonwood."

"I'd sw'ar it. When Injins is about he's always in, and a few at that, or I'm no snakes. But what become on him? Hope he did'nt go under!"

"That is more than I can say, as my friend here and I were carried off the field for dead, and have not been able to get the particulars of the battle since."

"He did'nt die, I'll bet my life on that! Ef he did, it's the fust time he ever knocked under to sich varmints."

"I suppose, then, you have seen none who were in the fight?"

"Never heared on't till now—so reckon I havn't."

"We fondly anticipated meeting some of them here."

"Its like you may yit; for ef they're about in this part o' creation, they're sure to come. But turn out them critters, for they looks hungry, and make yourselves at home here. And while I thinks on't, ef you've got any bacca, I'll trouble ye for a chaw."

As I had some of the desired article, I proffered it, and received his warmest thanks in return. We now set about removing our saddles and other appendages, and hoppling our horses; while the crowd, having stared at us to their satisfaction, and found nothing particularly remarkable in our persons or equipments, gradually sauntered away, until we were left entirely to ourselves.

Brown's Hole, at certain seasons of the year, becomes a place of considerable note, and presents many of the features of a western settlement on a holiday. It was interesting to us to note the avariciousness of the traders, and the careless indifference of the trappers, in disposing of their commodities. Dropping in daily—sometimes singly and sometimes in parties from two to ten, loaded with pelts and furs, in value from one hundred to several thousand dollars — the latter would barter them for powder, lead, tobacco, alcohol, coffee, and whatever else they fancied, receiving each article at the most exhorbitant price, without uttering a word of complaint. I have seen powder sold to the mountaineers at the enormous sum of from three to four dollars a pint; alcohol at double this price, the same measure; coffee ditto; tobacco two and three dollars per plug, and everything else in proportion. Money here was out of the question, as much as if it had never been in existence—furs, pelts, and robes being substituted therefor. Here I witnessed gambling on every scale, from the highest to the lowest—from thousands to units—while every doubtful or mooted point was sure to result in a bet before being decided. It was nothing uncommon to see a trapper "come in" with three or four mules, and furs to the amount of several thousand dollars, and within a week from his arrival, be without the value of a baubee he could call his own—furs, mules, rifle, everything, sacrificed to his insatiable love of gambling. The mountaineer over his cups is often quarrelsome, and an angry dispute is almost certain to be settled in an honorable way (?)—that is, rifles at thirty yards—when one or the other (sometimes both) rarely fails to pay the forfeit of his life. I had not been many days in Brown's Hole, ere I witnessed a tragedy of this kind, which even now, as I recall it, makes my blood run cold with horror.

The actors in this bloody scene were two trappers of the better class, of intelligent and respectable appearance, neither of whom had seen over thirty years, and who, as a general thing, were of very sober and quiet habits. They were from the same part of the country—had been boys together—had started together upon their adventures and perilous occupation, and were, moreover, sworn *friends*.

Some three days after our arrival, they had made their appearance, well packed with pelts and furs, which they immediately proceeded to dispose of to the traders. As their trip had been an unusually profitable one, they of course felt much elated, and taking a drink together, sat down to a friendly game of cards, to while away their leisure hours. More strict in their habits than most of their associates, they rarely gambled, and then only for diversion. On the occasion alluded to they at once began playing for liquor, and having at length drank more than their wont, proceeded to stake different articles. As the game progressed, they became more and more excited, until at last their stakes run very high. One was peculiarly fortunate, and of course the luck of the other was exactly the reverse, which so mortified and vexed him, that he finally staked all his hard earnings and lost. On this his companion took another drink, grew more and more merry at his own success, which he attributed to his superior skill in handling the cards, and finally bantered the other to put up his mules. No sooner said than done, and the result was the same as before. He was now, to use the phrase of some of the by-standers, who had crowded around the two to watch the game, "Han'somely cleaned out." He had staked all, and lost all, and was of course rendered not a little desperate by the circumstance.

"Why don't you bet your body fixins?" cried one.

Like a drowning man at a straw, he caught at the idea, and the next moment he and his companion were deciding the ownership of his costume by a game of euchre. As might have been supposed, the result was against him, and he was at last completely beggared.

Seizing the half emptied can of liquor by his side, he drained it at a draught, and in a tone of frenzy cried:

"Somebody lend me somethin! By——! I must have my fixins back."

"Luck's agin ye now," answered one. "Better wait till another time."

"No! now—now!—by——! now!" he fairly screamed. "I'll show Jim yet, that I'm his master at cards any day he pleases. Who'll lend me somethin, I say?"

None seemed inclined, however, to assist one so signally unfortunate; and having waited a sufficient time, and finding his appeal likely to prove fruitless, the disappointed man rose, and in a great passion swore he would leave "such outlandish diggins, and the heathenish set that inhabit them."

"Whar'll ye go?" asked his companion, in unusual glee.

"Whar no such —— scamps as you can find me."

"But afore you leave, I spose you'll pay your debts?" retorted the other.

"What debts?"

"Did'nt I jest win your body fixins?"

"Well, do you claim them, too? I thought as how you'd got enough without them."

"Claim all my property wharever I can find it," returned the other, more in jest than earnest. "Of course, ef you're goin to leave, so as I won't see you agin, I can't afford to trust."

"You're a villain!" cried the loser, turning fiercely upon his friend: "A mean, dirty, villainous thief, and a liar!"

"Come, come, Sam—them's hard words," replied the one called Jim, in a mood of some displeasure.

"Well they're true, you know it, and you darn't resent 'em."

"By——!" cried the other, his eyes flashing fire, and his whole frame trembling with a newly roused passion—"I dare and will resent it, at any time and place you please."

"The time's now, then, and the place hereabouts."

"And what the way?"

"Rifles—thirty paces."

"Enough, by——!" and both proceeded to get their rifles and arrange themselves upon the ground—a spot some forty yards distant from the encampment—whither they were followed by a large crowd, all eager to be witnesses of a not uncommon, though what often proved a bloody scene, as was the case in the present instance.

Selecting a level spot, the parties in question placed themselves back to back, and having examined their rifles, each marched forward fifteen paces, and wheeled face to his antagonist. Sam then called out:

"All ready?"

"Ready," was the reply.

"Somebody give the word, then," returned the first speaker, and at the same instant both rifles were brought to the faces of the antagonists.

For a moment a breathless silence succeeded, which was broken by the distinct, but ominous word,

"Fire!"

Scarcely was it uttered, when crack went both rifles at once; and bounding up from the earth, with a yell of pain, Sam fell back a corpse, pierced through the brain by the bullet of his friend. Jim was unharmed, though the ball of the other had passed through his hat and grazed the top of his head. Dropping his rifle, with a look of horror that haunts me still, he darted forward, and was the first to reach the side of the dead. Bending down, he raised the body in his arms, and wiping the blood from its face with his hands, called out, in the most endearing and piteous tones:

"Sam! Sam!—look up!—speak to me! —it's Jim—your friend. I did not go to do it. I was mad, or drunk. Sam! Sam! speak to me!—for Heaven's sake speak, if only once, and say you forgive me! Sam, why don't you speak? Oh! I shall go distracted! My brain seems on fire! You know, dear Sam, I would not murder you—*you*—my friend—my dearly loved friend—the playmate of my childhood! Oh, speak! speak! speak! O God! speak, Sam, if only once! It was the cursed liquor that did it. Oh speak! if only to curse me! O God! O God! he don't answer me!" cried the wretched man, turning an anguished, imploring look upon the spectators, as if they could give him aid, and then wildly straining the dead man to his heart.

"He'll never speak agin," said one.

"Oh no! do not say that!" shrieked the duellist, "Do not say that! or I shall go mad. I feel it here—here—in my head—in my brain. I killed him, did I? I killed him—murdered him—the only friend I had on earth? And you all stood and saw me do it. Yes, I murdered him. See! see! thar's blood—his blood—I did it—ha, ha, ha!" and he ended with a maniacal laugh, threw himself upon the ground, and hugged the corpse of his friend to his heart.

"Poor feller!" said one, "he'd better be taken into one o' the lodges, for he looks like he'd lost his sense."

"No, no, no! you shan't—you shan't part us!" cried the frenzied man, drawing his dead companion closer to his heart, as some of the party sought to carry out the suggestion just made. "No, no! you shan't part us—never, never, never! This is Sam, this is—Sam Murdoch—he's my friend—and we're goin a long journey together—ain't we Sam? We'll never part agin—will we Sam? Never! never!—O, never!—ha, ha, ha! Thar! thar! he continued, dropping the body, rising to a sitting posture, and staring wildly at some imaginary object: "I see, Sam—I see! You're in great danger. That rock's about to fall. But hang on, Sam—hang on to that root! Don't let go! Jim's a-comin. O God! who put that chasm thar—that mountain gorge—to separate us? I can't git across. Help! help! or Sam will die. Yes, he's fallin now! Thar! thar! he's goin—down—down—down! But heyar's what'll meet you, Sam. Comin! comin!" and whipping out his knife as he said this, before any one was aware what he was about, or had time to prevent him, he plunged it into his heart, and gasping the word "comin," rolled over upon the earth and expired beside his friend.

I had been a silent witness of the whole bloody, terrible scene—but my feelings can neither be imagined nor described. Speechless with horror, I stood and gazed like one in a nightmare, without the power to move, and was only roused from my painful revery by Huntly, who, tapping me on the shoulder, said:

"Come away, Frank—come away!"

Complying with his request, I turned, and together we quitted the ground, both too deeply affected and horrified at what we had seen to make a single comment.

The mountaineers, with whom such and similar scenes were of common occurrence, proceeded to deposit the dead in a rude grave near the spot where they had fallen. They then returned to the encampment, to take a drink to their memories, coolly talk over the "sad mishap," as they termed it, and again to engage in their usual routine of amusement or occupation. In a week the whole affair was forgotten, or mentioned only to some new comer as having happened "some time ago."

Upon the mind of myself and friend, it produced an impression never to be erased; and for a long time, apparitions of the unfortunate trappers haunted my waking senses by day, and my dreams by night.

CHAPTER XII.

RESOLVE TO DEPART—DISCOURAGING OBSERVATIONS—FAIL TO GET A GUIDE—SET OUT—UINTAH FORT—OUR JOURNEY TO UTAH LAKE—RESOLVE TO CROSS THE GREAT INTERIOR BASIN—FIRST DAY'S PROGRESS—CAMP—KILL A RABBIT—SUDDEN ATTACK FROM THE DIGGERS—REPULSE AND FORTUNATE ESCAPE.

WE had been a month in Brown's Hole, without having seen or heard anything concerning our old acquaintances—during which time another mountaineer had been the victim of a quarrel, though his death we did not witness—when I proposed to Huntly to set forward at once, and leave a place so little adapted to our tastes and feelings.

"But where do you propose going, Frank?" inquired my friend.

"To California."

"But can we find the way by ourselves?"

"We shall hardly find a place less to our liking than this, at all events," I replied.

"But we are safe here, Frank."

"I presume Charles Huntly does not fear danger, or he would not have ventured westward at all."

"Enough, Frank! Say no more! I am your man. But when shall we start?"

"What say you for to-morrow morning?"

"Agreed. But perhaps we can hire a guide?"

"We will try," I rejoined.

But our trial proved fruitless. No guide could be found, whose love of money would tempt him, at this season of the year, to undertake the conducting of us to California: while on every hand we were assailed by the mountaineers, with the most startling accounts of dangers from Indians, from snows, from floods, from storms, and from starvation.

"You never can fetch through," said one. "It's a fixed unpossibility."

"You're fools ef you undertake it," joined in another.

"It's like jumpin on to rocks down a three hundred foot precipice, and spectin to git off without no bones broke," rejoined a third.

"Ef you know what's safe, you'll jest keep your eyes skinned, and not leave these here diggins," added a fourth.

But these remarks, instead of discouraging us, produced exactly the opposite effect, and roused our ambition to encounter the formidable dangers of which all were so eager to warn us. To Huntly and myself, there appeared something bold and manly in attempting what all seemed to dread; and to each and all I accordingly replied:

"It is useless, gentlemen, trying to discourage us. We have decided on going, and go we shall at all hazards."

"All I've got to say, then, is, that it'll be the last goin you'll do in this world," rejoined the friend of Black George, who seemed uncommonly loth to part with us.

The next morning rose clear and cold—for the air in this part of the counry had become quite frosty—and agreeably to our resolve of the preceding day, we equipped ourselves and horses once more, and bidding our mountaineer friends adieu, set forward in fine spirits—shaping our course, to the best of our judgment, so as to strike the southern range of the Bear River Mountains, in the vicinity of the Utah Lake, which connects with the Great Salt Lake on the north.

To give our progress in detail, would only be to describe a succession of scenes, incidents, and perils, similar to those already set before the reader, and take up time and space which the necessity of the case requires me to use for a more important purpose. I shall, therefore, content myself with sketching some of the most prominent and startling features of our route—a route sufficiently full of perils, as we found to our cost, to put to the test the temerity and try the iron constitution of the boldest and most hardy adventurer.

While in Brown's Hole, we had succeeded in purchasing of one of the traders, at a high price, a map and compass, which he had designed especially for his own use, and similar to those we had provided ourselves with on starting, but which, together with many other valuable articles, had been left in our possible sacks at Fort Laramie.

On our compass and map we now placed our whole dependence, as our only guide over a vast region of unexplored country —or explored only by a few traders, trappers, and Indians—Fremont's celebrated expedition, which created at the time such universal interest throughout the United States, not being made till some three or four years subsequent to the date of which I am writing. And here, *en passant*, I would remark, that in determining our course for California, we had particular reference to the southern portion of it; for as every reader knows, who is acquainted with the geography of the country, or who has taken the trouble to trace our route on the map—we were already within the northeastern limits prescribed to this mighty territory.

Leaving the delightful valley of Brown's Hole, we dashed swiftly onward in a southwesterly direction, and our horses being in fine traveling order, we were enabled to pass a long stretch of beautiful country, and camp, at close of day, on the banks of a stream known as Ashley's Fork. Crossing this the next morning, we continued on the same course as the day previous, and night found us safely lodged in the Uintah Fort—a solitary trading post in the wilderness—which was then garrisoned by Spaniards and Canadians, with a sprinkling of several other nations, together with Indian women, wives of the traders and hunters, who comprised the whole female department.

Here we sought to procure a guide, but with the same success as before—not one caring to risk his life by an experiment so fool-hardy, as undertaking a journey of many hundred miles, with a force so small, over a pathless region of territory, and either peopled not at all, or by hostile tribes of savages.

The accounts we received from all quarters of the dangers before us, were certainly enough to have intimidated and changed the designs of any less venturesome than we, and less firmly fixed in a foolish determination to push to the end what at best could only be termed an idle, boyish freak. But as I said before, our ambition was roused to perform what all were afraid to dare, and we pressed onward, as reckless of consequences as though we knew our lives specially guaranteed to us, for a term of years beyond the present, by a Power from on high. I have often since looked back upon this period, and shuddered at the thought of what we then dared; and I can now only account for our temerity—our indifference to the warnings we received—as resulting from a kind of monomania.

A travel of some two or three days, brought us to a stream called the Spanish Fork; and pushing down this, through a wild gorge in the Wahsatch Mountains, we encamped the day following on its broad, fertile bottoms, near its junction with, and in full view of the Utah Lake. We were now in the country of the Utahs, a tribe of Indians particularly hostile to small parties of whites, and the utmost caution was necessary to avoid falling into their clutches. On either hand, walling the valley on the right and left, rose wild, rugged, frowning cliffs, and peaks of mountains, lifting their heads far heavenward, covered with eternal snows.

At this particular spot was good grazing for our horses; but judging by the appearance of the country around us, and the information we had received from the mountaineers, we were about to enter a sterile region, with little or no vegetation—in many places devoid of water and game (our main dependence for subsistence) peopled, if at all, the Diggers only—an animal of the human species the very lowest in the scale of intellect—in fact scarcely removed from the brute creation—who subsist upon what few roots, lizards and reptiles they can gather from the mountains—sometimes in small parties of three and four, and sometimes in numbers—and who, being perfect cannibals in their habits, would not fail to destroy us if possible, were it for nothing else than to feast upon our carcasses. Take into consideration, too, our education—our luxurious habits through life—our inability to contend with numbers—that the only benefit we could derive from our expedition would be in satisfying our boyish love of adventure—and I think even the most reckless will be free to pronounce our undertaking fool-hardy in the extreme.

So far, we had been very fortunate in escaping the savages; but from all appearances we could not do so much longer; and what would be the result of our meeting, God only knew. We were now on the borders of the Great Interior Basin, a region of country containing thousands on thousands of miles, never yet explored by a white man, perhaps by no living being! Should we make the attempt to cross it? We could but lose our lives at the worst, and we might perchance succeed, and find a nearer route to Western or Southern California than the one heretofore traveled. There was something inspiring in the thought; and the matter was discussed in our lone camp, in the dead hours of night, with no little animation.

"What say you, Frank?" cried Huntly the next morning, rousing me from a sweet dream of home. "Westward or southward?"

"Why," I replied, "there is danger in either choice—so choose for yourself."

"Well, I am for exploring this region left blank on the map."

"Then we will go, live or die," I rejoined; "for I long myself to behold what has never as yet been seen by one of my race."

The matter thus decided, we mounted our horses, and keeping to the south of the Utah Lake, crossed a small stream, and about noon came to a halt on the brow of a high hill, forming a portion of the Wahsatch range. Below us, facing the west, we beheld a barren tract of land, with here and there a few green spots, and an occasional stream sparkling in the bright sunlight, which led us to the inference that there might be oases, at intervals of a day's ride, across the whole Great Basin, to the foot of the Sierra Nevada or Snowy Range, which divides it from the pleasant valleys of the Sacramento and San Joaquin.

It was a delightful day, and everything before us, even the most sterile spots, looked enchanting in the soft mellow light. Descending the mountain with not a little difficulty, we set forward across the plain, shaping our course to the nearest point likely to afford us a good encampment. But the distance was much farther than we had anticipated, when viewing it from the mountain; and although we urged our beasts onward as much as they could bear, night closed around us long ere we reached it. Reach it we did at last; and heartily fatigued with our day's work, we hoppled our horses, and without kindling a fire, or eating a morsel of food, rolled ourselves in our robes of buffalo, and fell asleep.

The sun of the succeeding morning, shining brightly in our faces, awoke us; and springing to our feet, we gazed around with mingled sensations of awe and delight. Doubtless we felt, in a small degree, the emotions excited in the breast of the adventurer, when for the first time he finds himself on ground which he fancies has never yet been trod nor seen by a stranger. We had entered a country now, which the most daring had feared or failed to explore, and we felt a noble pride in the thought that we should be the first to lay before the world its mysteries.

The point where we had encamped, was green and fertile, abounding with what is termed buffalo grass, with trees unlike any I had before seen, and with wild flowers innumerable. Like an island from the ocean, it rose above the desert around it, covering an area of a mile in circumference, and was watered by several bright springs of delightful beverage.

Turning our gaze to the eastward, we beheld the snowy peaks of the Wahsatch Mountains, which we had left behind us, looming up in grandeur; while to the westward, nothing was visible but an unbroken, barren, pathless desert. Here was certainly a prospect anything but charming—yet not for a moment did we waver in our determination to press onward.

It will be remembered, that on leaving the village of the Mysterious Nation, Prairie Flower had taken care to furnish us a good supply of jerk; and this, by killing more or less game on our route, we had been enabled to retain in our possession, to be eaten only in cases of extreme necessity; consequently we did not fear suffering for food, so much as for water; and even the latter we were sanguine of finding, ere anything serious should occur. The only matter that troubled us sorely, was the fear our noble animals would not be as fortunate as we, and that starvation might compel them to leave their bones in the wilderness, and thereby oblige us to pursue our journey on foot—an event, as the reader will perceive, far more probable than agreeable.

As we had eaten nothing the previous night, we now felt our appetites much sharpened thereby, and looking around in the hope of discovering game, my eye chanced upon a rabbit. The next moment the sharp crack of my rifle broke upon the solitude, and the little fellow lay dead in his tracks.

Hastily dressing him and kindling a fire, we were already in the act of toasting the meat, when whiz-z-z came a dozen arrows through the air, some of them actually penetrating our garments without wounding is, and others burying themselves in the ground at our feet. Springing up with a cry of alarm, we grasped our rifles, though only one was loaded, and turned to look for the enemy. Upon a steep bluff, some thirty paces behind us, we beheld some fifteen or twenty small, dirty, miserable looking savages, with their bows and arrows in their hands, already in the act of giving us another volley.

"By heavens! Frank," cried Huntly, "it is all over with us now."

"Never say die to such dirty curmudgeons as them," I rejoined, more vexed than alarmed. "Quick! Charley—dodge behind this tree! and while I load, be sure you bring one of them to his last account!"

While speaking I ran, followed by my friend, and scarcely had we gained shelter, when whiz-z-z came another flight of arrows, some of them actually piercing the tree behind which we stood.

"Quick! Charley—they are looking toward our horses! (These were feeding within ten paces of us.) There! they are on the point of shooting them. Take the leader! For heaven's sake don't miss—or we are lost!"

As I spoke, the rifle of my friend belched forth its deadly contents, and the foremost of our foes, who was just on the point of discharging an arrow at one of the horses, shot it at random; and, with a loud yell, fell headlong down the bluff, and was dashed to pieces on the rocks below. Several others had their bows drawn, but on the fall of their companion, they also fired at random, and approaching the bluff, gazed down upon his mangled remains, uttering frantic yells of rage and grief.

By this time my own rifle was loaded, and taking a hasty aim, I tumbled a second after the first. The savages were now alarmed in earnest, and retreating several paces, just made their faces visible, apparently undecided whether to retreat or attack us in a body. This was an important moment; but fortunately for us, the rifle of Huntly was now again loaded, and taking a more careful sight than before, he lodged the ball in the head of a third. This created a terrible panic among our enemies, who fled precipitately.

Now was our chance, and perhaps our only chance, to escape; for we knew nothing of the number of our foe, nor at what moment he might return with an overwhelming force; and calling to Huntly, I darted to my horse and cut the tether-rope with my knife; and so rapidly did both of us work, that in three minutes we were in our saddles and galloping away.

As we turned the southern point of this desert island, we heard an ominous succession of yells, and some forty rods away to the right, beheld a band of at least fifty Indians, of both sexes, together with some twenty miserable huts. This was evidently their village, and, from what we could judge, they were preparing to renew the attack, as we had feared, when our appearance apprised them of our escape.

To the best of our judgment, they were Diggers, and on this oasis dragged out their miserable existence. Being divided from us by a ridge, neither party had been aware of the proximity of the other, until the discharge of my rifle at the rabbit. This it appears had alarmed them, and excited an immediate attack, from the fatal consequences of which kind Heaven had so providentially delivered us. We thought seriously of giving them a parting salute—particularly as they seemed to grieve so much for our departure—but on second consideration, concluded we would reserve our powder and ball, not knowing how necessary to self-preservation these might yet become; and so taking off our hats, and waving them a kind farewell, we dashed away over the plain.

CHAPTER XXIII.

A BARREN DESERT—NO WATER—ALARMING CONDITION OF OUR HORSES—CAMP—A LITTLE REFRESHED—A SANDY DESERT—INCREASED SUFFERINGS — DEATH OF MY FRIEND'S HORSE—A DRAUGHT OF BLOOD—CONSULTATION—RESOLVE TO PRESS ON—DEATH OF MY OWN HORSE—AFOOT—A TERRIBLE NIGHT—HOPE—IN SIGHT OF AN OASIS — GRATITUDE — ALMOST SUPERHUMAN EXERTIONS—A STREAM—INSANITY—EXHAUSTION—RELIEF.

OUR progress through the day was over an arid waste of calcareous formation, devoid of all vegetation, with the exception of a few tall, stiff, wire-like weeds, that grew here and there, where the soil appeared a little moist and loomy. Deep ravines, or cracks in the earth, in some places to the depth of it might be a thousand feet, cut across the ground in every direction, and rendered everything like speed, or traveling after night, out of the question. These gullies, when very narrow, we forced our horses to leap—but frequently had to ride around them—on account of which our progress westward was slow and tedious. The sun here seemed at least twenty degrees warmer than on the highlands we had left behind us; and not having come to any water, we began about mid-day to feel the oppression of a burning thirst, while our well fed and well watered animals of the morning, showed alarming signs of experiencing the same sensation, by lolling their tongues, occasionally smelling the earth, and snuffing the dry air. Oh! what would we not have given, even then, for a bucket of water, cool from some deep well!

We found no place to noon, and consequently were forced to push forward, in the hope of reaching an oasis for our night's encampment.

On, on we went, our thirst increasing to a great degree, while the sun rolled slowly down toward the west, and yet nothing around and before us but this same dull, arid waste. We now began to experience the effects of our rashness, and, if truth must be told, to secretly wish ourselves safely clear of our undertaking, though neither breathed a word to the other of the thoughts passing in his mind. Our horses, too, seemed very much fatigued, and required considerable spurring to hasten them forward.

The sun had now sunk within an hour of the horizon, and yet the same cheerless prospect lay before us. We looked back, and far in the distance, like a mole-hill, could faintly trace the outline of the oasis of our last encampment; while beyond, the snowy peaks of the Wahsatch glistened in the sunbeams. Advancing a couple of miles, we found ourselves compelled to camp for the night, without water, and with nothing for our horses to eat; and the fact of this was anything but cheering.

"What is to be done?" asked Huntly. "We can not long exist without water, and our poor beasts are already suffering to an alarming degree, and will not be likely to hold out more than one day more at the most."

"Well, I fancy by that time we shall come to a spot similar to the one behind us."

"Then you think we had better go forward?"

"I dislike the idea of turning back. Besides, we should probably fall into the hands of the savages, and death here looks full as tempting as there."

"But our horses, Frank—poor beasts! see how they suffer."

"I know it, and would to Heaven I could relieve them! But we cannot even help ourselves."

"Do you think they can go through another day like this?"

"I am unable to say."

"Oh! it would be awful to be put afoot in this desert!"

"By no means a pleasant matter, I must own. But, my friend, this is no time to get alarmed. We have set out, after being duly warned, and must therefore make the most of the circumstances we have brought upon ourselves. If our horses die, we must use their blood to quench our thirst."

"Heavens! Frank," exclaimed Huntly, startled with a new idea, "what if another day's travel like this should still leave us in the bare desert, with no haven in sight?"

"Why, I should consider our case nearly hopeless; but we will trust to having better fortune."

We now ate some of our meat with but little relish, and throwing ourselves upon the earth, at length fell into a kind of feverish slumber. A heavy dew falling during the night, refreshed us not a little. At the first streak of daylight, we were again in our saddles, and found, much to our joy, that although our poor beasts had eaten not a morsel since the morning previous, they, like ourselves, were considerably invigorated by a night of repose. Setting forward again, as cheerfully as the circumstances would permit, we traveled some two or three hours at a fast amble; but now the sun began to be felt rather sensibly, and our beasts to flag and droop, while our sensations of thirst seemed increased ten-fold. If this was the case in the morning, what would be the result ere another night? We shuddered at the thought.

About noon, the appearance of the ground began to change for the worse, which, in spite of ourselves, was productive of no little alarm. Gradually it became more and more sandy, and an hour's further progress brought us to a desert more barren than ever, where not a living thing, vegetable or animal, could be seen, over a dreary expanse, that, for all we knew, might be hundreds of miles in extent.

To add to the horrors of our situation, our horses were evidently on the point of giving out—for as they buried their feet in the white, hot sand, they occasionally floundered, and reeled, and seemed inclined to lie down—while our own throats, lips, and tongues began to swell, and the skin of our faces and hands to blister and crack. I recalled to mind the accounts I had read of bones being found in the great Arabian deserts, and I fancied that many years hence, some more fortunate traveler might so discover ours.

Cheering each other as well as we could, we kept on for another hour, when the horse of Huntly reeled, dropped upon his knees, and fell over upon his side.

"Oh God!" cried my friend in despair, "we are lost—we are lost!—a nd such a death!"

"Our last hope is here," I rejoined, dismounting and plunging my knife into the dying beast; and as the warm blood spouted forth, we placed our parched lips to it, and drank with a greediness we had never felt nor displayed for anything before.

This gave us no little relief for the time, and added vigor to our already drooping and weakened frames. But what could it avail us? It might relieve us now—might prolong our lives a few hours—only to go through the same terrible tortures and find death at last. Unless we could reach a spring by another day's travel, or come in sight of one, our case was certainly hopeless; and to carry us forward, we now had nothing to depend on but our own limbs and strength, while our path must be over a bed of hot, loose sand, where every step would be buried ankle deep.

"Well, Frank," sighed Huntly at length, "what are we to do now? I suppose we may as well die here as elsewhere."

"No! not here, my friend; we will make one trial more at least."

"And have we any prospect, think you, of saving our lives—of seeing another green spot?"

"Why, you remember when on the Wahsatch, we saw some hills away in the distance; and unless it was an optical illusion, I have a faint hope of being able to reach them before this time to-morrow."

"God grant it, my friend!—for though I fear not death more than another, there is something horrible in the thought of leaving my bones here in the wilderness."

"Well, well, cheer up, Huntly! and trust in Providence to carry us safely through."

A farther consultation resulted in the decision to await the night, and if my horse proved able to proceed, to let him carry our sacks, rifles, &c., while we were to keep him company on foot.

By the time the sun had fairly set, we resumed our journey; but after a laborious travel of half a mile, my horse gave out. Taking from him a portion of the jerked meat, our rifles, and such small articles as we could not well do without, we left him to his fate, with many a sigh of regret.

It was a clear, starlight night, and the air just cool enough to be comfortable; but unlike the preceding one, we no longer had the refreshing dew to moisten our bodies and renew our strength. Still we succeeded better than I had anticipated, and, by exertions almost superhuman, placed many a long mile between us and our starting point, ere the first crimson streak in the east told that day was again dawning. To add hope to our drooping spirits, we now found the ground becoming more and more solid, and ere the sun peered over the mountains which were almost lost to view in the distance, we set our feet once more upon hard earth, similar in appearance to that we had quitted for the sands. Struggling on a mile or two farther, we ascended a slight elevation, and, joy inexpressible! beheld far away before us a ridge of green hills. All the extravagant, unspeakable delight of the poor, ship-wrecked mariner, who has been for days tossed about by the angry elements, without food to save him from starvation, without water to slake his consuming thirst, on beholding, in the last agonies of despair, the green hills of his native land suddenly loom up before him—all his unspeakable emotions, I say, were ours; and silently dropping upon our knees, our hearts spoke the gratitude to our All-wise Preserver which our tongues were unable to utter. True, the famished, worn-out mariner might die in sight of land—and so might we in view of our haven of rest—yet the bare hope of reaching it alive, gave energy to our sinking spirits, and strength to our failing limbs.

Again we pressed forward, our now swollen and bloodshot eyes fixed eagerly upon the desired spot, which, like an ignis-fatuus, seemed only to recede to our advance. The sun, too, gradually rolling higher and higher, till he reached the zenith of his glory, and began to descend toward the west, poured down his scorching rays (for they seemed scorching to us in the desert), dried up, as it were, the very marrow of our bones, blistered our parched and feverish skins, and caused our limbs to swell, till every step became one of pain almost unbearable. All our previous sufferings were as nothing, seemingly, compared to our present; and when we reached the bank of a stream, which wound around the base of the hills, the sun had already hid himself for the day, and we sunk down completely exhausted!

Huntly, for the last two or three miles, had shown symptoms of confirmed insanity,—had often raved about home, which he declared was just below him in a pool of clear water, which he, being chained to a rock, was not permitted to reach, although dying of thirst—and had often turned to me, with much the look of a ravenous beast about to spring upon his prey—so that, with the greatest difficulty, in my then weak state, I had succeeded in getting him to the stream, where, as I said before, we both sunk down in a state of exhaustion. Had the stream been a mile, or even half a mile farther off, we must both have perished in sight of that water which alone could save us. Weak and worn out as I was, I still, thank God! had my senses—though sometimes I fancied they were beginning to wander—and I knew that for either to indulge his appetite freely, would be certain to produce death.

As my friend seemed too feeble to move, and as I was in a little better condition—though now unable to walk—I crawled over the ground to the stream, which was not deep, and rolled into it, restraining myself even then from tasting a drop, until my body was thoroughly soaked, and I felt considerably revived. After a bath of some five minutes, I took a few draughts of the sparkling element, and never in my life experienced such a powerful and speedy change for the better. Almost instantly I felt the life-renewing blood darting through my veins, and I came out of the water, as it were another being.

Hastening to my friend, I partially raised him in my arms, and dragging him to the stream, tumbled him in, taking care to keep a firm hold. In a few minutes I had the satisfaction of seeing him slowly revive. Then scooping up the water with my hand, I placed it to his lips, which he drank eagerly. Gradually his strength and consciousness returned, and with feelings which none but one in my situation can ever know, I at length heard him exclaim—

"Water! water! Thank God! Frank, we are saved!" and falling upon the breast of each other, overcome with emotions of joy, our tears of gratitude were borne away upon the river which laved our feet.

Eating sparingly, ever moistening our food, we at last found our former strength much restored; and fording the stream, we threw ourselves upon the grassy earth, and *slept soundly* that night *upon its western* bank.

CHAPTER XXIV.

EFFECTS OF OUR JOURNEY—THE MYSTERY SOLVED — EXPLORATION — GAME — A SUPPOSED DISCOVERY OF GOLD — TRAVELS RESUMED — IN SIGHT OF THE SIERRA NEVADA — INDIANS — REACH THE MOUNTAINS — ASCENT — TEN THOUSAND FEET ABOVE THE SEA — SNOW — SUFFERINGS — AN INDIAN HUT — HOSPITALITY — IN SIGHT OF THE SACRAMENTO — ARRIVAL AT SUTTER'S.

On the following morning, we found our limbs so stiff and sore, as scarcely to be able to move about. With great difficulty we gained the river, and bathed ourselves in its cool, refreshing waters, as on the evening previous. The result of this seemed very beneficial; but still we suffered too much from our recent almost superhuman exertions, to think of leaving our present locality for a day or two at least.

Looking back over the desert which had nearly cost us our lives, we could barely perceive the shadowy outline of some of the highest peaks of the Bear River and Wahsatch Mountains; but not a trace of that ridge whereon we had stood before entering this unexplored territory, from whence we had beheld distant oases and streams, none of which, save the first, had been found on our route. How this could be, was a matter of serious speculation, until Huntly suggested the fact of our having looked more to the southward than westward. His observation struck me quite forcibly; for I now remembered having examined our compass, shortly after leaving the Indians, and of altering our course to the right, although previously I remembered, too, feeling somewhat surprised at the time, that we had become so turned, but had afterward forgotten the trifling circumstance—at least what then appeared trifling—though, as events proved finally, a circumstance of life and death.

This then solved the mystery! We had come due west, instead of west by south, and consequently had missed the very points we thought before us, and which would have saved the lives of our poor beasts.

For two days we remained on the bank of the stream, which we not inappropriately named Providence Creek, without venturing away the distance of thirty rods during the whole time. On the morning of the third day, we found our limbs so pliable, and our strength so far recruited, as to think ourselves justified in resuming our travels, or at all events in making an exploration of the ridge above us.

Accordingly, ascending to the summit of the hill — which was densely covered with a wood somewhat resembling ash, though not so large — we made out the uplands here to cover an area of five miles in breadth by twenty in length, running almost due north and south, and composed of two parallel ridges, full of springs of fine water, some of which ran outward and formed the stream we had first gained, and others inward, forming another in the valley between, both of which, taking a southerly course, united on the way, and entered at last into a beautiful lake, barely visible from the highest point, and which also appeared the grand reservoir of the surrounding country.

Our present locality was a rich and beautiful desert island, and had our horses been here, they would have fared sumptuously on the green, luxuriant grass of the valley. To the best of our judgment, this spot had never before been visited by human being, as no signs indicative thereof could be found. The only game we could discover, were a few ground animals resembling the rabbit, and some gay plumed birds. We killed a few of each, and on dressing and cooking them, found their flavor, especially the former, very delicious and nutritive.

In this manner we spent a week on Mount Hope, as we termed the ridge, making explorations, killing game, &c., and at the end of this time found our wonted health and spirits nearly restored. We knew not what was before us, it is true; but as kind Providence had almost miraculously preserved us through so many dangers, we no longer had dread of our journey, nor fears of our safely reaching the valley of the Sacramento, at which point we aimed.

One thing in our rambles struck us quite forcibly—that in the beds of nearly all the streams we examined, we found a fine yellow substance, mixed with the dirt and sands, which had every appearance of gold. As we had no means of testing this, we resolved to take some along as a specimen, and should we escape, and our surmises regarding it be confirmed, either return ourselves, or put some hardy adventurer in possession of the secret. If this were indeed gold, it must of course have its source in some mine in the vicinity; and this important discovery alone, we felt, would amply compensate us for all we had dared and suffered in venturing hither.

The next morning, like each of the preceding, being clear and serene, we resolved to depart, and again try our fortunes. Looking toward the west, we beheld in the distance another camping ground; and hastening down the western slope of the hills, we made our way directly toward it, over a slightly undulating country, less sterile in its appearance than the desert we had crossed the previous week. We were not able to reach it till after nightfall, and suffered more or less through the day for want of water. Here we again found a rich soil, wooded with what I believe is termed the sage tree, and watered by several delightful springs and streams, in some of which we bathed, and of which we drank, much to our relief.

To follow up our progress in detail, would be to take up more space than can now be spared for the purpose, and, in a great measure, to repeat, with trifling variations, what I have already given.

Suffice it, therefore, that our journey was continued day after day—sometimes over sandy deserts of two days' travel, which blistered our feet, and where we again suffered all the horrors of burning thirst—sometimes over rough, dangerous and volcanic grounds, along side of giddy precipices, and yawning chasms, and adown steep declivities, where a single misstep would have been fatal—sometimes across streams too deep to ford, and which we were obliged to swim—subsisting, a part of the way, on roots and such game as we could kill, (our supply of jerk having given out,) and sleeping at night on the sands, in the open air, or perhaps under the shelter of some overhanging rock—occasionally drenched with a storm of cold rain, without a fire to dry our wet garments, and suffering more or less from hunger, and drought, and weariness, and violent rheumatic pains.

Such was our pilgrimage, over an unexplored country; and yet through all our sufferings, save the first, when we lost our horses, our spirits were almost ever buoyant, and we experienced a rapturous delight known only to the adventurer.

Some six weeks from our leaving the Wahsatch range, we came in sight of the lofty peaks of the Sierra Nevada, which we hailed with a shout of joy, similar to that of a sailor discovering land after a long, tedious voyage, and which awoke echoes in a wilderness never before disturbed by the human voice. Five hundred miles of an unknown region had been passed, almost the whole distance on foot, and now we stood in full view of our long looked for desideratum. During this time we had not seen a human being—always excepting our unfortunate friends, the Diggers—which led us to the inference, that the larger portion of this Great Interior Basin was uninhabited—or, at all events, very thinly peopled.

From this point to the Sierra Nevada, our course now lay over a rough, mountainous country, well watered and timbered; and on the second day, we came upon one or two miserable, dilapidated huts—which, from all appearance, had long been untenanted—and a mile or two farther on, saw a small party of savages, who, on discovering our approach, fled precipitately to the highlands—we probably being the first white human beings they had ever beheld.

About noon of the third day we came to a beautiful lake, and going round it, reached the foot of the mountain chain, bounding the Great Basin on the west, just as the sun, taking his diurnal farewell of the snowy peaks above us, seemingly transformed them, by his soft, crimson light, into huge pillars of burnished gold. We now considered ourselves comparatively safe, though by no means out of danger; for our route, over these mighty erections of nature, we were well aware, must be one of extreme peril. Unlike the desert, we might not suffer for want of water—but, unlike the desert, too, we might with cold, snows, storms, and from hostile savages.

On the succeeding day we began our ascent. Up, up, up we toiled—through dense thickets of dwarfish, shrubby trees—through creeping vines, full of brambles, that lacerated our ankles and feet, (we had long been shoeless,)—up, up, up the steep mountain sides we struggled—over rocks which sometimes formed precipices that only yielded us here and there a dangerous foot-hold—occasionally leaping across canons, in which the torrent of the mountain rolled murmuring over its rocky bed a thousand feet below us—on, on, up and on we pressed eagerly—sometimes suffering with fatigue, and with cold, and with hunger—up and on we bent our steps, for two, long, wearisome days, ere we reached the regions of eternal snow.

At last we stood upon the very backbone of the Sierra Nevada, ten thousand feet above the sea, surrounded by a few cedars, loaded with snow and ice, the former underneath us to the depth of many feet—and gazed downward, far, far below us—upon the broad, barren plains, fertile uplands, lovely valleys, and bright, silver streams and lakes—with feelings that are indescribable.

A mile or two farther on, we came to a pleasant valley, through which rolled a beautiful stream. Here, collecting a supply of drift-wood, we kindled a bright fire, and disposing ourselves around it, toasted our already swollen and frost-bitten feet, made our supper of a few roots and berries which we had collected on the way, and occupied most of the night in constructing some rude moccasins out of a quarter buffalo robe which we fortunately had brought with us.

Thus for several days did we continue our perilous journey — passing through scenes of danger and hardship, that, if detailed, would fill a volume—sustained, in all our trials, by a holy Being, to whom we daily and nightly gave the sincere orisons of grateful hearts.

Once, during our mountain journey, we came very nigh being buried in a furious snowstorm; and but for the providential shelter of an Indian hut, ere darkness settled around us, this narrative in all probability had never been written. The hut in question, stood on the side of the mountain, and was constructed of sticks, willows and rushes, well braided together, in shape not unlike a modern beehive. The tenants were an Indian, his squaw, and two half-grown children, all miserable, and filthy in their appearance. Our sudden entry (for we did not stop for etiquette) alarmed them terribly, and they screeched and drew back, and huddled themselves in the farther corner. However, on making them friendly signs, and intimating we only sought protection from the storm, they became reassured, and offered us some nuts of a pleasant flavor, peculiar to the country, and which, as I learned, formed their principal food. We spent the night with them, and were treated with hospitality.

On leaving I presented the host with a pocket-knife, which he received with an ejaculation of delight, and examined curiously. On opening it, and showing him its uses, his joy increased to such a degree, that, by signs, he immediately volunteered to act as guide, and was accepted by us without hesitation. He proved of great service, in showing us the shortest and best route over the mountains, and as a kind of bodyguard against other savages, whom we now occasionally met, but whom he restrained from approaching us with any undue familiarity.

On arriving in sight of Sutter's settlement—situated near the junction of the Rio Sacramento and Rio de los Americanos, or River of the Americans—we gave a wild shout of joy, and our guide made signs that he would go no farther. As he had been with us several days, and had proved so faithful, we could not bear he should part from us without a further testimonial of our generosity and gratitude. Accordingly, drawing from my belt a silver-mounted pistol, I discharged it, showed him how to load and fire it, and then presented it to him, together with a belt-knife and a good supply of powder and ball; and he went back with all the pride of an emperor marching from the conquest of another kingdom.

Hurrying forward, with feelings which are indescribable, we passed through a beautiful valley, green with blade and bright with flowers—through an Indian village, where every person appeared neat and comfortable, and well disposed toward us—and at last, ascending a slight eminence, just as day was closing, beheld before us, not half a mile distant, an American fortress, though in a Mexican country, and garrisoned by Indians.

In fifteen minutes more we had passed the dusky sentinel at the gate, and entered an asylum of rest from our long pilgrimage. We were received by Captain Sutter himself, who, gathering only a brief outline of our adventures and sufferings, expressed surprise to see us here alive, shook our hands with all the warm-heartedness of an American *friend*, and gave us a most cordial invitation to make his citadel our home, so long as we might feel disposed to remain in the country.

―――o―――

CHAPTER XXV.

OUR APPEARANCE — SUTTER AND FORT — LEAVE IN THE SPRING — REFLECTIONS — A YEAR PASSED OVER — ON OUR RETURN — THE ANTELOPE — CHASE — LOSS OF MY FRIEND — TERRIBLE FEARS — DESPAIR — FEARFUL RESULTS, ETC.

WORN-OUT and starved-out — our garments all in tatters — our frames emaciated — our faces long, thin and sallow — with sunken eyes and a beard of some two months' growth — we presented anything but an attractive appearance on our first arrival at Sutter's. But with the aid of soap and water — a keen razor — new raiment, and a couple of weeks' rest — we began once more to resemble civilized beings, and feel like ourselves.

Captain Sutter we found to possess all the refined qualities of a hospitable American gentleman. He had emigrated to this country, from the western part of Missouri, a year or two previous to our arrival, and had already succeeded in establishing a fort, on a large grant of land obtained from the Mexican government. He had succeeded, too, in subduing and making good citizens the surrounding Indians, many of whom were already in his employ — some as soldiers, to guard his fortress — some as husbandmen to till his soil — and some as *vaqueros*, or cow-herds, to tend upon his kine and cattle; so that everything around gave indications of an industrious, wealthy, and prosperous settler.

The fort itself was a large, quadrangular *adobe* structure, capable of being garrisoned by a thousand men — though at the time of which I speak, the whole force consisted of some thirty or forty Indians, (in uniform) and some twenty-five American, French, and German *employes*. It mounted some ten or twelve pieces of ordnance, and was well supplied with other munitions of war, most of which, together with a large number of stock, agricultural and other stores, Sutter had purchased from a neighboring Russian establishment, prior to its being withdrawn from the country. Its internal appearance — its arrangement of carpenter and blacksmith shops, store-rooms, offices, &c. — so closely resembled Fort Laramie, as to make further description unnecessary.

Here we remained through the winter, amusing ourselves in various ways — sometimes in hunting among the mountains, exploring the country, and fishing in the streams — and at others, in making ourselves masters of the Spanish tongue, which was spoken by many of the Indians and all of the natives. This last, however, was more for our benefit than amusement — as we had determined on a visit to the seaport places in the lower latitudes of Mexico, so soon as the annual spring rains, being over, should leave the ground in a good condition for traveling.

It was some time between the first and middle of May, that, mounted upon a couple of fiery horses — which, decked off with all the showy trappings of two complete Spanish saddle equipments, had been pressed upon us as a present by our generous host — we bade adieu to the noble-hearted Captain Sutter and family, and set out upon our southern journey.

As we rode along, it was with feelings of pleasant sadness we looked back over the eventful past, and remembered that about this time a year ago, two gay youths, fresh from college, were leaving friends and home for the first time, to venture they scarce knew whither. And what of those friends now? Were they alive, and well, and in prosperity? Had their thoughts been much on the wanderers? Had they looked for our return? Had they wept in secret for our absence, and prayed daily for our preservation? Ah!

yes, we well knew all this had been done; and the thought that we were still keeping them in suspense—that we were still venturing farther and farther away—could not but make us sad. But, withal, as I said before, it was a pleasant sadness; for we secretly felt a delight in going over new scenes—beholding new objects. Moreover, we were now in good health; our constitutions felt vigorous; and this tended to raise our spirits.

What an eventful year had the past one been! Through what scenes of trial, privation, suffering, and peril had we not passed! And yet, amid all, how had we been sustained by the hand of Omnipotence! How had we been lifted up and borne forward over the quicksands of despair! And when all appeared an endless, rayless night, how had our trembling souls been rejoiced by the sudden light of hope beaming upon our pathway, and showing us a haven of rest!

But where would another year find us? In what quarter of the habitable globe, and under what circumstances? Should we be among the living, or the dead? The dead! What a solemn thought, to think that our bones might be reposing in the soil of the stranger—thousands of miles from all we loved, and from all that loved us! What a startling idea! And yet, in our journeyings, how indifferent, how careless had we been of life! With what foolhardiness had we even dared death to meet us! And still, with all the frightful warnings of the past before us, how recklessly were we plunging on to new scenes of danger! Why did we not turn now, and bend our steps homeward? Had we not seen enough, suffered enough, to satisfy the craving desires of youth?

Home! what a blessed word of a thousand joys! With what pleasing emotions the thought would steal upon our senses! What a world of affection was centered there! What happy faces the thought recalled, and how we longed to behold them! Longed, yet took the very course to put time and distance between us and them! And this to gratify what our sober reason told us what was only a foolish, boyish passion—a craving love of adventure!

Home! In that word I beheld the loved faces of my parents. In that word I beheld the welcome visages of my friends. In that word, more than all, I beheld the sweet, melancholy countenance of Lilian!

Lilian! how this name stirred the secret emotions of a passionate soul! Had I forgotten her? Had I, through all the varied scenes I had passed, for a moment lost sight of her lovely countenance—of her sweet eyes beaming upon me the warm affections of an ardent soul? No I had not forgot, I never could forget, her. She was woven among the fibers of my existence. To tear her hence, would be to rend and shatter the soul itself. Thousands of miles away, she was not absent. She was with me in all my trials, sufferings and perils. Present by day, with her eyes of love. Hovering around me in the still watches of night, as it were the guardian angel of my destiny. Lilian was loved. Time and distance proved it. Loved with a heart that could never forsake—never so love another. I had done her wrong. But should God spare my life, and permit us again to meet, how quickly, by every means in my power, would I strive to repair it.

Such and similar were our thoughts, as we again bent our steps upon a long journey. But I will not test your patience, reader, with more. Neither am I going to weary you with a long detail of common-place events. In other words, I am not going to describe our journey to the south. Like similar journeys, it was full of fatigue, with here and there an incident, or a curiosity, perhaps a danger—which, were I making an official report to government, would be necessary to note—but over which you, doubtless, would yawn and call the writer stupid.

Suffice it, then, that with me you let a year pass unnoted. That you imagine us having gone a thousand miles into the heart of Mexico, and, heartily sick and disgusted with our travels, the people, and for the most part the country, you now find us on our glad journey to the north—fully determined, in our own minds, from this time forward, to let such as choose go among barbarians worse than savages, so they seek not us for companions. From this sweeping clause of condemnation, let me save the Mexican ladies; who, for the most part, exercise Christian virtues worthy of a better fate than being yoked and bound to such lazy, filthy, treacherous brutes as hold over them the dominion of lord and master. But enough! The bare thought of the latter puts me in a passion; and so to get an even temper once more, let me consign them to oblivious contempt.

You will fancy, then, that a year has passed, and that we, having so far escaped with our lives, are now on our return to Upper California, thence to shape our route to Oregon, and then, ho! for the far distant land of our childhood.

Little did we dream in that happy moment of contemplation, of the terrible calamity about to befall us. Little did we think that our hearts, bright with hope and joy, were soon to be clouded with woe unutterable—grief inconsolable. And why should we? We who had been through so many perils, and made so many miraculous escapes, where death seemed inevitable—why should we now, comparatively safe, already on our return, for a moment harbor the thought that a misfortune, before which all we had suffered sunk into insignificance, was impending us? How little does man know his destiny! Poor, blind mortal! what presumption in him to attempt to read the scroll of fate! But let me not anticipate.

It was a bright, warm day in the spring of 1842, that we arrived at Pueblo de los Angelos, where the Great Spanish Trail comes in from Santa Fé. We had been on the move day after day for nearly a month, during which time we had traveled some five hundred miles, and our horses were very much fatigued in consequence. Besides, their shoes being worn out and their feet sore, we resolved to remain here a few days, to have them shod, recruited, and put in a good traveling condition, while our time was to be spent in hunting, and examining the country round about.

Giving our beasts in charge of a responsible person, with orders to see them well attended to, we set forward with our rifles, and taking the Spanish Trail, which here ran due east and west, we followed it some two miles, and then leaving it to the right, struck off into the mountains known as the Coast Range.

About noon we came to a point where the country assumed a very rough and wild appearance. Cliff upon cliff rose one over the other, above which, still, a few peaks shot up far heavenward, capped with everlasting snows. Tremendous precipices, deep caverns, and wild gorges, could be seen on every hand, full of danger to the unwary explorer.

Making a halt, we were already debating whether to advance or retrace our steps, when, as if to decide and lure us forward, a fine antelope was discovered on a rock above us, not over a hundred yards distant, coolly eyeing us from his supposed safe retreat. Scarce a moment elapsed, so quick were the motions of each, ere our pieces, speaking together, told him too late of his error. He was wounded, this we could see, but not enough to prevent his flight, and he turned and bounded over the rocks up the steep.

"By heavens! Frank," cried Huntly, with enthusiasm; "here is sport in earnest. Nothing to do but give chase. He must not escape us. Dart you up the mountain, while I, by going round, will perhaps head him off on the other side. At all events, we will soon meet again."

On the impulse of the moment, I sprang forward in one direction and Huntly in another. To the great danger of my neck, I clambered up the steep activity, over precipitous rocks, gaping fissures, and through a dense brushwood, and stood at last upon the spot where we had first seen the goat. Here was a small pool of blood, and a bloody trail marked the course of the animal; and I pressed on again, rightly judging, from the quantity of blood left behind, that he could not hold out any great distance. But the distance proved farther than I had anticipated, and half an hour found me completely out of breath, on the brow of one of the lower ridges, without having come in sight of the antelope. Here the trail, more bloody than ever, took a downward course, and I counted on finding the chase between me and the foot of the hill. At this moment I heard, as I fancied, the shout of my friend; and thinking it one of delight, on being the first to reach the goat, I gave an answering one of joy, and descended rapidly on the red trail.

Within fifty yards of the the valley, I discovered the object of my search, lying on his side, pierced by two bullets, and in the last agonies of death. Applying my knife to his throat, I made an end of his sufferings, and then looked eagerly around for my friend. He was nowhere to be seen. I called—but no answer. This somewhat surprised me, as I felt certain of having heard his voice in this direction. Thinking he could not be far off, I repeated his name at the top of my lungs, but with no better success.

Although somewhat alarmed, I consoled myself by thinking I must have been mistaken in the sound I had heard, and that at all events he would soon make his appearance. With this, I seated myself on the ground, and throwing the breech of my rifle down the mountain, occupied myself in loading it.

Minute after minute went by, but no Huntly appeared, and I began to grow exceedingly uneasy. For a while I fancied he might be watching me from some near covert, just to note the effect of his absence; but when a half hour had rolled around, and nothing had been seen nor heard of him, I became alarmed in earnest.

Springing to my feet, I shouted his name several times, with all the accents of fright and despair. Then darting down to the valley, I ran round the foot of the mountain, making the woods echo with my calls at every step. In half an hour more I had gained the point where we parted — but still no Huntly. God of mercy! who can describe my feelings then! Nearly frantic, I retraced my steps, shouting till my lungs were sore—but, alas! with no better success. There lay the antelope, as I had left it, showing that no one had been there during my absence.

Until the shades of night began to settle over the earth, I continued my almost frantic search; and then, thinking it possible Huntly might have returned to the settlement, I set out for Los Angelos, with the speed and feelings of madman.

When I arrived there, it had long been night. To my eager inquiries, each and all shook their heads, and replied that my friend had not been seen since we departed in the morning. Who could describe, who imagine, my anguish on hearing this! Huntly, my bosom companion, was lost. Captured it might be by guerillas, or by Indians. Destroyed, perhaps, by some wild beast, or by falling down some precipice, or into some chasm. Gone he was, most certainly; and I wrung my hands in terrible agony, and called wildly upon his name, though I knew he could not hear me. So great was my distress, that it excited the pity of the spectators, several of whom volunteered to go back with me and search for him with torches. The proposition I accepted eagerly, and that night the mountains sparkled with flaming lights, and their deep recesses resounded the name of my friend, and cries of anguish. All night long we searched faithfully, and shouted with all our might. But, alas! all to no avail. My friend came not—answered not—perhaps never would again.

When daylight once more lighted that fatal spot, and those who had assisted me, declared it useless to search longer—that Huntly was either dead or a prisoner—my anguish exceeded the strength of my reason to bear, and I became a raving maniac.

For two months from that date, I had no knowledge of what transpired; and when, by the grace of God, consciousness again returned, I found myself in a feeble state, a close prisoner at Pueblo de los Angelos.

To a noble-hearted Mexican lady, wife of a Mexican military officer, for her kindness to, and care of, a forlorn stranger, is due a debt of gratitude, which, perhaps, I may never have power to cancel; but which, it is my daily prayer, may be found written upon the eternal pages of the Great Book of All-Good.

In June, a sad, emaciated, almost heart-broken being, I resumed my journey to the north. But alas! alas! poor Charles Huntly! His fate was still unknown. His last words to me, spoken gaily, "*At all events we shall soon meet again,*" had never been fulfilled.

CHAPTER XXVI.

ON THE ROCKY MOUNTAINS — HOMEWARD BOUND—SAD REFLECTIONS — RAPID DESCENT—TWO ENCAMPMENTS—MEET OLD FRIENDS — INCOG. — THEIR FRIENDSHIP TESTED—MAKE MYSELF KNOWN—FRANTIC JOY—VISIT THE SICK—PAINFUL AND UNEXPECTED MEETING.

I stood upon the summit of the Rocky Mountains. I stood upon that point of land which divides the rivers of the Atlantic from the Pacific oceans. Upon that mighty barrier, which bids its gushing rivulets roll eastward and westward. Where, springing from the same source, as children from the same parents, they are separated by the hand of fate, to end their course thousands of miles apart.

I stood upon the great dividing ridge of the North American Continent, and cast my eyes over a mighty expanse of territory. But with what feelings did I gaze around me! Were they feelings of joy! No! they could not be joyous. There was one absent from my side, that made them sad. I needed the bright eye, noble face, commanding form, warm heart, and strong hand of one who was now perhaps no more. Had *he* been by—my now melancholy gaze had been one of intoxicating, enthusiastic rapture. In every hill, in every tree, in every rock, in every rill, I would have beheld something to make my heart leap with delight—*for now I was homeward bound.*

What a strange creature is man! It is said that he sees with his eyes—but I contend that his heart gives color to his vision. If not, why do the same scenes, unchanged in their appearance, to him present different aspects? Why does that which to-day he beholds *coleur de rose*, to-morrow wear the sable hue of gloom? Is not the scene the same? Are not his eyes the same? Ay! but yesterday his heart was light and bounding with joy—to-day it is dark and oppressed with grief. All the change, then, lies in the heart.

Yes! here I stood—*alone*—my face set eastward—my steps bent to the still far distant land of my youth. What had I not been through, what had I not suffered, since quitting that roof under which I had known nothing but happiness and ease? In little more than two years, I felt I had lived an age, and even fancied my hair growing gray at twenty-two.

Yes! I was wending my way to my native land; but should God permit me to reach there alive, what an unenviable lot was mine, to make the home of my friend the house of lamentation and woe! And Lilian, dear Lilian, to whom, would to God, I could bring nothing but joy.—I must be doomed, too, to make her weep, to fill her bright eyes with tears, and robe her fair form in funeral weeds. Alas! alas! what bitter necessity! How my soul groaned in anguish at the thought, until I envied the supposed cold death-sleep of him I wept.

Such were some of my thoughts and feelings, as I commenced descending the eastern slope of the Rocky Mountains. I have said nothing of my route hither, since leaving Pueblo de los Angelos, and for the very reason there was little or nothing to say. My horse had borne me hither; my hand had guided him; my food had been such as came in my way; my sleep had been mostly upon the hard earth in the open air; my route had occasionally been pointed out to me—occasionally had been taken at a venture: I had sometimes had companions—sometimes had traveled by myself; and, lastly, was here now, alone, and that was the most I knew. Oppressed with a burden of grief almost insupportable, I had taken little note of external objects. With a sort of instinct, I had day after day, pursued my journey, perfectly reckless of that life which to me seemed more an affliction than a comfort. I had been surrounded by dangers at all times; I had been less cautious than previous in guarding against them; and yet here I was—alive—in fair bodily health—preserved how, and for what purpose, God only knew.

It was near the close of August, and the day was clear and cold, the sun, some three hours advanced toward noon, streamed over the scene his bright light, but without much apparent warmth. The north wind, sweeping down from the icy peaks of the Wind River Mountains—looming up in rugged masses away to the left—seemed to chill my very blood: and spurring my noble horse onward, I dashed down the long slope before me at a fast gallop.

A little after nightfall, I came to a romantic valley, shut in by hills, through which a bright stream rolled, and foamed, and murmured over its rocky bed. Here I beheld the fires of two encampments. The one nearest the bank of the river, was evidently a party of emigrants; for by the dim light, I could just trace the white outline of several covered wagons, and a few dark, moving objects near them, which I took to be their animals. I could also see a few figures flitting to and fro, some round the fire-lights, and some more distant—engaged, to all appearance, in preparing the evening's repast, and settling themselves down for the night. The other encampment, separated from the first some thirty or forty rods, consisted of only one fire, around which were squatted a small group of mountaineers. To this I directed my horse, and, on coming up, said:

"Gentlemen, will you permit a solitary traveler to mess with you for the night?"

"Well, we won't do nothin else," replied a voice which I fancied was not unfamiliar to me.

Although this answer signified I was welcome to join them, yet not a man moved, nor appeared to notice me at all. This, however, did not disconcert me in the least, as I knew so well the morose, semi-social habits of the mountaineer, that, to gain a grunt of assent to my request, was the utmost I could expect. I therefore dismounted, and, approaching the fire, scrutinized the faces of the party closely, as, rolling out clouds of tobacco smoke, they remained fixed like posts in a circle, their eyes apparently seeing nothing but the flames. Judge of my astonishment, reader, on discovering in this party of five, two of my old acquaintances — Black George, and Teddy O'Lagherty. My first impulse was to spring forward, and make myself known at once. But on second thought, I concluded to remain incog., and see what would be the result.

Removing the saddle and trappings from my horse, I hoppled and left him to crop the green grass of the valley. Then drawing near the fire, I squatted myself down in the ring, just far enough back to have a shade upon my face. The trappers were engaged in conversation of more than ordinary interest, and appeared not to notice me; while, for my own part, I determined not to interrupt them.

"Think she'll hev to go under," observed Black George, with an ominous shake of the head. "Thar's many places better to be sick in nor this here."

"Ah, jabers! but it's har-r-d now, so it is," rejoined Teddy, looking very solemn. "Howly murther! but I wish mesilf a docthor now — barring the physicing, that I don't like at all at all — if ounly to make the face of that swaat crathur glad, by tilling her I knows her mother's ailment. Ochone! but she's the purtiest live one I've saan since laving ould Ireland, where I wish mesilf back again. I could love her, for looking so much like me young masther, that's dead and gone, pace to his bones. Ochone! this is a sorry world, so it is."

"How she looked, when she axed for a doctor of me," observed another. "Ef I hadn't left soon, I'd a done somethin womanish, sartin."

"Augh!" grunted Black George, knocking the ashes from his pipe; "sich sights as them aint fit for us mountaineers."

"Of whom are you speaking, friends?" I now inquired, deeply interested.

"A beautihful lady, sir, and her mother as is sick," replied Teddy, turning toward me an eager look.

I instantly shaded my face with my hand, as if to keep off the heat, and saw I was not recognized.

"And where is the lady you speak of?"

"In the wagin, yonder. The ould lady is sick, and they've not a spalpeen of a docthor among 'em, and the young miss is crying like she'd break her heart, poor thing! For the matter of that, there's two young females, now, that's crying — but only one saams to be the daughther. Maybe it's a docthor you is, now, by your wee look and thinness?"

"I was educated to the profession, but have never practiced."

"Troth, it's no difference — ye must go an' sae the lady — for it's Heaven sin: ye here, I'm knowing mesilf."

"But, T—(I was on the point of speaking his name)—but I have no medicine."

"Divil a bit difference for that. Ye must be afther saaing her, if ye's a docthor—and can spaak the Latin names they gives, whin physic's short—if onnly to comfort the young lady that's dying of grief."

"Well, well, I will go," I said, finding myself fully in for it, and my curiosity being a good deal excited, also, to see the lady whom all agreed in describing as beautiful.

"Ah! that's a good sowl ye is now!" said the warm, generous-hearted Teddy, who seemed as much interested for the fair stranger, as if she were his own sister. "It's a good sowl ye is, now, to go and sae her! Faith! ye puts me in mind of a young masther I once had—voice and all—barring that he was a wee bit bether looking nor you is."

"Indeed! And what was your master's name?"

"Och! I had a pair of 'em. One was Misther Huntly, a lawyer—and the other, Misther Leighton, a docthor. It's the docthor ye puts me in mind of now."

"Well, what became of them?"

"Oh! sir," cried Teddy, wiping the tears from his eyes, "they got killed, sir. The divilish, murthering, baastly tiefs of Injins killed and ate 'em. Ochone! ochone!" and he rung his hands at the bare thought, and sobbed for very grief.

"Why, you seem to take it to heart as much as if they were related to you."

"And so would you, an' ye'd a knowed 'em, sir. They was two sich swaat youths! Perfict gintlemen, and jist from college, as I heard 'em say mysilf. Ochone! but I'd a died for 'em asy, and no questions axed, an' they'd a towld me to."

"Leighton! Leighton!" repeated I, musingly, as if trying to remember where I had before heard the name. "Leighton! fresh from college, say you? Was the one you term doctor, from Boston?"

"Ah, troth was he!" cried Teddy, jumping up in excitement. "Then ye know him, sir, it may be, by your way of spaking, jist?"

"I know enough of him," I answered, now fully determined on putting Teddy's friendship to the test.

"Arrah! sir, and what d'ye maan by saying the likes of that, now?"

"What do I mean? Why, my meaning is very simple. I know that this fellow you are so fond of lauding, is not a whit better than I am."

"And I maan ye're a dirthy, spalpeen blaggard—docthor or no docthor—jist for spaking in that contimptible manner of the finest gintleman as was iver saan and no exceptions made to your dirthy self, that's not worth the snap of me finger! Whoop! ye blaggard! don't be grinning that way at your bethers—but jist come out here like a man, ye cowardly tief! and sae what I'll taach ye! Whoop!"

Here the Irishman jumped up and cracked his heels, and made several warlike demonstrations with his fists, much to my amusement and satisfaction. The trappers, too, gathered themselves upon their feet, in anticipation of a fight; and as I showed no disposition to reply to Teddy, Black George turned his dark visage to me, and said, gruffly:

"Come, young chap, you've got to chaw them words you've jest put travelin, or git licked afore you ken say beans."

"What have I said?" I replied, finding the matter becoming serious, and pretending to exculpate myself. "I merely intimated that Mr. Leighton was no better than myself; and what more could I say, when of course I think myself as good as anybody?"

"Yes, it's all very well, boy, for you to talk," returned Black George; "but heyar's what knows a insult from a beaver, I reckons; and ef you don't chaw them words in less nor two minutes, and own up you aint no equal to him you've spoke aginst, I'll ram some fodder down your gullet you won't swoller easy—ef I don't, I hope I may be dogged for a dirty skunk all my life!" and he ended by shaking his fist rather nearer my face than was agreeable.

"Yes, and now be takin thim back!" roared Teddy, making preparations to spring upon me, "or I'll turn ye inside out, and shake ye as I used me masther's carpet-bag, that's dead and gone—not the bag, but the masther, ye blaggard ye!"

I now found, that to restore myself to the good graces of my friends, I should be obliged to own myself a falsifier, or make myself known. As I had fully tested their friendship for my absent self, I chose the latter.

"Gentlemen," I rejoined, mildly, "I can prove everything I have said; and even you will acknowledge it, when I tell you who I am. You behold before you, not the calumniator of Francis Leighton, but Francis Leighton himself, your old friend."

Had a bomb suddenly fallen and burst at their feet, it could not have caused more surprise and wonder with Teddy and Black George than did this simple declaration.

At first they both took a step or two back, and then springing forward, each caught me by an arm, and, drawing me close to the fire, peered eagerly into my face. One full, penetrating glance sufficed.

"Him, by ——!" cried Black George.

"Howly Mary!" shouted Teddy, throwing his arms around my neck, and weeping like a child. Then taking another long look into my face, he sprang away, and shouting, "Be howly St. Patrick! it's him—it's him!— me young masther's alive!" he danced and capered around me, with all the wild gestures of joyful insanity—sometimes weeping, and sometimes laughing, and occasionally catching hold of me, as if to assure himself of my identity, and that it was no vision, no hallucination of the brain.

Black George, meantime, pressed my hand warmly, and said, in a voice slightly tremulous with emotion:

"Boy, I never reckoned seein you agin. Thought you'd gone under—I'll be doggone ef I did'nt! You fit well—I'll be dogged ef you didn't! But whar d'ye float to, and whar's your partner?"

Some half an hour was now spent in questions and answers, during which I learned that Fiery Ned and Rash Will had both been killed at Bitter Cottonwood; that Daring Tom had been severely wounded, and shortly after left for the States; that Carson had escaped, and was at the present time acting as guide to Fremont; that Teddy had been on a trapping adventure with Black George and two or three others; that, having recently made a trip to St. Louis, they were now on their way to the mountains; and that neither myself nor Huntly had been heard from since that eventful night—in consequence of which they had supposed us killed or made prisoners. In turn I gave them a brief outline of my own adventures, up to the loss of my friend, at which both expressed deep sympathy, and Teddy wept freely.

"Spaking of Misther Huntly," said Teddy at length, "puts me in mind that you havn't yit saan the sick woman, your honor."

"True, Teddy—I had forgot. Lead the way!"

At the word, we quitted the trappers, and set forward to the larger encampment, where I found some six or eight heavy covered wagons, arranged in a circle. In the center of the area stood a group of men, conversing in low tones, and glancing occasionally at one of the vehicles, around which several women were collected, the faces of all, as far as I could see, expressive of deep sympathy and sorrow. Close to the wagon, in which on a rude bed the invalid was lying, were two young females, apparently of the better class, one of whom, clasping the thin hand of the sick person, particularly arrested my attention, by her display of violent grief. The other appeared to be weeping also; but the faces of both were from me, so that I could only conjecture.

Taking the lead, Teddy forced his way through the crowd, and lightly touching the shoulder of the one who held the invalid's hand, said, in a gentle tone:

"Here's a doctor, marm."

The next moment I found myself the cynosure of many eyes, while the one addressed, turning short round, gave one glance, and uttering a fearful scream, sank to the earth in a swoon. What this meant I was at a loss to comprehend; for her features had been in the shade of the same light which revealed mine to her.

"Nervous excitement," I said to myself; "joy at beholding a physician at hand;" and springing forward, I bent down to raise her.

Already had my arms encircled her slender form—already was I on the point of lifting her from the earth—when the light of a torch flashed full on her pale countenance. One look! one sudden start! one exclamation of agonized wonder! and I remained fixed, with eyes half starting from their sockets—speechless—motionless—seemingly transformed to stone—my arms encircling—merciful Heaven!—the lovely form of—*Lilian Huntly!*

CHAPTER XXVII.

INDESCRIBABLE FEELINGS — QUESTIONS FOR THE METAPHYSICIAN—DIGRESSION—PAINFUL AFFLICTIONS OF MY FRIEND'S FAMILY — WESTERN FEVER — CAUSES INDUCING EMIGRATION — AN IMAGINARY CITY — A MYSTERIOUS LADY AND DAUGHTER, ETC.

THERE are feelings that cannot be described. There are emotions too deep for utterance. There are times when the mind has power to paralize the body. When racking thought forces us to live an age in a minute. When we see and know all that is going on around us, and yet seem to be separate from the world—to exist in a world of ideality—a spiritual state. When our whole life, like a map, seems laid before us, and we behold at a single glance, in a second of time, what has taken us years to enact. When, leaping over the past and the present, we seem to pierce the great vail of the future, and behold our destiny.

May not this be a foretaste of death? May we not so see, and feel, and know, when the spirit shall have become separated from its frail tenement of mortality?

I have said there are such feelings and emotions; but they can only result from the most powerful causes. Neither do they effect all in the same manner. While a few experience the sensations just described, to others the same or similar causes may be productive of death, insanity, or the death-like swoon of utter forgetfulness.

Of the former class, was I—of the latter, Lilian. The same emotions which forced her to unconsciousness—paralized my physical powers, and forced me to a consciousness beyond the natural.

Bending over her—my eyes seemingly glazed, and fixed upon her sweet face, now pale and death-like — I remained spellbound—all my animal faculties suspended.

I heard a trampling of feet, as several persons hurried to our assistance. I heard voices expressive of alarm and dismay—and, above all, the voice of the invalid calling Lilian by name. I was conscious of being removed—of seeing the idol of my heart raised and borne away also. I felt my limbs chafed by half a dozen hands, and water dashed in my face. I saw thus, felt thus, comprehended all—and yet my mind was wandering far away to other scenes.

Have we power to think of more than one thing at the same time? I contend that we have—or else that thought, swift beyond comparison, sets before us different scenes, with such rapidity, that we *seem* to behold two at once—sometimes half-a-dozen—and yet, each perhaps, as opposite and distant as the north and south poles.

While I comprehended what was going on around me, my mind flew back to youth—to the time when I first felt a passion for Lilian—and traced every event of my life up to the present moment. Even the dream—wherein I had seen her bowed down by poverty, and finally murdered by my supposed rival—was not overlooked; and it now recurred to me as a vision of prophecy. Something fearful had happened, and I had been warned of it in my sleep.

How is it that in our sleep events are made known to us, that really are, or are about taking place? Can it be that the spirit then roams at will, in all the freedom of disembodiment, and returns freighted with intelligence to communicate to the physical senses? Let the philospher and metaphysician answer! Enough for me the effect, without at present seeking the cause.

And here, to keep my narrative straight before the reader, let me digress one moment, to place him in possession of facts which I gleaned afterward—partly from Lilian—partly from her companions of the journey.

It will be remembered, that in the opening of this story, I mentioned my own father, and the father of my friend, as being wealthy merchants in the city of Boston. Shortly after our departure—it might be on that very night of my singular dream—news of the failure of three large houses in New York, gave Huntly the astounding information that he was not worth a thousand dollars beyond his obligations. I am not going to describe his feelings, nor those of his family, on finding themselves thus suddenly plunged from a state of unlimited wealth to one of comparative poverty. The effect upon the elder Huntly, was to ruin him in his own estimation for life; and it soon became apparent to his friends, that he would not long survive the shock. All his energy, his ambition, went with his property; and a cloud of melancholy and grief settled over his once bright and joyous countenance. Several warmhearted friends, among whom was my father, came forward and offered to assist him—but all to no avail. He refused assistance—declaring it the chastening hand of God, to prepare him to depart to his long home. Oppression of spirits brought on physical debility, and the winds of the succeeding autumn sung a dirge over his grave.

A father and husband dead—a brother and son away, perhaps dead also—made the home of Lilian and her mother a house of mourning indeed; and what they suffered for the next two years, I must leave to the imaginations of those who have felt a similar visitation of the hand of Providence.

After paying the debts of the estate, a remnant of property remained, to which a few friends, on pretence they owed the deceased for this favor or that, generously added more; so that, although comparatively poor, they were in a measure above want. They left their fine mansion, to reside in a small but pleasant house, owned by my father, but for which he would receive no rent. Here they remained for eighteen months, laboring under a weight of affliction which those only can know who have lost friends by death, been suddenly reduced from affluence to poverty, and seen the cold, stinging look of scorn and contempt upon the lips of those heartless beings who were wont to play the fawning sycophant, and utter words of flattery and deceit as worthless as themselves.

During the winter of 1841-42, much was said concerning Oregon; and, as generally happens with every new place to which public attention becomes particularly directed, there were not lacking exaggerated accounts, which set it forth as the real El Dorado of the world. Whether these owed their origin to the prolific brains of certain romantic editors, or to the more designing ones of speculators, or to both combined, (the most probable) matters not; but the effect was to set on foot a tide of emigration, which, had it continued to the present time, without check, would have made Oregon a populous country.

Among those who had caught this "western fever," as it is frequently not inappropriately termed, were a few wealthy farmers in the vicinity of Boston, with one family of whom Mrs. Huntly had an intimate acquaintance. Being on a visit there in the winter, she soon learned, much to her surprise, that they were already making preparations to start, on the opening of spring, for this great El Dorado—this *Ultima Thule* of western emigration. Several of their acquaintances were going to join them, and, above all, an eccentric lady of wealth and refinement, who, with her beautiful daughter, had for the past year been the lioness and belle of the aristocratic and fashionable circles of Boston. Of this lady—who was known as Madame Mortimer, as also her daughter, who had received the subriquet of Belle Eva, the latter being her Christian name—Mrs. Huntly had more than once heard; and it was with no little surprise, as may readily be imagined, she now learned of her determination to venture upon such a long, tedious, and dangerous journey; and she mentally said, "When such a personage resolves to leave all the allurements of civilization, there must be something worth going for;" and this, probably, proved one of the strongest arguments to induce her to make one of the party herself. In addition to this, her country friends were enthusiastic on the subject of Oregon, of which they had received the most glowing, and of course exaggerated accounts, and were eager in urging her to join them. Oregon City a name which sounded well to the ear, was to be their destination. Of this they already had maps, whereon the beautiful streets and squares looked very enticing. Here each and all were to make their fortune; and in the visionary excitement of the moment, they overlooked the sober fact, that Oregon City then existed on the map only, drawn up by some speculator, and that its handsome streets and squares were simply imaginary locations in an utter wilderness.

But why prolong—why enter into detail of the hundred little causes which, combined, decided Mrs. Huntly (a lady whose main faults were an enthusiastic love of new projects, an overweening confidence in her own judgment, and a wilful adherence to her own decisions, right or wrong,) in joining this ill-timed expedition, contrary to the advice of her friends and of Lilian—the latter of whom consented to accompany her that she might not be separated from her only parent. Enough, that she had so decided; and that early in the spring succeeding, having disposed of all her effects, she and Lilian, in company with Madame and Eva Mortimer, (whom the fashionable world of course considered insane,) and some eight or ten families, had set out on their long journey to the far, Far West.

And here, apropos of Madame Mortimer and her lovely daughter, of whom much remains to be said at no distant period. Although they had appeared in the fashionable circles of Boston, reputed wealthy, nothing of their private history was known; and of course, as regarded them, curiosity was excited to a great degree, but without avail. They had been met among the *bon ton* of New York, and invited to Boston. They had accepted the invitation, had passed the ordeal of fashionable criticism, had conducted themselves on all occasions with strict propriety, and had departed, right in the face of all the gossips, without a single one being the wiser for his or her inquiries.

As to who and what they were, and how connected with the foregoing and succeeding events of this life-history, the reader who continues to the end of the narrative will doubtless be enlightened.

It is needless for me to touch upon the journey of my friends westward. Like all emigrants who seek Oregon for a home, they had experienced severe trials and vicissitudes, which upon them had fallen the more heavily, from being the first hardships they had ever known. Some three or four days previous to my joining them, Mrs. Huntly had been taken sick; and although Lilian had been greatly alarmed from the first, yet with the others the matter had not been thought serious, until the evening in question, when her symptoms had taken an unfavorable turn. Having no doctor among them, application for one had been made by Lilian to some of the trappers—who chanced to be passing—and this, providentially, had brought us once more together, after the long and eventful separation of more than two years.

Having now, reader, put you in possession of facts important for you to know, I will return from my digression, and go on with my narrative.

———o———

CHAPTER XXVIII.

RECOVER FROM MY PARALYSIS — THE INVALID — CAUSE OF ILLNESS — REMEDY — HAPPY RESULTS — JOY OF LILIAN — AN EVASION — FAMILIAR FACES — STRANGE MEETING — REFLECTIONS.

It was several minutes before I recovered from my paralysis; and this was doubtless much accelerated by Teddy, who, having tried various ways to restore me, at last threw his arms around my neck, and placing his mouth close to my ear, shouted:

"I say, your honor, is it dead ye is, now—or is it dead ye's jist agoing to be—by the way ye's stare so, and says nothing at all, at all!"

With a start, as if suddenly awakened from a dream, I looked around me, perceived myself the center of all eyes, and heard my name several times pronounced, coupled with that of Lilian, as here and there one, who had gained the secret of our strange behavior, sought to explain it to others. To most, my name was already familiar, as the companion of young Huntly, and son of the wealthy Leighton of Boston—and this, probably, had no tendency to lessen curiosity.

My first feeling on regaining myself, (if I may so express it) was one of confusion, that I had so publicly laid myself open to gossip; my second, indignation at being so stared at; my third, alarm as to what might be the effect of all this upon Mrs. Huntly; and to her I immediately turned, without a word to the others. Perhaps the reader, if a lover, is surprised that my first alarm was not for Lilian. Ay! but, dear sir, I saw at a glance that Lilian was in good hands, and in a fair way of recovery, and it would have been injudicious, at that moment, to draw any more attention to her.

Mrs. Huntly I found lying upon a feather bed, in a large, covered wagon, underneath which was attached a furnace for warming it; so that, all things considered, the patient was more comfortably situated than I had expected to find her.

In appearance, she had altered much since I last saw her. Her naturally rather florid complexion, and full, round face, had given place to pallor and thinness, and here and there I could trace deep lines of care; but I failed to note a single symptom portending immediate danger. Grief, fatigue of travel, and many anxieties of mind, together with a touch of influenza, had brought on a splenetic affection, something like what is vulgarly termed "hypo." She had fancied herself very ill, and in fact nigh unto death; and I saw at once, that could she be persuaded the crisis had passed, and that the danger was over, she would speedily recover—and upon this I acted with decision. The cause of her grief and of her being here I did not then know—for the information which I have given the reader on the subject, was not obtained till afterward—and I saw it would not do to question her. It was necessary I should appear cheerful, whether I felt so or not; and accordingly I approached her with a smile. Instantly her eye brightened as it met mine, and I perceived, to my great satisfaction, that the alarm occasioned by the swoon of Lilian, had proved beneficial, in drawing her thoughts from herself to another, and arousing all her dormant faculties. Extending her hand as I approached, she said, with a sigh:

"Ah! Francis, I never thought we should meet thus."

"True," I replied, "I had thought to meet you under other circumstances—though I presume all has happened for the best."

"You find me very low, do you not?"

"You *have* been ill," I answered, emphasising the word have; "but everything I see has turned in your favor."

"How!" she exclaimed, quickly, raising her head, and fixing her eyes intently upon mine; "would you imply that I am not in a dangerous condition?"

"I would not only imply it," I rejoined, with energy, pretending to judge by her pulse, "but I will assert it as an indisputable fact. If in a week from this you are not as well as you ever were in your life, I will give you leave to call me an imposter."

"Really, Francis, you surprise me!" she said, with animation. "In fact, I believe I do feel better. But I *have* been sick—you admit that?"

"O, most certainly," I said, rejoiced to perceive the beneficial effects of my mental prescription. "You *have* been very sick, and within an hour have been nigh unto death; but thank God! the crisis has passed, and you have nothing to do now but recover as fast as possible."

"But what is, or has been my ailment?"

Here I remembered the suggestion of Teddy, and quickly mumbled over a long string of Latin names, with scientific explanations, much to the satisfaction of everybody but myself. The spectators who had crowded around to hear what I had to say—being, with but two or three exceptions, good honest farmers and farmers' wives—nodded approvals to each other, and gave me many a respectful glance, equivalent to telling me, that my first case, without a single dose, had, with them, established my reputation as a skillful physician. O, the humbug of big sounding words! I would advise doctors and lawyers to use them on all occasions.

News of my decision, regarding the patient, flew rapidly from one to another—lighting each countenance, before gloomy, with a smile of pleasure—until it reached the ear of Lilian, who, just recovering from the effects of her swoon, uttered a cry of joy, and, much to the surprise and satisfaction of those engaged in restoring her, suddenly sprang away from them and rushed to her mother.

"O, mother," she cried, "I have heard such good tidings!"

"All true, every word," returned her mother, gaily. "My physician has pronounced me out of danger;" and she playfully pointed to me.

"God be praised!" cried Lilian fervently. "What a miracle is this! and how it relieves my anguished heart!"

Then turning upon me her sweet, pale, lovely countenance — her full, soft, blue eyes, moist with tears—she partly extended her hand, and gasped my name.

The next instant, regardless of the time, place, and the presence of others, she was clasped in my arms, strained to my heaving breast, and my lips were pressed to hers in the holy kiss of mutual love. It was a blissful moment, notwithstanding all we had both suffered. But it was a moment only; for the next she sprang away, blushing and abashed at what she doubtless considered her own boldness.

"You're a wonderful docther, your honor," whispered Teddy in my ear. "i' Faith! ye jist looks at 'em, and jabbers a few Lathin names, and they're betther'n they iver was—afore they've time to know what ailed 'em, jist—and, troth! a hugging ye at that, too, the purtiest one among 'em. Is it knowing thim ye is—or does the likes of her kiss by raason of yees being a docthor? Jabers! it's what I'd like done to mesilf, now, in any perfishion."

"Hush! Teddy. These are the sister and mother of my lost friend."

"Howly St. Pathrick in the morning! ye don't say!" exclaimed Teddy, staggering back with surprise.

"Hush!" I whispered in his ear, catching him by the arm, with a grip sufficient to impress the importance of my words. "Not a syllable concerning Huntly, as you value your life!"

"Och!" returned Teddy, placing his finger to his lips, winking his eye, and nodding his head—"I'm dumb as a dead nager, I is."

This caution was not made any too soon; for the next moment Mrs. Huntly exclaimed:

"But, Francis, where is my son—where is Charles—that he does not make his appearance?"

"O, yes, my brother?" cried Lilian.

I was suddenly seized with a serious fit of coughing, so as to gain time for a reply. It would not do to let them know the true state of the case, and I could not think of telling them a falsehood. A happy thought struck me, and I answered:

"Charles is not with me."

"Indeed! Where is he, then?" cried both in a breath.

"We parted in California; I left him going eastward; and, for what I know, he may be now in Boston."

"God help him, then, when he hears the awful news, and finds himself homeless and friendless, poor boy!" cried Mrs. Huntly, with a burst of grief, in which Lilian joined.

I now inquired what had happened, and learned, in the course of conversation, much of that which I have already given the reader.

"Poor Charles!" I sighed to myself, "it is well if thou art dead. Better be dead, than return to thy once happy home, only to find thy friends gone, and thyself a beggar!"

With Lilian and her mother, in their misfortunes, I sympathized deeply; but fearing these saddening thoughts might prove injurious to Mrs. Huntly, I hastened to console her by saying:

"We should bear in mind that all are born to die; that riches are unstable; and that whatever happens, is always for the best, though we be not able to see it at the time."

"That I believe to be the true philosophy of life," said a middle-aged lady at my side, whom, with her daughter, a meet companion for Lilian, I had more than once noticed, as possessing superior accomplishments; but, under the excitement I was laboring, I had failed to closely scan the features of either. I now turned at once to the speaker, and was immediately introduced, by Lilian, to Madame Mortimer and her daughter Eva.

"Strange!" I said to myself, as bowing to each, I became struck with the familiarity of their features. "I have seen these faces before, methinks—but where I cannot tell."

The name, however, perplexed me—for I had no remembrance of ever before being introduced to a Mortimer.

"Your countenance seems familiar," I said, addressing the elder lady.

"And so does yours, sir!" she replied; "and for the last half hour, I have been trying to recall where I have seen you—but in vain."

Suddenly the whole truth flashed upon me.

"Were you not in New York with your daughter, some two years since?" I inquired, eagerly.

"I was."

"At the National Theatre, on the night it was burned?"

"I was."

"Did not some one rescue your daughter from the flames?"

"Good heavens! yes! I remember now—I remember!" she exclaimed, a good deal agitated. "It was you, sir—you! I thought I knew those features!" and excited by powerful emotions, she seized both my hands in hers, and pressing them warmly, uttered a "God bless you!" while her eyes filled with tears of gratitude. Eva was too much affected to trust her voice in the utterance of a single word—but her look spoke volumes.

What a strange combination of startling events had this night revealed to me! How mysteriously had Providence arranged and put them together for some great design! Who could have imagined that the mere act of saving a fellow creature's life—a stranger at that, in a strange city—and leaving her without knowing her name, or even her residence, for a long journey of many thousand miles—was to have a direct bearing upon my future destiny, and that of my friend? Yet such was the fact; and however unimportant the incident might have appeared at the time to the reader—however irrelative to the main story—yet on that very circumstance, unknown to any, was depending many of the important events which followed those already described, and which in due time will be given.

It was with sensations peculiar to each, that these matters were narrated and commented upon for the next two hours; and doubtless not one who heard the strange and romantic story of how I saved the life of Eva Mortimer, but felt his most trivial act to result from the hidden design of a Higher Power. As for myself, such a chaos of ideas crowded my brain, as made it impossible for me to describe what I thought, or what feeling had the preponderance, unless it were a mingling of pleasure and sadness. But one thing seemed wanting to make me joyful; and that, alas! was my friend. Had he been present, notwithstanding all adverse circumstances, my heart would have bounded with rapture. And he! what would have been his feelings, thus to have met, in *propria personæ*, the idol of his dreams! thus to have been placed *tete-a-tete* with Eva Mortimer—the beautiful unknown!

———o———

CHAPTER XXIX.

STANDING SENTINEL—DROWSINESS—INTERRUPTION—SUDDEN APPEARANCE OF PRAIRIE FLOWER—HER WARNING, SURPRISE, AGITATION AND ABRUPT DEPARTURE—ALARM THE CAMP—HOSTILE PREPARATIONS—ATTACK—REPULSE—VICTORY—ARRIVAL IN OREGON—CONCLUSION.

It was late in the night, and all had become still in the encampment. The animals—consisting of mules, horses, oxen and cows—had been driven together and tethered, and were taking their repose. In the area, formed by the wagons, two fires were burning, at one of which sat Teddy and myself, half dozing, with our rifles resting against our shoulders. We had volunteered our services as sentinels for the night—but our watch could hardly be termed vigilant. In the surrounding vehicles, the emigrants were already giving evidence of that sound sleep which indicates health and weariness, and a cessation of the physical and mental faculties. I was, as I said before, in a half dozing state. I had been conning over the many singular pranks of fortune connected with myself, and particularly the wonderful revelations of the last six or eight hours. I had been musing upon the complicated web of man's existence and already had my thoughts began to wander as in a dream.

A rumbling sound, like the roaring of a distant waterfall caught my ear. Gradually it grew louder and nearer, until I fancied I could detect the pattering of a horse's feet upon the hard earth. Nearer and nearer it came, and I found my impression confirmed. It was a horse at full speed—but what could it mean? Suddenly Teddy sprang up, and tightly grasped his rifle. We now both darted outside the circle of wagons: By the dim light we beheld a horse and rider rapidly dashing up the valley. The next moment the beast was reined in to a dead halt, some twenty yards distant.

"Who goes there?" I cried.

"A friend," was the answer, in a clear, silvery voice. "Be on your guard, or you will be surprised by Indians!"

Heavens! I should know those tones! Could it be possible!

"Prairie Flower!" I called.

"Ha! who are you?" was the answer; and the next moment the coal black pony, and his beautiful, mysterious rider, stood by my side.

"Prairie Flower! and do we indeed meet again!"

"Who are you?" said she, bending down to scrutinize my features. "Ha! is it indeed possible!" she continued, with no little agitation, as she recognized me. "How you have altered! I—I—but I have no time to talk! I must not be seen here. It would cost me my life. I may see you again. Be on your guard! How strange! I never thought to see you again. I must go!"

These sentences were uttered rapidly, almost incoherently, while the voice of the speaker trembled, and there seemed a wildness in her manner. On concluding, she tightened her rein as if to depart—but still lingered as if to add something more.

"Heaven bless you, Prairie Flower! you are always seeking the good of others."

She sighed, turned her head away, and strove to say, carelessly:

"Your friend—I—I—is well—is he?"

"Alas! I cannot answer."

"Ha! what! how!" she cried, quickly, turning full upon me, and grasping my arm, which chanced to be resting on the neck of her pony. "Explain!" and I felt her grasp tighten.

I hurriedly related our last parting.

For some moments she did not reply, while her whole frame trembled violently.

At length she withdrew her hand, tightened the rein again, and gasped the single word,

"Farewell!"

Ere I had time for another syllable, her horse was speeding away like the wind; and ere I had recovered from my surprise, both were lost in the darkness.

So sudden had all this happened, that I felt completely bewildered. Was I dreaming? A word from Teddy aroused me. Despatching him to the trappers, to ask their assistance, I flew back to the larger encampment and gave the alarm. Instantly the whole camp was in commotion: and amid the screams of women and children, the men grasped their arms, and sprung from their coverts excited and pale, but ready to meet danger without flinching, in defence of those whose lives they prized above their own.

I hurried round the camp to quiet the fears of the weaker members, by telling them there was little or no danger—that the Indians, if they came at all, finding us ready to receive them, would not risk an attack. In this, much to my surprise, I was shortly aided by Lilian and Eva, both of whom displayed a heroic coolness, and presence of mind, and fearlessness of danger, for which, among all the virtues I had allowed them, I had given them no credit whatever. Had I been required, before this event, to select the most timid of the party, I should have pointed them out first. Modest, unassuming, retiring in their manners, weak in physical powers, unused to hardships and dangers, with a superior refinement in thought and feeling—I had supposed them the first to shrink at any alarm. Judge of my astonishment, then, when I saw them gliding over the earth, as over a soft carpet, and, with scarcely an appearance of fear, by their acts and language, shaming the more frightened to silence. The arrival of the trappers, too—well armed—and their seeming indifference to danger, reassured all in a measure, and served to restore order and quiet.

Hastily organizing, we marched outside the wagons, and took up our position so as to watch and guard any point of compass, not knowing at which the foe might make his appearance and onset.

All relapsed into silence, in which manner an hour was passed, and we were beginning to think the alarm false, when one of the men espied a dark object, as he fancied, slowly nearing him.

Without a second thought, crack went his rifle, and instantly, as if by magic, a dark spot to the north of us became peopled by some fifty savages, who, finding themselves discovered, and doubtless thinking this the alarm of the sentinel, uttered frightful yells, and sprang forward, in a body. Rushing to the point of attack, we hastily formed a line, and placing our rifles to our shoulders, silently waited until not more than twenty yards divided us from the main body of our enemies.

"Fire!" cried a voice; and instantly a dozen rifles poured their deadly contents among the dusky horde, with good effect, as could be told by several frightful groans of pain.

This was a reception the savages had not counted on, and they in turn became alarmed. Suddenly pausing, they uttered yells of dismay, and discharging their pieces at random, the balls of which whistled past us without a single injury, they turned and fled precipitately. The victory was ours, and to Prairie Flower we owed our lives. The remainder of the night we kept to our arms, but were not again disturbed, and by sunrise the whole party was on the move up the mountains.

As I could not think of parting with my friends (above all with Lilian) in the wilderness, I resolved to accompany them to their destination; and then to — to — I scarcely knew what. Teddy of course went with me, and the trappers, out of friendship, bore us company many days.

I shall not weary you, reader, with a detail of all the little incidents of our tedious progress to Oregon city. Suffice, that it was such as all emigrants experience in a greater or less degree, and was attended with a succession of scenes similar to those described throughout these pages. As I had predicted, the health of Mrs. Huntly was gradually restored; and within ten days from the commencement of her convalescence, she declared herself as well as at any period of her life, and that the word of her young doctor, as she jokingly termed me, was equal in effect to the combined virtues of the whole *materia medica*.

The return of Mrs. Huntly's strength and spirits, brought pleasure to the eye and bloom to the cheek of Lilian, which my daily presence, as I was vain enough to flatter myself, did not tend to dissipate.

Be that as it may, (and I leave the reader to judge) this long journey, so full of hardship and peril, however unpleasant it might have proved to her and to others, I must ever look back to with pleasure, as one of the happiest periods of my so far eventful life.

Crossing the Rocky Mountains at the well known South Pass, we continued on the regular Oregon route—passed Fort Hall—went down the Snake river and over the Salmon Mountains to Fort Boise—through the country of Shoshones, or Snake Indians, over the Blue Mountains to Fort Walla Walla, on the Columbia—down the Columbia, over the Cascade range, to Oregon City, on the pleasant little Willamette—where we all safely arrived about the middle of December.

At this period, as I before remarked, Oregon City existed only in name—being with the exception of a few log houses, (erected during the summer and fall previous, by a few emigrants who had reached here in advance of our party,) a complete wilderness. The appearance of the place, so different from what they had expected to find it, disheartened my worthy friends not a little; and had such a thing then been possible, I believe they would at once have returned to their native land. But this was out of the question; there was no help for their oversight now, only by making the best of a bad bargain; and so, after having grumbled to their hearts' content—wished Oregon for the thousandth time at the bottom of the sea, and themselves back home as many—they set to work in earnest, to provide themselves homes for the winter, declaring that spring should see them on their way to the States.

With proper energy, properly directed, a great deal may be accomplished in a very short time; and in less than two weeks from their earnest commencement, no less than eight or ten cabins were added to the few already there. In these the different families removed, Teddy and I taking up our abode in that appropriated to Mrs. Huntly.

Although without any effects save such as had been brought with them, and short of provisions also, yet, by one means and another, all managed to get through the winter as comfortably as could be expected; and instead of preparing to return, spring found the majority of the new settlers entering lands, determined on making this their future residence, be the consequences what they might.

Some three or four, among whom was Madame Mortimer and her daughter, were still disaffected, and would gladly have retraced their steps; but they could not find companions enough to make the journey safe, and therefore, against their will, were forced to remain.

Oregon City I found beautifully located on the eastern bank of the Willamette, and, from what I could judge, destined, at no very distant period, to become the great mart of the Far West. Here I remained through the winter, and as it proved open and mild, employed my time in hunting and fishing, and conversing with the only being I truly loved. Had my friend been with me, I should have looked upon the place as a perfect paradise; but thoughts of him—of what might be his fate—would steal over me in my most joyous moments, and cloud my brow with gloom. These singular changes were noted by Lilian and others with feelings of surprise, and frequently was I questioned by the former regarding them—but I ever avoided a direct answer.

Neither Lilian nor her mother knew the true cause of Charles Huntly's absence; and though I often meditated telling them, yet, when it came to the point, I ever shrunk from the painful task of making both wretched. He *might* be living; and the bare possibility of such a thing, I thought sufficient to justify me in keeping them in blissful ignorance of what I supposed to be his real fate. Both fondly anticipated seeing him the coming summer—not doubting he had gone east, and that so soon as he should receive tidings of their locality, he would set out to join them. I had no such hopes—but I dared not tell them so.

———o———

It was a lovely day in the spring of 1843. On the banks of the romantic Willamette, under the shade of a large tree, I was seated. By my side—with her sweet face averted and crimson with blushes, her right hand clasped in mine, her left unconsciously toying with a beautiful flower, which failed to rival her own fair self—sat Lilian Huntly. It was one of those peculiar moments which are distinctly remembered through life. I had just offered her my hand and fortune, and was waiting, with all the trembling impatience of a lover, to hear the result.

"Say, Lilian — sweet Lilian! will you be mine?"

Her lily hand trembled—I felt its velvet-like pressure—but her tongue had lost the power of utterance. It was enough; and the next moment she was strained to my heart, with a joy too deep for words.

"And when shall it be—when shall my happiness be consummated, dear Lilian?" I at length ventured to ask.

For a time she did not reply; then raising her angelic face, and fastening her soft beaming eye, moist with tears of joy, upon mine, she said, in a low, sweet, tremulous tone:

"*On the day when we are all made glad by the presence of my brother.*"

"Alas!" groaned I, mentally, "that day may never come!"

———o———

The fate of Charles Huntly—of the mysterious Prairie Flower and others—will be found in "Leni Leoti — or, Adventures in the Far West — a Sequel to Prairie Flower."

THE END OF PRAIRIE FLOWER.

CPSIA information can be obtained at www.ICGtesting.com
Printed in the USA
BVOW011406180911

271419BV00002B/83/A